Caeia March was born in the Isle of Man in 1946. She is the author of several short stories, published in *Everyday Matters 1*, *The Reach*, *Girls Next Door* (The Women's Press, 1985) and *Politics of the Heart: A Lesbian Parenting Anthology*, and of articles: in *Spare Rib* ('Diary of a Feminist Teacher', under the name of Kate Elliott); *In Other Words* ('Writing as a Lesbian Mother'); *Taking Reality by Surprise* ('Mental Filming'; 'Image Making'; 'Editing') (The Women's Press, 1991); *What Lesbians Do in Books* ('The Process of Writing *Three Ply Yarn*') (The Women's Press, 1991). Her poetry is included in *Dancing the Tightrope* (The Women's Press, 1987) and *Naming the Waves*. She has published two novels with The Women's Press, *Three Ply Yarn* (1986) and *The Hide and Seek Files* (1988).

She currently divides her time between London and Cornwall, and is working on another novel, a collection of poetry, and a collection of short stories.

CAEIA MARCH

Fire! Fire!

The Women's Press

First published by The Women's Press Limited 1991
A member of the Namara Group
34 Great Sutton Street
London EC1V 0DX

British Library Cataloguing in Publication Data
March, Caeia, *1946* –
  Fire! Fire!
  I. Title
  823.914

ISBN 0–7043–4282–0

Typeset by MC Typeset Limited, Rochester, Kent
Printed and bound in Great Britain by Cox & Wyman,
Reading, Berks

The author and publishers wish to thank the following
for permission to quote from their work:

How Much Is That Doggie in the Window (Merill) ©
Warner Chappell Music Ltd
(How Much Is That) Doggie in the Window (Merill)
© 1952 R 1980 Golden Bell Songs (USA and Canada)
All rights reserved. Used by permission.

Sweeter for Me Joan Baez. Used by permission of
Carlin Music Corporation, Iron Bridge House, 3
Bridge Approach, London NW1 8BD and © 1976,
Gabriel Earl Music, USA.

Turn Around (Harry Belafonte/Alan Greene/Malvina
Reynolds) 60% © Clara Music Publishing INC, USA.
Reproduced by permission of EMI Music Publishing
Ltd, London, WC2H 0EA.

It has proved impossible, despite great effort, to contact the copyright holders of the remaining 40% of
Turn Around.

Acknowledgments

The acknowledgments here differ from those in my previous novels. My writing process has been interrupted by ME (Myalgic Encephalo-myelitis) for almost three years.

My thanks go first to my partner, Keri Wood, for her love and sense of humour during my long bouts of invalidity, and for believing that I would regain my health; to my sons for understanding that I needed to bring forward my long-term plans to live by the sea; to Penny Holland and Pat Hextall, who, in their different ways, gave me care and comfort – Penny, who telephoned daily to ask how I was – and Pat, who planned wonderful mystery tours into the countryside around London.

Fire! Fire! was begun in the mid 1980s. Thanks are due to Hania Dolan who, in the Women's Studies Group at The Albany, Deptford, asked if we could examine women's lives in feudal times in this country. As tutor I then turned my research and reading towards producing teaching materials for the group. During that process several fictional characters emerged. I would like to thank Gillian Spraggs for support and encouragement with that early research into the seventeenth century.

Parts of this manuscript were later inspired by a book of poems called *Paper Talk* by Sally Flood. I'd like to thank Sally for permission to use that concept and to adapt it as 'Speaking Paper' throughout this novel.

Many women helped in several ways during the editing and re-writing of the various drafts. Special thanks to Cynthia Morris and Peg Wiseman for hours and hours of friendship, constructive comments on all my work and, specifically on *Fire! Fire!* from the early manuscripts to the final drafts. To Bernardine Evaristo and Ruth Harris for encouraging my work, and to Bernardine, Ann Bellingham and Margaret Chinn for reading later drafts and offering positive help and detailed feedback. To Pat Angove, Sandy Chapman, Elaine Hawkins, Judy Kirk, Suzanne Nield, Ros Pearson and Marcia White, for many useful and exciting conversations about my work during the development of *Fire! Fire!*

My thanks to all the readers who have written to me saying that they've enjoyed my work, and I'd especially like to thank Priscilla Doherty – the first reader to write to me, years ago – who generously gave her time to help me proofread *Fire! Fire!*

Lastly, for her unique blend of humour, fun, patience and professional commitment, my thanks go to my editor, Sue Gilbert, with whom I've been delighted to work during the past year.

Fire! Fire! is fiction. None of the characters are taken from women or men known personally to me. The places, however, are sometimes drawn from those parts of city, country and coastline which I know and love.

Caeia March, 1991

One

If Sumach trees don't lie, it was the very end of summer. Leaves that changed between my visits to the DSS flamed for me that day: surfer-board orange and sizzling red.

It was a lovely day, with autumn in the air. I didn't mind waiting at the bus-stop. I loved that small tree, in someone's tiny front garden. It loved me too, in all weathers, and all seasons.

P'raps once I'd been home, got over the fact that the DSS had lost my file *again*, I'd walk to Epping Forest. It called me. I would visit the old log seat where Maria and I used to kiss. After all she'd died over a year ago and I couldn't live in the past for ever.

Seasons changing? It was May when Maria died. All around me the seasons continued – summer autumn winter spring-summer. Now almost autumn again. The will to grow is strong. Rose-bay willow-herb will cover a patch of wounded land in London; brambles will stitch together the sides of a deep cut quarried in the country. Given time the earth will renew herself: grass and wild flowers, heather and trees. I followed her lead: I collected time like seeds, planted minutes and grew them into hours, days, weeks, months, seasons.

The bus queue was mostly pensioners using bus passes, and young women with babies, and their buggies folded and hooked over their arms. There hadn't been buggies in my day, but the young women were loaded with carrier bags, like I'd been.

Just then, a news vendor arrived along the road, set up a stand, and shouted: 'Iran–Iraq latest, Iran–Iraq latest.' No one besides me at the bus-stop seemed to take the slightest notice.

This summer, '87, tension in the Gulf had been increasing.

My mind searched the shapes of people ahead of me, wondering if they thought England was at war, and if any of them did, whether they too had a son involved.

> Turn around and they're four
> Turn around and they're young
> men
> going out of the door
> going out to the war.

The young women knew each other. They chatted together, occasionally grumbling about the wait for the bus. I wanted to natter to Maria next to me. To talk to her about the Gulf, about life, about plans and autumn and a definite shift in the angle of light. But Maria was gone. The other side of night. I wanted what I couldn't have: to talk with her. A simple thing I couldn't have: to talk with her.

A breeze rustled some litter by the bus-stop. I felt Maria close by. Then I thought someone spoke to me. Must be one of the pensioners behind me. I turned round, but she was busy chatting to her friend. No one in the queue was speaking to me. No one at all. I shivered, though it wasn't cold, and a voice that wasn't Maria's spoke right into my ear, very softly. I kept very still, didn't glance round. No one was aware of me. I could easily have been invisible.

'I am Wind,' said the voice. 'Came to see if you needed a friend.'

I shuddered, remembering Joan of Arc, on telly – she got voices and they burned her at the stake. Now *I* was hearing things.

The bus didn't come.

'I said, I am Wind,' repeated the voice.

Wind? In our house we said 'roses'. Maria's were quiet but environmentally unfriendly. Serious 'roses'. Maria caused

2

the gap in the ozone layer.

'You haven't answered me,' said the voice. The same voice. A kind voice. 'Tonight I'll be following Moon. Lovely sky out there. Come tonight, on a night ride. Use your imagination.'

Confused, I couldn't speak. The voice again: 'Stay calm, Denny. Don't panic. Stop and listen to me. I can show you stars, the Milky Way. Come, ride with me tonight.'

'No thanks. Take a rain check,' I felt myself reply. Then I spun around, shocked in case I'd spoken aloud. Not in front of this lot, please.

No one paid me any more attention than they did the news vendor, still calling.

I was truly spooked, swallowed hard. Maria seemed very near.

The voice returned: 'I saw that you planted primroses. You did well. They're difficult to germinate from bought seed, you know. In my job description, of course. They'll be a picture in the spring.'

'Will it take me till next spring?'

'I think so. You can't hurry such things. You start to heal the hurts, to go forward, slowly. Turn a corner.'

'How'd you know?'

'Talked to Death. Part of the job. Know it from all sides, in my professional capacity.'

'No. Not 'professionals'. Had enough of them in my teens.'

'Oops, just trying to help. Wrong words, wrong time. I don't find bus queues conducive to a genuine conversation, d'you? It's my word of the week, this week, 'conducive'. I found it in a Sunday supplement left lying about. It's my hobby you know Denny, recycling words from patriarchal rubbish. I breeze about all over the place collecting. You wouldn't believe the words I can come up with. Take 'job description' for example. Found that on an office window-ledge. Rustled a few papers that day, I can tell you.'

'You like the sound of your own voice that's your trouble.'

'True – some of the time. Well I'd better breeze off. Between you me and a sweet-wrapper swirling round this bus stop, I'd say you're sailing along.'

'Why don't you just shut up? Take up your words and go? It's my son that's the sailor, not me. Somewhere in the Gulf and I don't know where. Just go. Go away and leave me alone. I don't need you stirring me up. Got it?'

'Oops miscommunication. Prone to that also as you'll find out. But I'll call again tomorrow, if not tonight. I want to take you stratosphering, wonderful experience. Do you the world of good. If you've the energy. Oh look, here comes the bus. I'm off. Bye.'

In an instant, the bus queue mutated. An insect mutant turtle robot, with walking-stick antennae that probed the bus, and buggywheel eyes that revolved round on long, thin metal attachments. We clanked and lumbered forward, a strange thing of flesh and metal. We were all aliens, joined to each other, in a zigzagging carapace, fantastic and fabulous.

Afterwards, we were just a crowd of boring humans stifled in a London bus.

It smelled of old upholstery, diesel fumes and BO. I found a third of a double seat next to a huge man who stank of drink.

I couldn't see out the windows in any direction. So I closed my eyes and imagined the cool, green forests of old Epping from pictures in our local library. At home I had old local maps that I'd borrowed and they fascinated me. Maps were one of my passions, had been since I was little.

Back home I tried to forget the voice of Wind in the bus queue and the sensation of replying, though I was sure I'd not spoken aloud. I unlocked our back door and whistled for Roof, who was at the end of the garden, chiding the Wren.

Ours was a typical Victorian mid-terraced house, one of dozens like it in NE London, with a bathroom in a tiny brick box on the back of the kitchen. We shared years in that house, Maria's house. Me, Maria, her daughter Cheryl, and my twins – boys but not identical – Graham and Phil.

We loved the house, our life and each other, Maria and I. It was the only time of stability and contentment I'd known.

4

I grabbed a sandwich then walked with Roof the two and a bit miles to Epping Forest. There, all around me, leaves were patched with an odd assortment of colours, pale yellow, old mud, and beigey browns. What a bodged-up job. Bits of this and bobs of that, uneven stitches with raggy scraps of green. D'you need some help, forest? Being made redundant?

We came to a clearing. I'd loved this special place, though without Maria the area was like a dance floor empty of dancers. I looked at our old log seat and, for the first time since Maria died, sat down there.

Roof ran to the shallow stream, fished for sticks, brought them to the seat for me to throw, then amused herself, dashing up and down the sloping bank, into and out of the water, alternately shaking and soaking herself.

She was a large dog, a mixture of something tall and shaggy, perhaps some Airedale, and highly intelligent, perhaps some sheepdog. The only dogs she feared were Alsatians. She'd have taken off the arm of any unknown man who approached me, though she wanted to make friends if we met other women walking with their dogs. We knew our own routes, and we'd never had any bad experiences in the forest, but I took the fear inside me from the streets to the woods.

No splashing at the stream. Roof had gone.

I heard leaves rustle and twigs being snapped the other side of the water. Then voices, low and confidential. Where was Roof? I was just about to call her when two women appeared. I sat completely still, my gaze fixed on them, but they seemed not to notice me. One woman was in her thirties, wearing a long skirt, with a shawl and long hair. The other was much younger, in her teens, wearing a mini, heavy ankle boots and leggings. Her hair was short, spiky, a careful punk cum haphazard urchin cut.

They were strangers to me. I gripped the edge of the smooth log seat. I had the same sensation as at the bus-stop, that Maria was close by. Her presence was all around me.

Roof came back. She nudged soggily against my legs, and I

5

didn't want to speak, my gaze fixed on the two women, so I simply rubbed Roof's wet ears. Why hadn't she barked at all? Why didn't she take any notice of them?

They walked on, and away from us, out of view, still talking as if they knew each other very well. I could hear the swish of the older one's skirt and judge the weight of the young one's boots on the earth. I leaned back against the log seat and closed my eyes. I don't know why, but it seemed to be the right thing. Then just behind me, I heard a young woman's voice, a kind voice, olde-worlde, broad Essex:

''Tis my chance to talk to you.'

I took a deep breath, but kept my eyes shut tight.

'Why? Who are you?'

'Roarie's the name. Born with a roar they cannot quiet. Was my desire to talk to you the winter past. Alas, 'twas not your wish.'

'I was grieving for Maria and my two friends who died when she did. I didn't talk to anyone, anyone at all. I wasn't ready, I suppose.'

'I have a plan. I need you. Shall you listen out for me this winter?' The voice was soft, urgent, with a sense of mystery, but I wasn't frightened. I don't know if I was speaking aloud. Only that we seemed to be talking to one another, though I had my eyes closed. She was somewhere behind my seat. I sensed that I mustn't turn around. So I simply nodded.

She said: 'Mary By-the-Well waits for me. I must go now. I shall come back. I need you.'

She didn't say anything else and after a moment or two when I was sure she'd gone, I opened my eyes. Roof was sitting looking at me, her head on one side, quizzical. I stood up. Roof wagged her tail, meaning: 'Can we go now? I'm starving.'

'Good girl,' I said. 'Come on Roof, let's go home, eh? I must be going mad. I talked to Wind at the bus-stop and now I'm meeting phantoms in the forest. Did I imagine all that? Surely I didn't speak out loud, did I?' Roof didn't answer.

I knew that grief did all kinds of weird things to people. I'd read loads of women's mags, and even one or two library books on the subject – they depressed rather than helped me.

I handed them back unfinished.

I waded my way out of the forest with Roof, taking our favourite route. Her body was almost hidden in tall grass. Her tail was aloft, a banner held high on a demo. Every day was a demo for her: she loved me.

A fine wind came whispering, scattering the first leaves. It should have been romantic, even idyllic.

It couldn't be. Maria was gone.

Two

      I picked up a newspaper from the news-stand on the corner as I turned off Forest Road, and read that Iraqi aircraft had struck 'several large maritime targets'. They meant oil tankers. My bloody silly macho son, Phil, caused havoc at home when he decided to go off and earn some money on a tanker. He and Graham had such a set to about it. Graham said that Phil's politics stank. Phil retorted that Gray would never amount to anything because he didn't have any grit. Graham shouted back that Phil was a free spirit and if he wanted to get himself blown to pieces that was up to him but why didn't he give a thought to how Mum would feel, i.e. me.

    I tucked the paper under my arm to catch up on the details later. First I wanted a cup of tea and to write a letter.

The little back bedroom was over the kitchen and bathroom and looked down into the back garden. I had a small table by the window. I always sat there to write to Beatrice, my friend in New Zealand, which she called Aotearoa.

    We had been friends for years, working side by side in the printers and stationers. When the firm went bust, we were both made redundant. She had decided to return home. Her mother was seriously ill.

    I found my writing pad, airmail, large thin blue paper, and my fountain pen. The best words for Beatrice always came out of that pen. I began to write . . .

    Instead, the girl from the forest came through, straight on

to the paper, as if the pen and I had nothing to do with it.

'To keep you company is my aim.'

'Roarie?'

'I am the weaver's daughter. Anne Brewster, who runs the alehouse, is my aunt.'

'Brewster!! I know that name.'

'One line in your printed book. A pox on't.'

'You're real. The girl from the forest; you're real.'

''Tis true. Yet 'tis not safe to live deep in the woods. Wild hogs. Be more wary where you tread.'

'I am. Roof warns me if anyone's approaching. Except for you.'

'I hear her whenever you arrive in the forest. Loud voice. No wonder they took her for a boy.'

'How did you know that?' Rufus had bundled into my life along with all the other things – animal, vegetable, and mineral – that the twins had collected, come by, gained possession of. By means mostly fair, sometimes foul. Her name tag said Rufus. No one ever claimed her, though we went to the police. She was, from the start, a lovable rag-bag of a dog, all limbs and ears and a tail that wagged fast enough to launch a space shuttle.

'Plenty I know about you,' said Roarie, adding to, not solving the mystery.

'Do you think I needed keeping company?'

'Is it not true?'

'It is. I have been very lonely but I'm toughening up.'

''Tis your desire to survive. Mine to be a comfort.'

'How can you? I've to come to terms with it myself.'

'Trust me. People do trust me.' She paused. ''Twas the journey was my problem. Speak across to your time. My voice – 'tis in my time. 'Tis a heavy task – wearisome. I shall speak through your hand.' I looked at my pen. She had not said quill. Did she know the name for pen?

'This is my pen.'

'You shall write, in your time, in your voice.'

'I don't know how. I don't know how to translate.'

'Shall work on't. You and me. Time is *now*. You have many voices. You speak with Wind, Dog, Bird.'

'How do you know so much so young? How old *are* you?'

'Fourteen. Same age as you when . . .'

'I don't want to talk about that today . . .'

'You shall know me, my friends, my people, my times. Shall find old maps, paintings.'

'In galleries, you mean? Museums? Paintings of your places, your times?'

'As you wish, Denny. As you may. 'Tis my way to listen. Wind, animals, servants, labourers. Listening, 'tis the key. Not with ears. With heart. Ears not necessary. You shall pick up your . . .' She faded. I closed my eyes trying to hear her. 'Pen. Listen, 'tis the key. Our story dies in prison. You shall unlock us. Time is now. Now you grieve for Maria.'

'How do you know? What's happ iing to me? I . . . I seem to be on a bridge. You one si␣, Maria the other. You're right, I am grieving. People say it will ease with time. But I grieve for Daphne too and Bronwyn. Too much loss. My skin burns. I'm burning. Help me.'

'Fire and Burn: the twin sisters. Talk in two voices, wear matching cloaks. You shall meet them both. Time is soon. But first is one who inspires me: Candace Barton. First is to meet her. Trust me. Follow me.'

'Sometimes your voice fades. It's hard to follow, I mean understand.'

'No you don't. You mean *follow*. They wrote me one line. One line in a printed book. I am angry, very angry. One line. 'Tis not enough. Shall make a new bridge. Me and my people shall journey; shall speak and be known. A bridge of words.'

'A bridge of words?' I closed my eyes, and thought of Maria's favourite painting: a bridge over a lake with water-lilies, by the painter Monet. The bridge was an important idea to Maria. So was the water-lily, from her years of yoga. Through her I had already seen paintings of Roarie's times, before the industrial revolution took hold. Green landscapes, rural, with people working in the fields. Rivers and streams; water-mills; barns and hayricks. Use your imagination, Wind had said. But where would it take me? Would I be better or worse off? And was I imagining all this or was it real and if so, was this some sort of time travel? I didn't believe in all that stuff. Did I?

Last winter, alone and not wanting to go out and face the world, and having no job anyway, I sat for hours watching school programmes and OU sessions on the telly. The history, geography, geology and ecology ones were my favourites. Land-use patterns, old maps, times gone by.

Often I didn't understand the technical details, but mostly I was taken right out of myself, into other worlds. I was always glad when the next programme came on, so the telly became a real friend. I'd had no schooling beyond fourteen, not to speak of, but I enjoyed learning from the telly, and there wasn't any teacher standing over me, waiting for me to make a mistake, sarcastic to me or scornful of things I didn't know.

That's where my interest in seventeenth-century maps began. My local library in Walthamstow was marvellous. The maps and books passed the time for me. But I hadn't in a million light-years expected to hear Roarie Brewster.

She answered me: 'You shall touch old trees in forest. See with hands. Feel water.' She broke off. I could hear sobbing. I was very shaken but I couldn't leave my small table and I couldn't put down my pen.

'Forgive me,' said Roarie. 'Water and Air mean Death.'

Did she mean typhoid? Plague? She couldn't mean acid rain, pollution, not in her times. She wouldn't have those words.

'Trial by Water. Many women 'swam'. Trial by Air. Women hanged. My friends at Harland Heights, servants, hear tales of Scotland. Death by Fire.'

'Witches. I read in Maria's books. Nine million.'

'Should say women, Denny. Punished for being women. Now come, meet Candace Barton . . .' The words trailed off. I looked at my fountain pen. Nothing.

Must think. Listen. Concentrate.

'I am so weary. Fading. Shall return . . . Fading. Study all your old maps.'

I dashed down to the living room for the maps. But, side-tracked, I was drawn to an alcove, the Monet print with

the bridge, and below it, a shelf of framed photos. I picked
one up. Daphne Ellis, a Black woman, her arm around
Bronwyn Griffiths, a white woman.

My two dead friends. I held them to me. Then I let out the
grief, the rage at the waste. They'd had so much going for
them. I sat and rocked, howling, holding the photo to me.

Presently, I pulled myself together. Made tea. Carried it
up to the back bedroom, where Roof waited patiently. She
had her head on the floor between her outstretched front
legs. Her tail whammed a couple of times on the carpet as I
arrived.

I leafed through some books on the seventeenth century
with pictures in, that I had from the library.

Then I spread the maps along the single bed, on top of the
quilt that Bronwyn had made. I knelt, poring over the maps.
One of them was old London around the river. I forced
myself back into the sixteen hundreds. I looked at the map
closely, thinking of a dowser I'd seen on telly, pendulum
poised over a map. Surely there wasn't anything in all that
stuff? Two hours passed. I shifted back to the table. Picked
up my pen.

It is 1666 in London in the months following the Great Fire; a
freezing night on the south bank.

Candace Barton, a Black woman in her early twenties,
strides from her lodgings, towards Long Southwark. On the
river, bonfires are alight. People mill around them on the ice.
It is so thick that the fires don't melt it, though some are half
as tall again as a person.

Two beggars hold out their hands. Candace has two
farthings. She drops one in each palm. A woman thanks her,
clutching a shivering child inside her shawl. A man on
crutches, his legs twisted and his feet splayed, also thanks
her. They both smell terrible. Candace hurries, pulling her
cloak tighter around her. A small Black child sneaks up and
tugs her cloak.

'What are you doing here, Gabriell?'

'Watching the fires.'

''Tis no place for you. Does Bess know?'

He shakes his head: 'She works late.'

'Come. 'Tis a dark night.'

She takes his hand. They step over a dead dog. Across their path fall oblongs of light from alehouse doorways. Tobacco smells mingle with rum, ale, bread and broth. Gabriell is hungry. He hurries along keeping tight hold of Candace. She is his other mother.

They pass through a low archway, down several unlit alleys. Gabriell stumbles over a snoring drunkard. Candace tugs him, to avoid slurries of vomit. In the alley there is gutter mess, and night soil. They both retch.

Finally another alley opens into a courtyard ringed with horse-boxes. There are lanterns but the light is poor. A mare whinnies from a stable door.

They enter one of the stables. Three Black men, obviously friends, are talking and laughing while grooming the horses. One is Richard Thomas, innkeeper, who loves horses and takes a turn in the stables; the second is Richard's brother Sam. The third, John Wild, now puts down his horse brushes and steps towards Candace and Gabriell.

'Up you come,' says John Wild, lifting Gabriell high on to his shoulders so they have to dip down to go out of the stable. In the adjacent horse-box he swings Gabriell up on to his dappled grey mare, Naomi, so that Gabriell sits astride bareback.

Under the cover of this activity, out of earshot of John's friends, Candace whispers: 'What news?'

'Arrival.'

'Good.'

Presently Gabriell is lifted down, laughing. Candace and John wait, talking together as Gabriell strokes Naomi's head. Old, wet stable hay smells high, acrid. By the end of winter it will be pungent. The mare nuzzles Gabriell, knows him.

Calling goodnight to the other two men, they leave John Wild with Naomi, and cross the yard.

Up a back wooden stairway they reach Bess' door. Candace stoops to go in. Inside, a wick light casts a dim glow, but a bright fire burns in a brick fireplace.

Furniture is sparse. A bed with a wooden frame bears a

lattice of tight loom cord, with a thick mattress. The pale brown linen cover is fresh, clean. Some blankets are folded, dark grey.

A table, three chairs, plain wood, dark. On the table, tankards of steaming soup, crusts of bread in a shallow basket, a jug of ale. The air is warm, free of smoke; a wooden shutter cuts down the wind. No glass, only a square hole.

From a door opposite, Gabriell's mother, Bess, arrives. The women embrace warmly, kissing. Bess gives Gabriell some soup and thick bread.

''Tis good?' she asks, as he eats hungrily. Standing beside him, she rests her hand lightly on his shoulder: ''Tis from the batch for the tavern, this morning.' From below they hear loud laughter, bawdy voices, an occasional scream.

Gabriell falls asleep quickly after his food. The women sit by the table talking. Their work is to plan the escape along the 'underground' of many fugitives, a few white, mainly Black. They have heard that the Ellisons – a Black man, his sister and her child – have arrived safely at a remote farm to the south. They will work and hide there until they have to move on. Nowhere is truly safe. They came to the docks in a pirate ship the previous month. The rest of their loved ones are dead, in shallow graves on the sugar plantations.

Bess is now nineteen. She is twelve when she comes with her mother on a slave ship from the West Indies to the great slave port of Bristol. Both Bess and her mother are pregnant by the plantation owner.

They come as illegal cargo on the ship. No English man is supposed to purchase slaves to own on English soil. Ships approach the coast of England with fear and dread, sailing in from the Atlantic. Many of the ships bound for Bristol never arrive. Strong sou'westerlies gathering force drive them off course, towards the vicious rocks of the Cornish coast. It is called the shipwreck coast. Cargoes from Africa, America, the West Indies and the Mediterranean all lie submerged. Lost goods are recorded in the ports, alongside the names of the ships and their captains. But it is not in the interest of the shipowners to record illegal cargoes. The sea hides its

14

secrets of contraband.

On the sea bed, between caskets of unrecorded jewels, ivory, rum, porcelain, wood carvings, silk, brocades, molasses and wine, there are the tangled bones of the sailors, pirates, smugglers, captains . . . and slaves. Men, women and children. For the fine houses of England have also their unrecorded humans. Children severed from their mothers, brought as pets; girls, pregnant, brought as servants; adults, brought as maids and footmen. Their bones lie meshed in rusting chains.

Bess knows this because she hears about this hidden contraband when she arrives in Bristol, aged twelve. For days after her journey in the hold, the ground sways as if she is still on board. She is purchased by a wealthy Bristol trader, friend of the shipowner, and with her mother she is sent to his huge house in the country. She understands much of the language because she has been raised on an English-speaking plantation, though with her fellow slaves she uses a different version. In the country near Bristol, she listens, giving nothing away. The accent is difficult, but she is bright, quick to learn. The new master has lost two such human cargoes already. This is his third attempt. Bess spits in the soup before it is served to him.

When Bess is thirteen her mother dies in labour. With her own child Gabriell strapped to her back, Bess rides to London. She knows horses. She has also heard that in London, on the south bank, it is possible to merge into the chaos of streets, alleys and alehouses.

Bess lives now as a free Black woman, working for the alehouse owner, Sarah Thomas, one of the roughest, loudest, strongest women on the south bank.

. . . The words trailed off. Frustrated, I stared at my pen. Nothing happened. I read and reread the words in front of me. Lines of fairly neat writing on airmail paper, in fountain pen. Candace and Bess. They were not in the Essex records with Roarie Brewster. How could they be, if they lived on the south bank? And Roarie's whole life was reduced to one line.

Tearing my hair, I took up my copy of *William Holcroft: His Booke – Local office-holding in late Stuart Essex*. It was a library book. I found the section in the introduction on Sir William Batten, commissioner for the navy after the King was restored to the throne. This man lived in some splendour in Walthamstow and 'his possessions included a Black servant called Mingo'.

For a while I let my thoughts wander from Candace and Bess to Mingo. Was Mingo male or female and how did s/he arrive in England?

How had Candace arrived and what was her story? No wonder the 'underground' needed to be so secret. Maria always talked about learning the three Rs: Resistance, Rebellion, Revolution. Her involvement in the seventies: Namibia, Angola, Mozambique. Learning to cry: 'Azania Azania Now!! Free Nelson Mandela.'

Back to the underground. Had the Ellisons survived on the remote farm in Sussex? Was there any connection between them and Daphne? Her name was Ellis, not Ellison.

I didn't know what was happening to me, but I had to find out more. 'Come on, walkies,' I called to Roof. We spent the afternoon in Epping Forest, waiting for Roarie, who didn't appear.

Back home I paced up and down, after my meal, then returned to the old maps and sat poring over them until I felt I knew every alley of London, south bank, in Roarie's time. I was very tired but decided to have one last try before bed.

'I waited. Alas you were gone to the forest.'

'What happened? You faded. Right in the middle of Bess.'

'I am your storyteller but I know not the words for the women that night. The place, I do know. The river. The ice. The cold and the fires. 'Tis the words of the two women take flight.'

'And you had no right to intrude?'

'You follow me.'

'I follow that you're white. That Candace and Bess are Black women, your friends, perhaps, and there are things they don't tell you. Things they can't share with you. Won't share with you, er, and er, it's hard to translate but it's to do

16

with respect not just about eavesdropping on private, I mean, personal stuff. Am I making sense to you?'

'Yes. 'Tis the reason I chose you. To Speak Paper.'

'I'm honoured.'

'Our lives shall be told. But the way is hard.'

'I'll do my best. If you fade, I'll wait.'

'Candace and Bess love one another. This I can tell you.'

'You mean they're lovers?'

'Did you think you and Maria invented it, Denny, in your times?' I couldn't answer. Could hear her laughter. She added: 'After their passion, they sleep in one another's arms, this night.'

I didn't say anything, ask anything. My mind ran round the world in eighty seconds. Across time and place. I saw a mother in Mozambique. A Black woman, carrying her wounded son, his arm hanging down. I saw my own son on a tanker, shells exploding in the water, throwing jets in the air high as flames; I saw Soweto, young people, unarmed, being fired upon; I saw Mothers of the Disappeared in Argentina. I saw the Falklands. I saw the people of Nicaragua, trying to rebuild their homes beside their children's graves.

I saw two women, their arms around each other, their babies on their backs, three-year-olds holding fast to their free hands. I saw my own hands.

'Now 'tis late. Time for bed. Meet me the morrow on the manor of Chingford Meade. I bid you goodnight.'

Three

Roarie is the eldest of six children who live in the weaver's cottage at the edge of the manor of Chingford Meade. It's the largest of three cruck houses near the end of a lane only just wider than a footpath. They can't drive a cart along because of the trees on either side. The path dips where it crosses the dry bed of an old stream that used to run into the River Ching. In winter the ditch fills with snow – it usually floods with muddy water when the weather improves. Then the younger children play and muck in it until they're put to work in the fields.

The whole family except Roarie has been hit by rickets. Her dad's a tiny man who can scrabble under the loom to tie the threads; her mother is bent over from a life of toil in the fields and carrying heavy bundles of firewood or cloth on her back; and her brothers and sisters are small and frail with bones that mend and break, mend and break many times over due to rickets.

Roarie steals food for the family when there isn't enough at home. She has an appetite twice that of her nearest brother, and feeds herself from raw vegetables sneaked from the strip fields, especially west field when the cabbages are planted there. It's the easiest field to reach from the fringe of trees along its west border, under cover of twilight.

Sometimes late evening when work is over and the younger children are almost asleep, Roarie follows the tree-line past the fields to Epping Forest. Her dad keeps pigs on the common land there, but piglets are reared in a pen behind the cottage, fattened for festivals or for tithes taken by the bailiffs.

She loves the forest, its secrets and its dangers. Wary of mantraps, she treads carefully. The dark deepens. The branches overhead creak and bump. Trees speak in their own way – the tangle of branches is an overhead spider's web of wood. Wind says its own words too, its own distinct sounds. Roarie hears chatter, rustle, snap and pause.

'Hide now, there's a hog a few yards away.'

'Where?'

'Climb. Quick.'

'Help me. Carry my scent away.'

'Yours to command. I'm off. Don't worry. I won't let them find out you're here. Mind out for mantraps. Stay on the paths.'

Wind changes direction. Hogs, ugly fierce beasts, lumber after Wind, charging forwards, missing Roarie's hiding place.

Up the tree, Roarie wishes she is years older, not a mere girl, noisily calling across the fields, known for her voice. She longs to be the leader of a powerful people's army, with her own company, calling them to muster like William Holcroft, one of the most famous of the King's Justices in these parts. Everyone has heard of him. He has well-known friends, like Samuel Pepys. But William Holcroft is not a man of the people. He sends petty thieves, poor folk, poachers, wandering vagrants, to the dreaded house of correction, in Barking.

She is not his people. Is not on his side. Longs to march with her own army against the landowners, such as Alistair Harland, friend of William Holcroft. Roarie dreams of setting fire to his house at Harland Heights, burning it to the ground, to stop the Harlands enclosing the forest. From her Aunt Anne, who runs the alehouse and hears all the local news, Roarie knows how 'enclosure' can be done.

Alistair Harland writes to William Holcroft – he is also verderer of the forest, for the King. Harland makes petition for permission to fence off tens of acres of Epping Forest and adjoining common land. Holcroft forwards a 'certificate' to Lord Chesterfield, who acts for the King himself. Alistair

Harland sits back, wining and dining, awaiting a reply.

No one cares about William Brewster, Roarie's father, who needs the forest to keep his pigs; nor about villagers like the Turners, the Claytons and the Wainwrights, who have held the right to firewood from the forest for generations.

Where shall our pigs be grazed? And our cows, our goats, if the forest around here is closed off? How shall we feed ourselves?

Roarie has friends at Harland Heights, servants, some Black, some white. Some can read. They know much of what's going on, and they pass the news to the village people on the manor through Roarie and the healer, Mary By-the-Well. But neither the servants nor the villagers have the power to stop the petitions nor the certificates nor the enclosures.

The Civil War is over, and the King reigns again. In the towns, in the villages, in the alehouses, inns and taverns, anyone who can write can scribble a few lines, fit them to a well-known tune, take it to a printer, trade it for a few pence. To the printers come the pedlars, buying up the ballads and ditties, selling them off fast for a penny or two.

On the manor of Chingford Meade, news arrives from far afield in ballads and broadsheets. Those who can read relay them. People learn the words; the tunes are known. Person to person, singer to pen, pen to printer, printer to pedlar, pedlar to people. When they tire of one song, they stick it to the wall and buy another. And another. Marshes, hills, woods, valleys are all being fenced off. Where shall the poor go?

'The King rides over the gentry,' says Anne Brewster. 'And they ride over us.'

'Aye. 'Tis true, sister,' replies Roarie's dad. ''Tis God's law.'

'If thou weren't runt of litter, William, I'd be picking thee up and shaking thee for thy words. 'Tis man's law, thou will o'wisp. But thou art too weak to know it. Get thee gone. Be off with thee. Go weave thy cloth. Thy words be not worth weaving.'

Later, when William Brewster is out of earshot, Anne sets

Roarie to kneading dough, all the while talking at her, not to her, about villeins and villains, the poor versus the powerful, on the manor of Chingford Meade.

Anne begins: 'The King declares, "Fence off your acres. Fell your fine oaks. The best shall be my fleet. Plough your woodlands – turf your fields – raise your flocks." ' She gestures with waving movements of her arms, but Roarie's arms are thick with dough, so she continues to knead as her aunt warms to the subject. ' "Seas of white wool shall cover my England. Enclosed or open, 'tis of no consequence to me. My rights to vert and venison shall remain." '

Anne Brewster places a plate on her head and twirls dramatically. Roarie is a good audience. Anne's ridicule of the King and her laughter are both infectious. Besides, Anne is a loud woman and enjoys centre stage. This is why she runs the alehouse, she says. Then, holding the plate as a crown, she sweeps across the kitchen in front of her favourite niece, adding in her deepest voice: ' "For I am the King. This is *my* country." '

Up the tree, freezing cold, Roarie thinks: 'Woe betide one who courses greyhounds in this forest. Is caught. The King's deer must roam free, for he himself shall hunt to kill. Aunt Anne does mock, and rightly. But a pedlar did trade with us this day, did tell of London town – of theatres, merriment, and coffee houses. The King insists on fun, much gaiety. So, come the first of May we shall dance, shall we not, round a ribboned maypole. Ne'er was dancing done amid the Puritans.'

She scrambles down from the tree, and returns to her teacher's cottage, without having raised her army, nor challenged the King.

Roarie is only eight when she is put to weed on the strips in north field, furthest from home. One day, taking a rest and eating her bread, too near the honeysuckle, she cries out, stung by a bee. Her rescuer is the healer, Mary By-the-Well, who removes the bee sting, treats the wound, and applies a tincture to ease the pain. From that time, the healer becomes Roarie's local heroine.

By the age of ten, Roarie is Mary's apprentice, though she still weeds for her father, and carries cloth to the mistress of Harland Heights and to Lady Chingford Meade of the manor.

Within a year Roarie has given up her bed on a high shelf in the arch of her father's cottage. Now she sleeps on a narrow single bed in an alcove of Mary's living room. She witnesses Mary treating the servants from Harland Heights, and from the Manor House, secretly at night. Women make well-worn tracks to and from the croft, though they risk the fury of their own mistresses if they are found out. Mary is not allowed to treat the servants in the great house, though she is the only one they trust. Instead they are compelled to have the master's friend, the doctor from Barking. They call him the Barking butcher.

In her yard and cottage garden Mary grows herbs which the village people rely on. She is the local midwife, calm in crisis, skilled and firm. To Roarie, who idolises her, Mary is quiet as the millpond on a cool grey afternoon. Her eyes are grey.

The millpond is deep, at the far west of the manor, where the mill-stream is dammed before it runs into the river. By the pond there is a paved area, with stones that catch and hold the warmth of the summer sun. There Roarie goes to watch the pond, when there isn't time for a walk in the woods but she needs to be away from her family and from Mary's cottage. Such times are the aftermath of anger; or death.

When Roarie is twelve, her mother has two stillborn babies, born together, joined at the shoulder. After the burial, Roarie sits by the millpond, watching, listening.

The sluice gate is lifted, only a minimum height. Roarie observes the water running from the millpond under the raised sluice, downstream to catch the fins of the undershot wheel. A very small flow can power such a wheel, a few feet lower than the sluice.

She hears the cogs engage, apple wood on apple wood, the whole mill grinding gear being set in motion. There is no one outside the mill. She is alone. She hugs her arms closely around her thin body. Her mother is home again. The younger children are about the cottage, and her father is back at his loom. From the stones by the millpond, Roarie can just make out the top of her father's cottage across the fields. She hugs herself and watches the water, as she rocks to and fro, not crying, no stranger to dead babies. Every year babies are born dead on the manor; or born alive only to live a few hours. That's why people have plenty of them, because they know some won't survive. Children are a gift, and when they grow they work in the fields; but they are also more mouths to feed. So the cycle turns, like the mill-wheel, birth and growth and death.

Roarie thinks: The water flows onwards, neither torrent nor deluge nor bursting in flood. More a mere measured amount, like the power of my Mary, Mary By-the-Well. She has a quiet voice and deep grey eyes, a low careful steady voice, of water's strength. Measured and forceful, turning power. Turning this manor's rules and ways round and round, when she names the Lord of the Manor – Lord Chingford Meade himself – as the father of her expected child, fathered against her will.

The night is chill, the firelight dim, as Roarie and Mary sit on the low truckle bed in the front room of Mary's cottage. Mary says: ''Twas not my wish to conceive this child. He was too heavy for me, riding upon me on his huge horse, on my way home here this April past. No. 'Twas not my want. But is my wish to let this child grow in my belly, give it life. Long and hard I prayed. Took down my herbs, to be rid of it. But changed my heart, my mind. 'Tis time I bore a child. I shall bear this one. I hope for a daughter.'

'I'm feared for you. 'Tis unmarried you be. In these parts people talk of the past. Of women "swam" and hanged. For no more than you be doing.'

'I shall speak out. My words shall be heard. The father shall be named: a curse on him.'

''Tis not your place to name Lord Chingford Meade. To stir up his wrath against you. My mother says you are a good healer, a fine midwife, all the women love you. She says let it rest, 'tis not your place.'

'My child is not the devil's baby, but the baby sired by

23

Lord Chingford Meade, against my will. My way is not to hide, but to speak. Loud and louder.'

'The drowning times. I'm feared of the drowning times.'

'All women are feared of the drowning times. 'Twas men's intent we should be feared. 'Tis their turnabout for in truth they do envy us our power to bring forth life.'

'The men will punish you. They will be angered. They will say you are the tongue of the devil – speak with his tongue. My mother told me.'

'I shall speak. Mark me. Thou wast born with a roar. Wouldst thou be quieted?'

'Never.'

'Never? 'Tis a long time. You shall not be quieted, neither shall I. Now sleep. We have much work to do. You shall help me deliver Lucy Turner of her latest child. You shall watch and learn. Time is come. I wish for you to live and work here, in my cottage, when I am gone.'

'Don't go. Don't leave me. I know not all there is to know. I need many years with you. You are my teacher.'

'We have not many years as 'twas my wish. 'Tis the fault of Lord Chingford Meade. He must be named.'

'I am not yet old enough nor yet wise to be midwife.'

''Tis true. Yet the herbs you do already know. Now sleep. Work waits on the morrow, early.'

Four

Mary By-the-Well speaks out, naming the father. The village people believe her. They all fear for her life, fear the fury and revenge of Lord Chingford Meade and the paid officials under him.

Two generations have passed since the witch hunts, but memories are clear and people have reason to be frightened. What will become of a woman who refuses to marry anyone, lives independently with her young apprentice, and now carries a child saying that it is sired by the most powerful man on the manor?

Times are changing, the manor is adapting to the restoration, gone are some of the old feudal ways. But power remains, in men like Lord Chingford Meade.

Clouds do not lift from village roof-tops for days as people wait for the trial by the manor court of Mary By-the-Well. Not Lord Chingford Meade tried for rape; but the healer for her accusation. Lady Chingford Meade has left the manor for her relations in Shropshire. But the village women do not leave. They wait.

A fine, soaking drizzle runs down the thatch, soaks the paths, puts the men gathered for the court session, men such as William Holcroft, in no mood for this brazen challenge.

The morning arrives for the trial. The largest room in the manor house has been cleared for this occasion. Mary stands in the courtroom, quietly thinking of Roarie who will have gone to the forest. Roarie is deemed too young to be allowed into the room.

Despite the rain, Roarie begins the day in the fields, hoeing her father's crops. Her mother lies at home, trying to recover from back pain. Roarie's sister Ginny looks after the other children.

Up and down the rows Roarie moves, thinking of Mary. The rain is relentless. Roarie imagines it falling on the millpond, imagines the women ducked and 'swam'. It is raining but Roarie feels Fire. The twin sisters Fire and Burn surround the field with a ring of white-hot fear. Roarie drops her hoe and runs. She runs along the known path, sprinting past west field, until she reaches a certain tree. She climbs fast, though the trunk and branches are slippery with rain and she is cold and soaked. Then on a high branch under a canopy of leaves, she crouches, praying for the soul of Mary By-the-Well, and for the souls of the men in court.

The rain stops. Mary is taken to the whipping post on the village green, in sight of the manor house. The local women watch, horrified. There hasn't been a public whipping for years. The men who tie Mary to the post are rough. She has her eyes closed. She seems to be praying but no one can hear her words.

Roarie's Aunt Anne runs forward angrily. William dashes from the crowd and with unusual strength pulls his sister back. Anyone who tries to free Mary By-the-Well will in turn be punished; that is the way on this manor.

Roarie's aunt frantically searches the small crowd of onlookers, families such as the Turners, the Wainwrights, the Claytons, the Millers and Sawyers. Anne cannot see her niece, Roarie.

Mary By-the-Well does not scream.

Some of the women are crying. A child yells: 'No, No'; is silenced by someone's hand across its mouth. The village men stare at the ground.

It is over. The body at the post is slumped and bleeding, the back of its clothes soaked with blood. The men who did this wipe their whips and stride back to the manor house and its buildings. Mary By-the-Well is to be left there. It has

26

stopped raining but it isn't yet midsummer and the nights are cold. Anyone who approaches the post will be arrested.

'In the name of God,' cries out Anne Brewster, 'who shall cut that woman down?' There is silence except for the treading of feet, turning away. To her brother, as they slowly leave the scene and walk to their homes, Anne says: ''Twas well that Roarie wasn't here. Lock her up tonight, William. She'll not be the one to leave Mary to bleed through the night.'

'I'm shamed for what I've seen, shamed for the coward I am.' He stops by the single-storey alehouse, Anne's home.

'William, we are all shamed. You are feared for your wife, for the life of your Martha.' Anne puts her hand to her throat. 'A hundred women swam and hanged not many miles from this manor. We be all cowards, this night.'

Roarie does not go home. In the dark she creeps as near to the post as she can without being seen, hiding by the corner of a barn. She has no knife to cut the bonds, nowhere to hide Mary, clean the wounds, feed her, quench her thirst. All night she keeps vigil, though the figure on the ground, whose arms are strained by the weight pulling on the ties on the post, does not move. From time to time she moans.

By dawn, Roarie is desperate and a short while later she leaves the village. She thinks that news of this event will travel fast. Can it already have reached the one person who can help? He has not been in these parts for a few weeks. Perhaps he is by the sea, or looting along the roads out into Essex. He works as far as Colchester.

Roarie travels on foot. The rain holds off, though it is very wet underfoot from yesterday's squalls. She reaches the millpond. It seems dead under grey skies. Is it an omen? Is Mary By-the-Well about to die? Before she can be taken to safety? Will she die from exposure, exhaustion, infection? Will she bleed to death? Will the baby die inside her?

Past the mill there is a coppice. Coppicing is winter work, between Michaelmas and Candlemas. Now in the early summer, the young thin growth is green, the leaves gleaming wet, not drying off as there is low cloud. After the coppice a track leads deep into the forest and Roarie follows it to a

27

copse atop a hill, with five oak trees. It happens there are five; not a magical number, just a number. One of these oaks is so tall that it can be seen for miles around.

Roarie likes to climb but has not before tried anything so reckless. Strong and lithe, her muscles trained from work in the fields, she is also angry and determined.

She climbs, hugging the tree, reaching from branch to branch, stretching up, hauling herself higher and higher. She dare not look down. But the rain does not return and although the bark is wet and scrapes her shins through her leggings, she makes headway. It is neither fun nor adventure.

As high as she dare climb, she looks over the countryside. Far away, it seems miles and miles, is the manor house and its buildings, surrounded by the fields and scatters and clusters of cottages. The people are too small to be seen from this distance. Long thin sections of forest that protect the fields from the wind meet the stream that fills the millpond, where the land slopes down to the River Ching.

In the south, is the River Lea, where a ferry is crossing, like a toy boat. Past the ferry, hidden by more forest, is London.

Roarie takes off the shawl that Mary gave her; a light, white creamy colour, new cheese. Carefully Roarie breaks off the longest, thinnest branch she can reach. It is strong, with green sap rising. She ties the shawl firmly to the end, wishing that it was winter with no leaves to get in the way. Slowly she pushes the branch as high as possible. Suddenly the wind catches the shawl, so it starts to fly like a flag. She wedges the broken end of the flag-pole against an upright part of the tree trunk, which is thin at this height. Then she crouches, takes off the belt that holds up her short skirt and, using the belt, ties the pole against the trunk. Now, so long as the shawl doesn't shred in the wind, nor work loose, and so long as the flag-pole remains firm, the signal is set.

It is done. All her energy is gone. Now fear creeps along her limbs. Fear of not succeeding; fear that the man who loves Mary might not be in the neighbourhood; fear that rain will return and make the wet flag useless; and fear of being unable to reach the ground again without falling and breaking a limb. The upward climb was easier, with a goal to aim for.

Without her belt she cannot wear her skirt, so she removes it and is left with her leggings and boots, though her leggings are torn and her shins are sore. Rolling the skirt in a tight ball, she throws it down to the ground. She thinks she could have brought some rope. She feels foolish.

The way down takes longer. At the foot of the tree she rests. She's hungry, and it's probably about midday, as the sky is bright light grey. She cannot hear sounds from the manor. The wind must be in the wrong direction. Suppose the signal does not work; or he does not see it, does not come.

She sits, waiting. If she were a highwayman like the man she's waiting for, she might be loved as he is, by Mary By-the-Well. She is too young for a woman like Mary, who sees her as just a girl, an apprentice, and Mary is a woman who will love only once in her life. How she came to be the woman for that man, Roarie doesn't know and cannot ask.

He is a fugitive, an outlaw. He must be extremely brave, thinks Roarie. He is supposed to belong to white people who brought him from the West Indies. He is Black, and in the local speech is called the blackamoor highwayman. But his name is John Wild. He takes that name for himself, saying that he will not be caught again. He is free now, the only one who can take Mary By-the-Well to safety.

If he sees the signal he will come. Roarie does not doubt him. But perhaps others might see it first and come searching. It's a risk, but there is no other chance of help that Roarie can think of, so she waits. If he comes it will be at twilight.

Waiting, she reasons to herself. Very few people come this way. The King will not be hunting – the servants at Harland Heights have mentioned that there are no plans at the house for a hunting party. This route is not used by travellers and wayfarers to and from London, but it is used by John Wild. It's one of his hiding places on the way to Cambridge.

As light fades from the forest, Roarie faces her second night in the open, and Mary By-the-Well her second night tied to the whipping post. There is no moon. It is not raining but the air is damp, though there is some wind, which is good for the flag. Roarie thinks maybe she's wrong; that it's a fool's escapade after all; that she's young and ignorant, hasn't used her brain, nor worked out a proper plan; and that John Wild hasn't seen the shawl.

Far away through the trees, the lights of Chingford Meade beckon, but Roarie hasn't memorised the route home in the dark. To stray would be to lose a leg in a trap; or be ravaged by hogs. Perhaps she should abandon the wait; and camp out all night in one of the outhouses of the mill, sheltered despite the rats. She is despairing, making ready to walk to the mill, when she hears hooves.

His horse, Naomi, is dappled grey, and whinnies as he pulls in the rein. He reaches down to help her mount behind him, saying, 'Come. You have courage, Roarie Brewster. We have work to do.'

He says that he saw the signal, and news has travelled fast through the area. His body is warm as she clings to his back, astride Naomi. Jealousy and relief compete for Roarie's soul, equal rivals. She will not see Mary for weeks, perhaps months, perhaps for ever. She doesn't know where he will take Mary, only that it will be safe. Are they already too late? Is Mary already dead? There has not been a child by John Wild, though Roarie hears them loving and laughing together in bed sometimes, as she lies alone in her thin bed.

He drops Roarie at the end of the lane leading to Mary's croft. He rides quietly to the village green.

Following him on foot, darting from shadow to shadow, Roarie watches as he dismounts and ties Naomi to a sapling. The place seems deserted. John Wild checks around him, reaching for his pistol. No one is keeping vigil. As he touches Mary, she moans. She is alive. He carries her to Naomi, places her over the saddle, and leads Naomi out of Chingford Meade, by the rein, taking the route south to London.

Roarie leans against the corner of a barn, out of sight, and lets herself cry.

Five

The new librarian at the enquiries counter, central library, was astonishingly blonde, with deeply tanned skin and dark blue eyes. Her previous job could have been holiday '87 tour guide, on package tours to Sweden. But her hair was spiky, very dykey.

Now it was a long time since I'd been able to pass as straight, or wanted to, so she recognised me too, and there we stood, dyke encounter of the unexpected kind.

So – I smiled.

So did she. 'Can I help you?'

I thought: Australia?

So – I smiled; 'Australia?'

'Aha.' She nodded, as well as smiled.

Serious smiling.

'My lover, Maria, she was from New Zealand.' I was surprised at my boldness.

'I'm from Sydney. Know it?' She had a wonderful smile.

'Not yet.'

Our laughter was interrupted by Joan, the other librarian, who looked up from her computer screen. 'Hi, Denny, how did you get along with the old maps?' Before I could reply she said: 'This is Freyja McLeod. Freyja, meet Denny Slater. You'll soon get to know each other.' She turned to Freyja, adding: 'Denny's a dog fanatic like me. We meet in the park. Excuse me, won't you, I've a mile of these to finish.' She returned to her screen and was soon oblivious to us.

Freyja looked over the counter. 'A very little dog?'

'She hates market day. I leave her at home. No, she's not little.' I handed her my card for reserved books. Then I asked: 'McLeod? You remind me of Mrs McLeod, Dr Duncan's wife. Are you any relation?'

'Yes. My gran. On Dad's side.

'I didn't mean to be nosy, but the likeness is unmistakable. Mrs McLeod is very well known around here for her charity work. She's often in the paper.'

'We haven't seen each other since I was so high. They've made me very welcome.' Her tone was relaxed; easy, without being too familiar. She had ear-rings with small double axes. The rest was body talk.

As she turned to search for my reserved books I heard myself say: 'Do you know anyone else, hereabouts?'

She returned with the books. What an attractive woman! A lovely solid dyke, taller and much broader framed than me.

'No. Not yet. I arrived last week. Gran said they needed someone urgently here at the library. So I came and stood in, and I'm applying for the temporary job that's in the paper, covering for maternity leave. Hope I get it. I have, er, unpaid leave from work, back home. Six months.' Her expression changed to hurt and loss. A broken relationship perhaps.

'I'm not often as bold as this, but why don't you come for lunch Sunday? It's not a proposition,' I blushed, she grinned, I rushed on, 'I know the area very well, could take you to Epping Forest, er, with my dog.'

'Sunday would be great. Thanks. I'd like that.' She dropped her voice, we leaned forward instinctively across the counter. She said: 'Last March my lover, Gemma, and my best friend Estelle, both died in Sydney. Gran suggested this trip to help me. I've been so numb, living in a tunnel. I wouldn't have blurted it like this . . . but . . . I'm not always good company.'

I thought of Roarie, how I'd met her suddenly and mysteriously, in the forest. Now for the second time in a very short space of time, I'd come up with another very unexpected meeting. I took a deep breath before I replied: 'Until today I haven't met anyone bereaved like me . . . Maria.' I paused. 'It's been well over a year. I wouldn't say I'm through it yet, but I am surviving.'

Her eyes were really very dark blue. Her face open, not lying. Her eyes full of deep pain and hurting at the edges.

We looked at each other gently as if to say: we like one another and yes, wouldn't a new friend be a good thing at this time?

'I'd love a walk in Epping Forest. What sort of dog *have* you got? I love dogs.'

'Big, soppy, Heinz fifty-seven, brown, sort of Walt Disney cartoon. Meaning large mongrel.'

'Crazy?'

'No, she's sane. I'm the crazy one. See you Sunday then. My address is on the card there, and the phone number. How about half-past twelve, and er, is vegetarian OK?'

'Yes, on both counts. Good. Shall look forward to that.'

'Me too. Bye Freyja; say bye to Joan for me when she's not computing.'

As I walked home, the news-stand on the corner read: Gulf – Latest. But for a little while my worry over Phil, whether he was caught up in the Iran–Iraqi conflict, receded as I thought ahead to Freyja's visit. I'd look up her name in Maria's old Goddess tomes.

For Freyja, I seemed to remember, was mother of the linen industry; the northern lights shone from her amber necklace.

Something to do with a magic cloak of bird feathers; and a very ancient name for Fire.

Later that week Graham phoned, his voice warm and kind, as if in the same room. Luckily the line was good. I asked how he was getting on.

'Fine, yeah, it's going well. There's a few old crocks like me.'

'Graham, love, you're only twenty!!'

He laughed. 'Most are straight from school. I'm old.'

'How about new friends?'

'Fine, yeah. I'm in lodgings with Tony. He's twenty-two.'

'Over the hill,' I said.

We both laughed.

'Mum, have you heard from Phil?'

'Not a whisper.'

'Thought you'd have had a letter.'

'By now, yes.'

'Nothing?'

'Not a dicky bird. I watch the telly news every day, the Gulf, and I wonder about him.'

'He must be all right. He's OK. You'd hear if not.'

'So I tell myself. I have to or go barmy.'

'To think I used to look up to him. Told Tony about him. And about you. That wasn't hard – Tony's gay.'

'Has he got family?'

'Yes and no. His parents don't like gays. I met his older brother, a plumber. He's OK. He was in the pub. Liked him but his wife's called Wendy!!'

'Get away.'

'Life's full of jokes. You OK? Did they find your file?'

'I'm fine,' I lied. 'Yes they did. Don't worry, I'm a tough nut to crack.'

'Shall I come and beat them up?'

'You and whose army? You can organise a sit in, if they lose it again.'

'Leave it to me.'

'I will. Any wild parties to go to?'

'Mum, I'm just a boring bank clerk.'

'Not any more. Have some fun.'

'You're not s'posed to say that.'

'I never say what I'm s'posed to. I don't do what I'm s'posed to, either,' I said. We laughed. I added: 'Life's now, not years hence.' . . . Better believe it, Denny.

'Got to go, no more tens. Love you lots, Mum.'

'You too. Bye, love.'

Afterwards I sat with the photos, my twins, chalk and cheese. Gray younger by five minutes but it might have been five years. Phil was taller, faster, streetwise. Gray, in his own words, trailed behind like Minnie Mouse. Until now.

My own brothers were so much older than me, there'd been no catching up to do. Hadn't been part of it. One had gone to Cleethorpes, working as a car rep: housing was cheap there. The other was in Dover, in admin for hover-crafts. Both were married with grown-up children. We sent cards at Christmas: could hardly call us close knit. I don't believe in Christmas anyway, but they wouldn't know what to do with a Solstice card.

Ahead of me was Freyja's visit. A new friendship. Beginnings. The first day of my future starts a minute from now. I slept well, not a rattle at my window. A calm night.

Mine is a long road. I imagined Freyja walking along counting the house numbers as I did when I came knocking in search of new lodgings. It was raining then, as well. I sheltered under a crab apple tree which spread its branches over the pavement. Rain rolled down the fat oval fruits. Female. Sexy. The droplets hung, catching the light. Beatrice looked after the boys that day. Hundred years ago.

By the time Freyja knocked on my door, setting Roof to a welcoming frenzy, she was covered in a layer of fine round prisms. We greeted each other, commiserating about the weather as our walk would have to be postponed. After lunch I dashed out the back for kindling and coal. We stayed indoors by a real fire.

She asked few questions about Maria. Perhaps she sensed that I didn't want to talk about how she died. Instead we began with our teenage years, as if to tiptoe around the graves, not land at once with huge footprints heavy on newly turned soil. This was a link, a sensitive start, a kindness, unlike some of my friends who'd stamped on the grave like a horde of reporters, destroying dignity, plundering privacy. Needless to say, I didn't count them as friends afterwards.

I don't know if Gemma was near to Freyja as we began, but Maria was close to me.

I also felt Roarie watching.

I thought: she is inside the mill, right at the top, astride a pile of empty sacks, near the pulleys. It's cold. Rain beats against the stone walls of the mill. The machinery is silent, unused today. Floorboards creak. Roarie shivers, and mice scrabble about, though the lid on the wooden hopper below is closed. One or two rats are scurrying.

In front of the living-room fire, I juggled with memories, real and painful. What would we find out about one another, Freyja and me? The crackling fire took on a sinister phantom life. In the sharp white flames I saw rats' teeth. In the coal. Burning bites being chiselled there.

Freyja said: 'You seem young to have two grown sons, Denny. Were you still at school?'

Her question seared my past. I handed her the packet of biscuits: 'It's a sordid little story.'

She waited. We crunched noisily, scattering biscuit crumbs around us. I was on the two-seater settee, she opposite me in the old armchair. She seemed to find the fire a comfort, as I usually did. But not today.

'I was in a gang. About eight or nine of us, all girls. Tearaways. We truanted half the time. We were from the same form in the secondary mod; all lived within three or four streets of one another. Yuppies live there now. I couldn't even rent a room there. East End kids we were.

'Anyway, we started these dares. I wouldn't have anything to do with the first one. The others had got into witchcraft. Goings-on in the cemetary after dark, pinching people's cats and the silver candlesticks from the church, things like that. I love animals you see . . .' I looked around the room for Roof, saw her sneaking out the door as if the vibes in the place didn't suit her.

'Come here Roof. It's OK. Come on.' She settled on the hearthrug, but kept a wary eye on me; very remarkable behaviour. I felt uneasy, but at least I wasn't talking about Maria's death, so that helped me.

Freyja was waiting patiently. I decided I really liked her, so I carried on: 'Two cats died and I was incredibly upset. I didn't want to leave the gang because we'd been together a long time, but I was very angry. Then two of them got nobbled by the churchwarden, ended up in juvenile court, got thrown out of school. Quite an achievement to get expelled from my school, I can tell you. They called it a sink school. Right?'

Freyja nodded. She passed the biscuits back. I shared one

with Roof.

'Shall I go on? Do you really want to know the rest?'

'Sure do. What happened next?'

'Well the rule we'd made was you had to take part in two out of three dares or forfeit your place in the gang. The second dare was easy. We started doing the old phone boxes. They weren't like they are now. They changed them on account of girls like us. We were proud of that later. I made a bit of money, paid Mum's rent a few times. Told her I'd got a paper round; it was easy. Loved it. The adventure, the risk. Didn't get caught.

'Then the third dare landed me with the twins. There was this guy at one of the garages. A dish. A real catch. We all had to chat him up and I pulled him. Luckily I only got the twins.'

'My God, my childhood was so ordinary in comparison. So how old were you?'

'Just fourteen when I pulled him at the end of May. Still fourteen when I had them at the end of the following March. Then it was all social workers and housemasters and head-masters and more social workers and home tuition and gawd knows what else. I wouldn't have them adopted, and I'm the baby of my family so my parents said they'd stand by me. My brothers always said I was spoiled. Though they also wanted me to keep the twins. Mum and Dad put up such a fight I can tell you. It's probably why Mum's so bitter now. She loves the lads, loves me, but hates lesbians and gay men.'

'But you weren't a lesbian as a teenager or you wouldn't have done the dare?'

'Right. I wasn't anything as a teenager until I suddenly became a mother at fourteen. Then I lived with Mum and Dad – till I was twenty-one. The twins were just six. Mum had had enough and I had had enough. It was really bedlam. Mum ended up wanting me to live in a nice glass dome near the telly, on the unit, like the sort they keep dried flowers in. Then she could say, "That's my daughter and those are my grandsons, isn't it amazing how different they are," and no mess, no bother.

'She was tired, worn out, I knew that, but you can't hear

properly, living in a glass dome. So we shouted. So she sellotaped the dome to the unit, with me and the boys inside it. Then we couldn't breath *or* hear, so we left.

'One of the gang was still around. Molly her name was. She was married, quite respectable. Her husband was a cabbie, you know, the black London taxis? Good money in those days. They were renting out rooms at the top of an old house they'd bought. It wasn't far from the printers and stationers on Forest Road where I found work later. Anyway I thought I'd give it a whirl, at Molly's place, because by then I was quite desperate to move away from home, with the twins.

'Molly's neighbour did childminding and so when the job came along on Forest Road I took it, and it worked out very well. That's how I met Beatrice, who became my best friend. Through her I met Maria, as they were both from New Zealand, and were already friends. But that was a while later. Meantime the boys were at school, and I had a roof over my head and a job.'

'They were six and you were twenty-one, that's a long time ago. How come the lesbian life? Through Maria?'

'Good question. You wait till I ask you all these things.' We both laughed. A natural break, like when the ads come on telly and you nip out for a pee, and to put the kettle on, which we did.

While Freyja was using the bathroom, which was off the back of the kitchen, I watched the rain run down the kitchen window. Looking back it did seem a dramatic series of events for such an ordinary bod as me.

We carried the tea things back into the living-room and, settling again by the fire, Freyja said: 'This is a lovely cosy house. I'd love a place like this.'

'Are you renting, back home?'

'Yes. A first-floor unit in a block. No garden but there's a communal area and I'm happy there.' She paused. 'I had some savings so I paid the rent in advance while I'm here; and I've a friend staying there while I'm away so that helps.'

'I'd like to stay here,' I said, 'but I'll have to move on before long. Never dreamed I'd be leaving. It'll be a wrench.'

38

'I'd assumed it was yours now.'

'Maria didn't make a will. We never gave a thought to death, too busy living. When she died, her daughter Cheryl inherited the house.'

'Ye Gods. Oh, I am sorry.'

'Maria was eight years older than me. When she died she was forty-two. Cheryl was twenty-two.'

'But you could have contested it.' Freyja's tone was indignant.

I leaned back; shoved my hands in my pockets; imagining Graham and Phil when tiny: I'd kiss their palms, fold their fingers around the kiss, whisper "don't lose it". Now, fold my own fingers around the memory of Maria's kiss? Safe in my hands where no one can see?

'Cheryl and I always got along well. I'd say we were good friends. She left home at eighteen to work in an insurance company in the city and share a flat with two friends. They're all straight, nice lot, I've met them. She has her life all organised. Her mother's death hit her very hard too. And neither of us has Maria to talk to, ask her what her wishes would be.'

'But Cheryl is young,' protested Freyja. 'She presumably earns good money, set to be a 1990s yuppie in a job like that. And she'd get mortgage relief on another house or flat. Low percentages they offer in those companies, don't they?'

'I know.' I swallowed hard. 'But I could never go to a solicitor against Maria's own daughter. I just couldn't. It isn't on . . . never was. I told Cheryl that from the beginning. She's been kindness itself to me – we love one another. She wants me to stay on here as long as I want to. She's as embarrassed as hell about it all.'

'She can afford to be.' Freyja snorted as if she had known me a long time and she was in my 'gang'. It was well over the top and I thought: so that's how it looks to outsiders, is it? Damn. Hurt and angry I said aloud: 'If you met Cheryl, and p'raps you will, she comes to dinner sometimes, you'd be a bit more sympathetic. OK she likes the big money, career, het company, everything I'm not into, but she's warm and loving too, surely the photos over there show that?'

Flinching at my tone, Freyja looked across to the unit with the maps on. Maria trying to tread warily, barefoot in the forest, had tripped, landing in a multitude of migrating frogs; Maria sprawling, squealing and laughing; Roof going mad barking; hundreds of frogs each no more than an inch long, hopping, determined to get to where they were going; and there was Cheryl catching her mother's eyes, laughing, the other side of 'frog crossing'.

'Besides,' I said, still very angry, and looking slyly at Freyja: 'How would you feel if I had inherited this house, then willed it to my sons, and Cheryl, the young woman of the case, daughter of the houseowner, got nothing?'

She put her head back, needing to laugh, not doing so, her hands fiddling nervously with the piping on the edge of the old armchair. 'One of ideology's little contradictions?'

'Well, that's it with my little contradictions for the moment. Where do you want to start with yours?'

'Touché.'

After a few seconds she said: 'With Mum and Dad, I think. And the fact that I was born in Sydney, but it should have been in London.'

'How come?'

'Mum's English. Dad's a Scot.'

She caught my glance, saw that I was still hurting from her attack on Cheryl and hesitated before changing tack.

'I hurt you over Cheryl.' A statement not a question.

I looked away, withdrawing. Prayed, please don't let this go wrong.

'I'm sorry,' she said. 'I've been stumbling over people for months. I hurt others all the time.'

I'd have attacked if I'd spoken so I kept quiet.

'I'm very raw,' she said. 'I expect you are too. I don't mean to hurt you.'

'I don't want to hurt you either. But . . .' I stopped. Did I have the grit to be really honest? 'If I take risks then get hurt, I attack. That's how it's been since Maria died. I want to get over that. I want to make a real friendship. But I'm afraid.'

'So am I. So do I . . . want to be friends. Make a real friendship I mean. You're my first friend over here. Apart

40

from Gran, and that's different. Do you want to talk about Maria?'

Just then the window rattled. Freyja looked around, then bent forward to tend to the fire. But I heard Wind's voice:
'Don't talk, listen,' said Wind.

'Not today. I'm not ready. But if you want to talk about Gemma I'd like to hear about her. And all your family.' I thought: I don't want to trample around on your family, in my boots. I should tread warily, barefoot. I added: 'I'd really like to hear about them – they've travelled around a bit, haven't they? I reckon you've a long story there.'

'Yes. It's all fresh in my mind because Gran and I were up late going over it all last night.'

Six

I settled back, patting the cushions beside me for Roof, rubbing her ears as I listened to Freyja.

'Mum comes from a big London family, the Abbotts. She met Dad while he was stationed in London during the war. Her family liked him from the start. They married, then Dad was abroad for most of the time. Mum drove an ambulance.

'After the war they kept trying for a child, but no luck. Then the Abbotts, including Mum and Dad, emigrated to Australia, later joined by Sadie and Sam, my aunty and uncle, who had seven children. Their eldest was fostered in Yorkshire and didn't go with them. Their next to youngest was a girl, my cousin Estelle, five years older than me. I was born in Sydney, 1957.

'So although Dad's a McLeod, the relations I knew as a child were all on Mum's side, the Abbotts. Estelle is technically my second cousin, but I thought of her as my cousin. We were very compatible, despite the age gap. All my teenage years I looked up to her, loved her. She was my best friend.

'By the time I was twenty-five, Estelle was divorced, a single parent with a little girl called Nonie. I'm Nonie's godmother. Anyway, Estelle was very short of money, so she took in a lodger. She brought her to my twenty-fifth party saying, "Freyja, meet Gemma. I've a feeling you two'll get on like a house on fire." I remember those exact words. Gemma stayed at Estelle's. I had my wonderful rented flat. It's across Sydney Harbour Bridge from the family, a bit of a blessing at times. I love them dearly but they all live too near one another to suit me.

'The Abbotts run a scrap metal yard, which they own and built up from nothing. Estelle was the admin and accounts person. If she needed extra help, Gem would give her a hand. Gem worked for a company of accountants. She was almost through her exams, only one or two to go. They trail on for years. She was a whizz with numbers.

'In the early days, my aunty did a stint in the office at the yard. She learned bookkeeping and accounts at night school. I loved her, much more than my own mother.

'I didn't know so much about the McLeods as a child, but I caught snippets of family gossip from time to time. We had photos of my Grandmother McLeod – like me in a magic mirror being turned into someone older. *She* fascinated me.

'She was born into a wealthy family in Norway. There was money on her mother's side. When she was ten – that was in 1920 – her parents came into a lot more money. They decided to travel from Norway, with the four children, to Orkney to see if they could trace some of their family tree.

'They stayed on Orkney a few months, I think, then made their way down the west coast of Scotland.' Freyja paused. 'Have you got an atlas, Denny? I'll show you.'

'Maps, Freyja!' I found the page. 'I'm in my element!'

'They settled here, opposite Lewis,' she said, pointing, 'and bought a house. Freyja – that's Gran – was about eleven, the youngest. Later, she met a local lad called Robert McLeod. She married him while still very young.

'The McLeods were highlanders who were cleared off their land in terrible times in the 1880s. Enclosures. The large landowners forced the crofters out, took over, put the hills to sheep grazing. They burned the crofts, razed many of them to the ground. The people fled. Some to America, some on from there later to Australia, when it was first being colonised.

'It horrified me as a child, when I first heard it. If they were too old or sick to get out, they were burned in the crofts.'

I said, 'The enclosures started earlier, in many places.'

'Did they? So violent. My father grew up knowing the history. Then, when he emigrated after the Second World War – in very different circumstances obviously – he said he had a sense of retracing the old migration routes.'

'Migration doesn't stop, does it? Routes south, routes north.'

'The Highlands. Orkney. Norway. I used to dream the routes. I'd love to follow them. I'm saving like crazy to make it happen.'

'You will. You have to dream first.'

'But I'm a very ordinary person,' said Freyja. 'Earning a living, going from day to day. In origin the Abbotts were all working class, and I have my aunty in mind, to keep my feet on the ground.'

'Ordinary people can dream. I do.'

'What do you dream, Denny?'

'It'd take a TV mini-series.' I chuckled then zipped my mouth shut, stroking Roof who was by now asleep, snoring, with her head on my thigh. Freyja laughed, and I thought: I bet you've some well-kept secret dreams. Wind on the heather, free and wild. Echoes. A boat from Orkney to Oban. 'Tell me about your gran. Where does her husband, Duncan the doctor, fit in?'

'There were hints of intrigue, whispers behind closed doors when I was little. Freyja McLeod, my gran, was linked to me, somehow. A sense of fate? Destiny? But, unlike Gran, as *I* grew up my longings were for other girls, not boys. Only Estelle knew about that, and she knew from the very beginning.

'Gran had a passion for a young man, her husband's cousin – a young medical student, Duncan McLeod. They began an affair, not at all hidden, and Robert, it was said, died of a broken heart. A decent amount of time later, Gran married Duncan.

'They left Scotland, came to London where Duncan's medical career took off. So they settled here.'

'She's known for her lefty views locally,' I said. 'Works hard for CND and cancer charities too. That's how come I'd seen her in the paper, saw the resemblance as well as the name.'

44

'Right. I mean left. Gran is just what I want. Whereas my mother became conventional, conservative, self-made and status seeking. Mum doesn't like me much. Not if she's honest. And I have to work hard to like her. Painful, but true.'

'What about your dad?'

'Loved him; liked him. No effort. He hated political arguments, such as my mum versus my aunty on class and voting – Dad wouldn't get drawn in. Used to make Mum mad.'

'Like my dad. Wants a quiet life.'

'What's he do, your dad, by the way?'

'Same job, different names. Dustman, Corporation Operative, Council Refuse Collector. Mum works in a café, been there years.'

'You were close to them, before the twins came?'

'And afterwards. They were very good to me. It's been a heartbreak. They don't like queers, as Dad calls us. How did your dad manage to stay out of the family firing line?'

'Tobacco. We're a non-smoking family.' Freyja smirked. 'At the first sign of debate, he'd fly to the garden and light up.'

'Smokescreen?'

'Mum called him the Flying Scotsman.'

We laughed, then she said: 'I'll introduce you to Gran soon, but she's very busy. I have to have a visiting card.'

'There's no rush.'

'No, there isn't. I love London, and Grandmother. I don't want to go back, except for Nonie and she's being very well cared for. Too soon for a long-term decision.'

Freyja watched the fire, thinking of home. I waited, not wanting to push the story in this or that direction.

Freyja began: 'The day that changed it all was my thirtieth birthday, 17 April, last spring.

'I could have taken the day off, annual leave, but Estelle and Gem had to work late – the auditors were due the following week. It was a race against time to do the accounts.

'I opted for the afternoon and evening shifts at the library. I drove there, humming to the car radio. Really happy. Friday: Freyja's day.

'I arrived in plenty of time for work. The others greeted me with flowers and cards. Thirty's a big one. Then at six, Gem called in. We'd planned everything. Her car was being serviced. She'd take my car, drive to the yard, help Estelle, bring Estelle back, pick me up. Off we'd go, the three of us, to wine and dine. My aunty had Nonie for the night, table was booked, all was fine.

'Gem bought me chocs to share around, which I did. Then the others left and there was just me and Gem for a few moments.

'We went down to the counter. She said, "I must dash, trust the bloody auditors to pick next week. What a rush. Best be off, back for you about eight. Glad it's Friday, what a week. OK then darling? See you soon."

'It seemed a perfect day. There was only one reader in the reference room, a very old man, a widower called Mr Simon. He more or less lived in the library.

'During the first hour people popped in on the way home from work, but Fridays were never very busy. People like to get home, start the weekend. I worked steadily, and when I'd finished checking the reserved books, I changed to computer work. Later, I switched it off, and time dragged, so I had a chance to think about being thirty, what it meant.

'That made me reflect about not getting on well with Mum, and what I might be able to do about it. There was still some tension about me being "out", even after all those years. I hoped the family party over the weekend would be a success.

'Then I thought about having left home, gone to university, about my work and my flat. Gem, Estelle and I were talking about buying a large house together. That way we'd all be able to live as we wanted: Gem and I could share; there'd be a room for Nonie; and Estelle wouldn't be left out.

'I always did like Friday evenings at work, because I had a bit of thinking time. There weren't interruptions, so I'd get through the computer chores faster. I'd even thought of doing a bit of writing, though that was maybe a fantasy.

'I glanced at the clock as Mr Simon left: seven forty-eight.

I began to tidy the desk for the Saturday staff, then I thought I'd phone Gem and Estelle. I reached for the phone.

'My brain told me I was silly. They'd be busy. I'd only slow them down by phoning.

'Suddenly, I went cold. The library was empty. I noticed that Mr Simon had left the door open. So I closed it. But I didn't warm up. I was cold inside.

'I was uneasy. Couldn't explain why. I reached for the handset. As I touched it, it rang. Gem's voice: "Darling, it's me."

'She sounded strange. I said: "What's the matter?" She didn't know. Some guy had been across from the road works. Advised them to go the long way round. Gem said: "We'll be a bit late."

'I was tense. Began to shiver. My voice wobbled. I said, "Gem, what else d'you know?" She said: "Nothing much. Estelle thinks she can smell gas, but I can't. Not at all. She imagines things. You know what she's like."

'I replied: "Gem, be careful. I don't like it."

'She said: "Nothing to worry about. See you soon." Then behind Gem, I heard Estelle scream. I shouted: "Gem? Gem? What is it?" She said: "Oh my God, Freyja, it's the yard. The yard's gone up. Freyja, I love you, Freyja."

'I was left yelling into an empty receiver: "I love you too. I love you too." I don't know if she heard me. I could hear both of them screaming. I knew exactly what was happening.'

Tears were streaming down Freyja's face. I felt I shouldn't move, should stay as quiet as I could, though I wanted to dash across to her, put my arms round her. Somehow I felt that wasn't what she needed; that she wanted to talk until it was all said; that it was part of healing, to tell the story. She'd said she wanted to talk. It now seemed a desperate want, a deep need.

I drew my arms into my sides, my feet together. My arms comforted my body, my legs and thighs touched each other. I made my edges leakproof: concentrated on not letting my pain leak out on to Freyja.

47

Freyja said, 'I put the phone down. I could see the office portacabin, the blazing yard, the two of them. I was certain. Don't ask me how.

'I picked up the phone, redialled. Fire, Ambulance, Police. Then Gem's mother, then Estelle's mum – my aunty.

'I was a robot. So distant, so calm. I told it over and over like a tape loop. Round and round. It wasn't me talking, just a machine inside me.

'Same at the funerals and memorial service. There was a lot to do. I went through all the actions, magnificent they all said. They said I was magnificent. That's a strange word.

'Then it was all over. Then I couldn't speak at all. I'd open my mouth and no words would come out. I couldn't touch a telephone. People were kind. But my voice had completely gone. Left with images. Pictures in my head. Flames everywhere, day and night. Dreams so vivid I'd wake trembling. But not screaming. I still had no voice.

'Every night I'd dream. Obvious things. Telephones and roadworks. And fires. Fires of all kinds. My name means fire, did you know?'

'Yes, I looked it up. It's like the Irish Brigit. Multiple goddess, part of her is Fire. I'd say that the Northern Lights shining from an amber necklace is Fire as well.'

'Not many people know that. It's more likely they'll think of Scandinavia as snow queens and spinning myths. I thought I'd go mad with the fires. Madness is there in all of us I think. Reality shifts this way or that, shifts too far, too fast, the world spins past and we can't catch hold any more and we can't jump off.

'Life hasn't slowed yet since the fire. I wrote to Gran McLeod about Gemma, our relationship, the fire. Had a long letter back. I'll keep it for ever, her reply. She sent me the return air fair, an open ticket they give you. She said she wasn't in any position to judge me, my life, not anyone else's. She said why not ask for compassionate leave. Surely they'd understand.

'As it happened, they didn't. Unpaid leave or resign. I don't know quite what I'd have done if I hadn't been able to come here to Gran.

'My aunty was almost off her rocker. All the grief she had pushed down when her mother died, and before than when she had to leave her eldest daughter with her mother when they emigrated, it was all there again, unresolved.

'Gem's parents couldn't help me. We tried to be kind to one another. But we couldn't. Too much grief and loss.

'Nonie was bed-wetting. Sleeping with the light on. Waking up screaming. She went to live with Ronnie, Estelle's closest brother. He's married and his daughter's not far from Nonie's age. I heard from Mum last week that Nonie's pulling through now.

'I'm a survivor, that much I do know. All the clichés: life goes on; life at the end of the tunnel; never too late to begin again. I've sublet the flat to a friend who's broken with her lover, needed somewhere urgently, suits us both. I don't know if I shall ever want to go back there. Memories.'

'I can understand that.' I spoke softly, in reply to Freyja's unspoken question as she looked across at me. 'I'll give this house a little while longer,' I said. 'Then I'll look for somewhere else. Need a job and a place to live. Haven't been ready for the upheaval, not till now. I admire you coming all this way. Are your Gran and Duncan easy to get to know?'

'Yes. They are the only ones, other than my aunty, who value my love for Gemma, the kind of value I need. I'm not in a position to demand it. You can demand it of strangers, governments and charters, but in your family, demand's not the right word.'

'No. It's not. I tried demanding it of Mum and Dad, over Maria. They just closed me out. Being "out" isn't the same as being closed out, is it?'

Seven

That night, after Freyja had gone, I slept badly.

Fire. People ran in every direction trying to escape. Screaming and choking on the smoke, we were jostling each other in our attempts to escape the fires. Hundreds of people, all refugees, landless, running. Eyes watering from the smoke, covering our noses with any cloth we had, we ran. My own cries filled my head, my mind, my ears, my mouth: 'Nowhere to run to; nowhere to run.'

I woke.

Roof nuzzled me, trying to calm me down. I was trembling, got up, put on all the lights upstairs, went down, made tea, put on all the lights downstairs. If there'd been a bonfire in someone's garden before I fell asleep, with the smoke wafting indoors, the dream couldn't have seemed more real. The smell of the trees blazing, the feel of the intense heat, were so vivid that I felt I'd been there.

I took the tea back to bed, leaving every light full on in the house. I slept, like Nonie, with the bedside light on. Each time I woke, it comforted me.

Night after night the dreams came.

Several nights later, I dreamed a variation of a dream that I'd had since Maria died.

In the dream, I'd find Maria face down on a stony beach, and I never saw her face, though I'd dreamed it many times before. Now, a new feature was added. Behind Maria the hills rose to a range of volcanoes. They rumbled, threatening and enormous. I couldn't see fire. Confusion was everywhere. I could hear a newscaster on telly saying: 'Rain is imminent, rain is immiment. Correction: fire is imminent.' The beach was in New Zealand, called by its Maori name, Aotearoa.

I always woke shaking from that dream, but it hadn't had fire in it before.

I couldn't phone Freyja, because she'd gone to York with her grandmother, to see the Jorvik exhibition, which had been booked even before we'd met. Her time off tallied with a long weekend, and she felt she owed her grandmother the time and company.

I wanted Freyja for a friend, but she'd brought more fire into my life, and I longed for relief, some balance. I wanted to Speak Paper to Roarie, but she didn't come near me.

The dreams continued. I could hear and see the sounds and pictures. Nothing fabulously beautiful about the fires. The flames weren't joyful reds and yellows; the people weren't merrily playing bonfires, with laughing children and happy families.

But I couldn't lie awake, either. I was very physically tired when I went to bed, as if grief itself was exhausting.

Just before I slept, I tried to shut out the fires. To cover them over with pretty stretches of bluebell woods in spring; chocolate-box happiness with thatched roofs and flowers. But it didn't work. I could hear screams from under the thatch, and thatch is a fire hazard too.

I did not dare tell anyone about the fires.

I went about my daily life as if I was quite normal. I signed on; did the shopping; went to the launderette. My washing machine was dead and I couldn't pay to get it resurrected. I took Roof for short walks, not going near the forest or the canal. I cleared some fallen leaves from the garden, and dug up the last of the potatoes. I fed Wren, who lived in the philadelphus at the end of the garden; and I watched television; and went madder and madder and madder.

I didn't know where I was in time or place. It felt like madness. I told myself that people who don't know the difference between real fires and imagined fires are mad. So I must be mad.

I began to dread something. I didn't know what, but I called it 'Them'.

I would burn with the fear that They would come and get me. I feared sleeping, and waking. It was last winter all over again. But worse, because this winter was filled with fire, in a way that last winter wasn't. Last winter was empty. I had slept a lot; cried a lot. I'd wanted to toughen up and I'd thought I'd succeeded.

Instead I'd given in to fire, phantoms, and nightmares. Now They would come and get me. Take me away like poor Connie in *Woman on the Edge of Time*; set my brain on fire with electrodes like Istina in *Faces in the Water*. They would separate me and Roof: we'd die in different pens in strange places, of broken hearts.

I didn't know who They might be.

One night I sat in the living-room, listening to a tape of Maria Tolly. She was one of my Maria's favourites. Having a woman with the same name singing in the room was like having Maria back.

The central heating was on, and the house was warm. No fire in the grate. I couldn't bear the sight of it. I sat in Freyja's armchair – not on the settee. It was too big, the gap beside me too obvious.

I was waiting. Waiting for Them. Now I had finally and completely gone mad and it would all be over soon. I wanted Them to come. They could take me away, fill me full of drugs, take me to the mountain in *Scented Gardens for the Blind*.

There I'd be all right. All my needs would be met. Food, toilet, being dressed.

I knew I was mad, because I thought the singer was my Maria. That proved to me I was mad. I needn't do anything else about anything. No more responsibility. No twins to raise; no lover to cope with; no friends to remember birthdays for. Friends were gone, all gone, cremated.

So I waited.

What a relief it would be. I wished They would hurry up. They would dull my senses. I could tell Them I didn't want fire dreams. They'd take it all away. I'd not have to face another day waking up for a nothing time without Maria. No more Roarie Brewster who had led me a silly dance and now left me in this state and was gone. Who did she think she was anyway? How dare she tease me like that?

I hadn't imagined her. I hadn't. She was real. She was there in the forest even if Roof hadn't noticed. She talked to me on paper. Powerful Paper Talk. So I must have learned to time travel like poor Connie without realising. Well, They understood about things like that. So I waited for Them.

The tape clicked off. I didn't move from the chair. Roof was on the rug by the radiator. She knew every hot spot in the house. Sometimes she'd lie on the floor where a hot water pipe ran along underneath. My mind zoomed around. It wouldn't stop in any particular time. I lived inside time, in the sheet of red and yellow flame.

'Denny, it's me, Beatrice,' came a quiet whisper.

'I'm missing you, Beatrice. I need someone to talk to.'

'I haven't forgotten you. How's Cheryl? Can't you talk to her?'

'She's fine, thanks for asking. She visits each week, but no, I can't talk to her, not like I talk to you. It's different. You're my best friend.'

'I meant it when I invited you here. You'd love this country. We could spent time together.'

'Time yes, but not money. My savings drop faster than water under a mill-wheel.'

I couldn't hear Beatrice's reply. I closed my eyes and saw moonlight illuminating the clear blue-black open sea, and people navigating using only the stars and patterns on the waves. A sense of vastness and eternity. The night sky a star map for the people below in canoes. The moon moved steadily across and behind the stars like a hand on a celestial clock, time in minutes not important, time and space wider and higher than I'd ever imagined they could be.

Waves were the depth of a canoe, the height of a person as far as the edge of the world in every direction. Beatrice's voice had seemed as near as when we worked in the stationers' shop. Now it had faded as far away as the horizon. The canoes moved on, following known routes, a hundred, two, three, four, five hundred miles, trading and exchanging gifts and ideas and words.

Beatrice's voice lay along the edge of the first prow as it moved up and down across the waves. I had to concentrate hard to bring it back. The height and depth of the waves changed all the time so that sometimes Beatrice's voice dipped down into a trough. I had to wait until the prow rose again, skimming across the lips of the sea, for the voice to come across uninterrupted.

Beside me the phone rang. I picked it up.

'Are you there, Denny?'

'Yes, but it's hard to hear you. It comes and goes.'

'Is Philip still in the Gulf?'

'Yes, I think so, but he hasn't written. Gray and I are worried. How did you know?'

'It's a small world. I met a woman from London over to see her relations. She knew Maria, the Women's Centre. She heard one of your sons was working on a tanker.'

'I contacted the Seamen's Union. At first I wouldn't ring them. Phil can't bear interference. He'd see that as invasion, you know, of his privacy. But I had to phone them. It's too urgent. They said he wasn't even a member.'

'I think of you often, Denny. You've friends on this side of the world, beaming in on you. Hang in there. This time will pass.'

'They say it's going to escalate in the Middle East. Iraq is stepping up the attacks.'

'Try not to lose hope, Denny. The UN's working for a cease-fire. Try to stay optimistic.'

'I'm trying. But you're a mother and it's hard. Beattie, I'm scared.'

No reply. Beatrice's voice had faded.

I tapped the receiver, shook it, blew into it. Her voice returned.

'Then it becomes clearer what people in war zones have gone through,' she was saying, 'waiting on some man's action, some man's decision. Sometimes I want to let them

54

all blow each other up and be done with it. Then I'm ashamed. What sort of a way to opt out is that?'

'Enough about Phil. How're your two?'

'Busy lives, complicated lives, but they're fine.'

'And your mother?'

'She's pulling through. She's lost all her hair with the therapy, but they think she's clear and the next month or so will tell us. I've learned a lot from her, Denny. Her will to live is amazing, even though the hospital said they didn't know if she'd be strong enough to stand the pain. We're all so proud of her.'

'Beattie that's wonderful!! They really think they can cure her? It's the best news in a long time. It's *wonderful*.'

'It is, isn't it. I miss you Denny, but I'm glad I'm here. I tell myself that every day.'

'How's Bill?'

'Up to his neck in politics. All the claims on the Waitangi Treaty, it's a mess. And with Bill's sister-in-law being Maori, her family are very involved. They're fishing people, deep-sea fishing rights.'

'I'm dreaming again about your country. The stone beach dreams again, but different. I was reading Maria's books: Maori goddesses – Mahuea, Rona. The beach dream's got volcanoes. I'm afraid to sleep. I was walking near the volcanoes. It was terrifying but I came through.'

'You wouldn't remember them in the mornings if you weren't strong enough to face them. They're healing dreams, Denny. Let them happen. Can you go and talk to someone?'

'You mean someone "professional". Yuk. Besides I can't afford it. Even with sliding scales, money's money. Have to go through it on my own. I'll write to you. This call's three guineas an ounce.'

'Yes, must go. But you're worth it Denny, every penny, every pound. I knew you needed me. I thought you'd been having bad nights. I heard you. We've always done this.'

'Not across the time zone.'

'We have now. Mind how you go.'

'And you, Beattie. Hug your mother for me.'

I sat, hand on the phone, receiver back in place. I couldn't remember when it had rung, when I'd answered it. I was thinking of her, hearing her voice, then talking with her. I couldn't tell how much was real, how much imagined.

I felt a creeping sensation along my legs, up through my body, up my arms, into my shoulders and chest. Heat, rising. Gluey heat, as if I was a glass jar of boiling jam just poured from the pan. The glass was so brittle it would crack at any moment. I daren't move. My skin was hot glass, my bones red hot jam-blood. With the heat the fear worsened.

'Oh Maria, help me,' I whispered aloud.

'You make it hard for me, sometimes,' said Wind, gently, entering the room. 'I'm sad to find you in such a state, Denny. Come on, let's go out. Take you away from here for a while. You've let yourself panic, shut in here, night after night with Roof. You haven't been out at night nearly enough since Maria died. Under curfew. Self-imposed. Come on, hurry up. Reclaim the night. It's wonderful outside. The sky is high and wild; there's a night full of stars. Get yer 'at 'n coat on, girl, put Roof on her lead, and off we go. And don't forget your front door key. The state you're in you're likely to lock yourself out.'

I walked with Roof, tugged by Wind, until we came to the canal. Roof was now off her lead, quiet and trusting. She showed her delight at being outside, walking loose-limbed, tail wagging, sniffing at all her usual places, stopping to lay scent now and then. Hansel and Gretel through the wicked wood left a trail. Together, Roof, Wind and I, we walked along the canal bank.

Bank, trees, roots, routes, earth.

Bank, money, dole, housing, hassle.

From time to time Wind touched my cheek in a cooling gesture. Wind took me to Water: the slow cold canal. Cool deep water.

Reclaim the night. The towpath was deserted and we walked north along the canal which ran parallel to the reservoirs.

I thought: it is 1664. These are the marshes where Roarie

56

gathers rushes for the wick lights in the weaver's cottage. Here, Mary's apprentice searches for wild marsh plants – roots, stems, leaves, flowerheads, for her remedies. In such a place, Freyja, Goddess of flax, would be at home. So am I, in my time.

Maria came to me, with her familiar feeling of nearness, no image or voice. Wind was unhurried, reassuring.

Looking up, I could make out the Milky Way, millions of miles overhead. When I looked into the canal, there it was again, the same colossal formations, a lurex umbrella blown inside out.

Beside me, the canal water flowed on, as if it knew how it came there, where it was going, and why.

'Roof.' I spoke quietly but the air was clear, so she heard me and came immediately.

'S'all right, Roof.' I knelt and put my arms around her. She was warm as a blanket. I sobbed and sobbed, muffled in her coat, and she seemed to hug me back.

'Am I really going mad?'

'What you need,' she said, 'is a fast walk home and a nice cup of tea. This canal bank is lovely, but enough's enough and you know what a coward I am? What if we met a geezer with an Alsatian? They're hogs not dogs and they only talk War. It's too reckless here. I'm for home.'

I didn't have a hanky, so I twisted the end of my nose a few times between fingers and thumb, sniffed and swallowed. When I stood up Roof was there with her biggest body on, getting her bottle up in case we met an Alsatian. I copied her, making myself as large as possible as we strode back together.

We made a fast pace along the towpath then up our side of the road bridge and along Ferry Lane, home.

Turning the key in the lock, I thought about Maria who was not home, waiting with the kettle on. I nodded a brief goodnight to Wind who floated along with us.

'Sleep well, get a good night's kip,' said Wind, who was prone to the occasional slang. 'I'm not in a howling mood. Not a rattle at the window nor a rustle down the alley shall disturb you.'

I woke next morning refreshed. I fed Roof and ate toast and honey, then settled at the table upstairs to write to Beatrice.

My books on old Essex, Chingford and Waltham Forest lay open where I'd left them. The maps and pages beckoned.

I picked up my pen.

'You took long enough. You're late. I've been working since dawn. You have a most slothful life, you people.'

'Says you.'

''Tis pity you cut off in such a manner. 'Twas my wish to take you to water. Does so little trust abide between us?'

'But I couldn't find you. You'd gone.'

'Small effort, on your part.'

'How did you know I need water?' I asked, ignoring her telling off.

'Were you not burning with fear?'

'Yes. I've been dreaming of hell fires, all kinds of fires.'

'Was so sad when you trusted me not. *Must* rest your trust in me. Cannot Speak Paper but through you.' Her tone changed and she began to plead. 'Please, my new friend, give to the both of us this chance. I need you. Now, please away for coffee, 'twill excite you.'

'But I already had some with my toast.'

'Please, while I gather my words. You shall study water-mills. I wish you to know my dear friend, Martha. Yes, the same name as my own mother. Shall meet you once again after your studies. Enjoy your coffee. Here, 'tis only for the rich. Meet me by the old mill.'

Eight

It is 1665, the middle of September.

Hard times, on the manor of Chingford Meade.

Plague sweeps through the manor as fleas brought by a travelling cloth merchant jump from husband to wife, brother to sister. The parish register tells the story. It isn't a happy one.

People say that Fire's twin sister, Burn, is tormented by the devil. Whenever she visits she causes a trail of devastation. When she takes on the form of plague, she is terrible to see. She touches men, women and children, so they burn red hot with fever and their groans can be heard everywhere. Boils and blisters and weeping sores appear on people's skin. The weakest perish first.

Burn is not like Fire. Fire can take the guise of love and warmth, filling people with laughter, lust and fun. But Burn only has sorrow and loss. She has nothing to give that is worth giving. No one gives her anything in return. Burn does not respect wealth. She has little or no regard for estate. She passes from person to person, house to house, from servant to master and mistress to maid. Wherever she goes she causes pain and grief and fear.

The manor house is empty. At the first hint of plague, Lord and Lady Chingford Meade flee, with their servants, to Shropshire, to spend the autumn and winter there, hoping to escape completely. There is no one to mind their animals, who wander away. Some are poached by the Turners, the Claytons and the Wainwrights. Some animals are attacked by hogs in the forest. Others wander into the marshes and drown.

The miller of Chingford Meade is dead. There is no one to take his place. His wife and children are buried beside him in the graveyard. The sluice gates are closed, the millpond almost silent except for a steady drip through a small hole. The mill is quiet too, apart from the scrabble of mice and occasional heavy footed scurry of a rat.

Carts trundle through the manor, rocking over ruts; and the people bring out their dead.

With ghoulish humour, Anne Brewster cries: 'Bring out yer dead; bring out yer dead. I said bring 'em out not throw 'em out.'

Roarie's sister Ginny is dying. Roarie makes possets and junkets to nourish her. Poultices for the boils, to no avail. Their mother and father and all their brothers and sisters are already gone. Roarie will be the last of the Brewsters on the manor if she escapes the plague. With her Aunt Anne, she buries the family, without much ceremony.

Roarie's real name is Anne, after her aunt. Truly speaking, her father should have taken the name Webber when he took up weaving, Webster if he'd been a woman. But he kept with Brewster because the Brewsters took him in when he was found an orphan, wandering on the village green. No one knows how he came to be there, only that he had been the youngest in his family and he became the adopted 'younger brother' of Anne.

The plague records already show Brewster, William, with his wife Martha and his youngest four children.

Orphaned now, Roarie tries to save her sister's life, and continues Mary's work as best she can.

Aunt Anne withstands the epidemic. She stays on at the alehouse, though the village population is depleted.

Burn moves away.

The people from the huge country house, Harland Heights, are in Scotland, staying with Alistair Harland's side of the family. A few servants remain, caring for the house and its own farm, separate from the manor, the manorial fields and the village.

On a dry autumn morning Ginny dies. A short time later, before midday, Roarie goes to the millpond. It is silent there. She watches a vole swimming, an arrow of water forming from the tip of its nose. Orphaned, with no brothers or sisters left now, Roarie sits dry-eyed and sombre, wondering why there is so much death in life.

At that moment, in London, two young women, Martha and Ruth, are standing together in a long queue stretching to the public plague pit.

Weeping, Ruth wheels a barrow forward with the wrapped bodies of her two young sisters. Ruth tips the barrow and watches as the small bodies roll over and over down into the pit, where they lie on top of others. She is so distressed she almost lets go the handles of the barrow. Martha leans forward and grabs one, hanging on to both Ruth and the handle as they steady themselves. The stench of bodies and lime fills the air. It is the worst way to die they can think of.

Martha takes charge as they turn from the gruesome sight, wrapping their shawls across their noses and mouths against the odour. It was her turn last week. They buried three of her younger brothers. Then her mother. At night, Martha's father, Samuel Faryner, drowns his grief in drink.

As they trundle through the narrow cobbled streets, Martha cannot blame her father. To her he seems a good man, working long hours. A faithful man, not given to womanising. A rare man, making the best of life in the sweating, stinking streets around him. He is lonely, and he loved her mother deeply, despite appearances.

They pass by Martha's house, one of a jumble of wooden buildings in Fish Street. There's no running water. It's carried from the pipe at the crossroads. Now they hitch up their skirts to avoid night-soil in the centre of the cobbles. It's been raining. The pungent mess swills down Fish Street to the river.

The streets are packed close, and the number of people living there is increasing all the time. Martha and Ruth press themselves against the nearest wall as a rich person's carriage approaches. Holding up their skirts, they lean back to avoid the night-soil that's being churned out of the ruts by the carriage wheels. Their own barrow is now blocking a doorway. They retrieve it, and Martha strides on, pulling it as she does each day when it's loaded with sacks of flour from Ruth's father's windmill. Martha's work is to deliver the flour to the King's bakers in Pudding Lane where her father works. It's near the abattoir which gives the lane its name – pudding is the inside of a dead pig.

Strong and tough we are, thinks Ruth, wiping her eyes on her shawl and keeping pace with Martha. It's not easy – Martha is taller and is hurrying. And such friends, since childhood, adds Ruth, keeping her thoughts to herself.

Aloud she calls: 'Martha, mark me, I should like to leave this place. Leave here, be a sailor. Let us go from here. Dress as men and steer our tall ships. Pirates. In the taverns are tales of women pirates.'

'Ruth Bates, Nathaniel's daughter, you lose your senses.'

'Two of my brothers – the plague killed them. Every voice Speaks Death this day. I desire to leave this place.'

'Come. Your head turns foolish. Make haste, Ruth. Your father waits for us. My father also. Barrow shall be loaded by noon. King's bakers shall curse for want of 't.'

Ruth sighs as they enter the mill to start work. Her mind strays to the taverns, listening to the sailors.

'Islands,' say the sailors, ''neath oceans. Mountains do smoke. 'Tis fire in belly of earth. Fire dost belch high as heaven. Yet do some islands sleep. Might wake this day, or night. Dragons deep in belly of earth do rumble, most fearsome.'

In the winter following the plague, Ruth's mother runs away with the coppersmith. Ruth misses her dreadfully, but thinks her father isn't much competition for the long sweet nights on offer to her mother in the coppersmith's feather bed. Nathaniel's idea of home comforts, as Ruth is used to hearing, are the roll on (grunt three times), roll off and fall asleep variety.

Nathaniel and Samuel are friends. Each night they can be found in the alehouse, pinching the barmaids, and laughing with the sailors. Their lusty singing can be heard in the street.

Martha sneaks up to Rising Hill Mill to be with Ruth.

Martha and Ruth keep house for their fathers now that their mothers are gone; but they vow they will never marry, bed with a man and have children like their own mothers. For sex, they prefer each other. There's no one they'd rather love or kiss or hold, day or night.

Samuel is warned at work about being drunk on the job. Everyone drinks, but Samuel is drowning his sorrows too long and too often.

It's a warm night in September 1666. Samuel is working late, trying to stop thinking about his wife, who died almost exactly a year ago.

Nathaniel is in the nearest tavern. Martha and Ruth are in bed at Rising Hill Mill. Above London the sky is dark and starry, with a chill in the air. Then in the hours before dawn, when a dull brown wash should be colouring the sky, a deep red glow begins over Pudding Lane where Samuel is drunk in the bakery. It becomes darker and brighter; clouds become dense, packed with smoke.

In the house of Samuel Pepys the maids are still busy finishing the preparations for many guests on Sunday. It's three a.m. as one of the maids is finally dismissed for bed. On her way to her room she is to close all the windows. Her feet are swollen with fatigue; her head aches for lack of sleep. As she closes the last window thankfully, she peers out. Seeing the red pall, she rouses her master, begs him to go and look at what's happening, and asks him what should be done.

However, as the maid later tells her brother, who travels from village to village selling broadsheets, her master says the fire seems far away and therefore of no great consequence. When he sends her off to bed, she's so tired she doesn't argue and daren't challenge him anyway. She sleeps like a dead dog till morning.

Not so Martha and Ruth.

Ruth wakes because there's a slight breeze. She shivers and pulls the covers up over herself and Martha. But her attention goes to the window, which is made of translucent horn as her father cannot afford glass. From the open casement there's an acrid smell. Getting up, Ruth wraps her shawl around her and peers out. Her room is above her father's room, so she can see the whole scene. She calls Martha.

The breeze that wakes Ruth is fanning the flames over Pudding Lane, and the mill being on higher ground gives a fine and horrible view. Over the King's bakery, flames leap high. Fire encases the buildings on either side.

Running to the window and looking out, Martha cries, 'Wind blows the fire towards us. 'Tis driving the fire to the mill.'

'Downstairs, hurry. I shall wake my father. Fetch our skirts and cloaks, some water and some bread. Make haste.'

However Nathaniel hasn't come home. They are on their own at the mill.

'What a stink. First the plague, now a great fire. Why? What have we done, Martha? What sign is this?'

Outside they find the alleys crowded with carts and barrows. People are trying to move and to find out what has happened. They yell news and call out to one another, ferrying belongings to relatives' houses. People duck to avoid bundles chucked from high windows. Cats mew pitifully, trapped in high rooms. Pigeons flutter overhead, or plummet with singed wings.

Wheels creak and dogs howl. Men, women and children stagger about under boxes that are too heavy. People fall, scramble to their feet, retrieve their burdens and try again. Babies cry, hungry because mothers cannot hold them to the breast and journey about. Toddlers are coughing, children choking on smoke. People's eyes are streaming. Old people, the lame and the sick, jostle along, some helped by others.

Underfoot, some are crushed and lie groaning in the gutters. Night-soil clogs against their legs. Older children fight as families move from house to house, street to street.

Martha and Ruth hold tight to one another, mingling with the crowds, horrified at the sights. They try to shield their mouths, noses and faces from smoke and sparks, but are carrying bundles of clothes and food, and dare not let go of each other for fear of being swept apart in the surging panic.

The pace of the crowd changes. People start to run.

Others yell: the river; the river.

Martha and Ruth keep up with the crowd. They're slowed by carts jammed in doorways; by blocked off alleys; by blazing wooden joists about to tumble; by flurries of frenzied birds, squawking in terror; by caved-in passages and toppling archways.

They run and dodge, clinging to one another. They cough and splutter. Their eyes sting from smoke.

Houses crack and cave in; flames surge into sudden gaps; balls of fire roll down from rooftops; and people dare not look back because the wind is changeable, driving showers of firedrops like hailstones.

At the river all is confusion. Rich people pay ferrymen for wherries and lighters. The poor, Black and white, stand in clusters, stranded. Wind is rioting. Arching fireballs fall into the crowd. People scream and shout.

Some of the rich take pity on the poor. Mothers with babies in arms and children clinging to their skirts are handed across the narrow gap of water on to barges. They sit among the trunks and furniture. Some lighters are so full of bundles and books that there's no room left for people.

'The ferrymen will be rich,' says Ruth.

''Tis a nightmare. What is to be done?'

'Look, Martha, at all the women and children. I cannot step aboard a ferry afore a mother with her child. I cannot.'

'Nor can I, Ruth. 'Tis an error to be here, at the river. We are strong, are we not?'

'What occurs to you, Martha?'

'Wouldst thou turn north with me? Make for open country? Skirt around this fire?'

''Tis a fine idea. To leave this place was my own dream, was it not?'

Turning, with their backs to the crowds at the river, they watch the great arch of fire, the flames rising between the steeples and towers, all burning. Wooden houses on London Bridge are blazing.

They move away from the river at the edge of the fire. They take their time now. Alive, unharmed and together, they pass gangs of ex-prisoners pulling down houses to stop the course of the fire. The King's men strut about, shouting orders as hordes of beggars are rounded up and set to work, reinforcing the groups of ex-prisoners and some militia men.

They make their way past rich people's houses where servants are set to dig trenches and pits in the yards to bury wine and caskets and trunks of gold. Servants are closely supervised so that they can't thieve their masters' goods.

A church looms up ahead with its huge doors open. More servants carry in expensive furniture. The stone walls of the church might withstand the heat. Martha and Ruth watch: barrow-loads of tapestries and furs; pictures and leather-bound books; more caskets of wine; spinets and other musical instruments.

Ruth tugs Martha's arm, 'They take in bedposts and fenders.' Ruth is fascinated and horrified in the same moment. Servants are calling: 'Yes, sire, no sire, where to next, sire?' as they shoulder brass and glass and lace and linen, all sorted and tied or wrapped.

'We see not all their riches till now,' says Martha. 'Come, mind your feet. No, Ruth. You cannot save her.'

Ruth looks at the body on the ground. It's a young woman, but she is already dead.

'Once my father set down all of us, together. I ne'er did tell you this. He said we must mark his words. If e'er we should be trapped by fire we should breathe smoke. We wouldst pass away afore fire burned us. Wouldst not feel pain. I wonder, shall I e'er see my father?'

'I know not.' Martha wonders about her own father as they leave the city, following a stream to a different river, the River Lea, then following the river itself until they come to a ferry.

The ferryman's widow rows them across. She listens to their story, likes them, takes pity.

''Tis a miller is needed,' she tells them, 'on the manor of Chingford Meade. 'Twill be a hard winter. The mill wants repair. No miller this twelve-month past. Plague took them;

miller, rib and children.'

With her arm, she points the way, gesturing with her hands to show the lie of the marshes, fields and woodland.

'Be alehouse on manor. Keeper be woman, known to me. Anne Brewster, loud and strong – her niece be healer. Roarie Brewster. Go to her, make greetings from a ferry-man's widow. Mistress Luck shall 'company.'

Nine

Beatrice wrote that she planned a holiday to Fiji. She enclosed photos of their new house, almost on the beach in North Auckland; and a copy of Patricia Grace's book – *Potiki*.

I held the book in my hands, remembering Maria. Her copy had been on loan to one of her friends who had read it in the bath and washed it to pieces. Maria had been hopelessly generous. Her things were all over the women's movement, and after she died women wanted to keep them, small parts of Maria herself, precious and rare. To have something, anything, brought her just that little bit closer.

I smoothed out Beatrice's letter and put it carefully in a folder with her name on it. For some reason I always kept a copy of my own letters to Beatrice. I'd take them out and read them, hers and mine, the story of our friendship. Many years of working with Beatrice, gone now, folded in neat pages of airmail paper. But recently I'd not been able to write without interference from Roarie.

Then I sat and read *Potiki* as if I was under an apple tree on the manor of Chingford Meade, watching the sun and light on the fields, the water passing under the mill-wheel.

I'd loved *Potiki* first time round, more so this time. In Aotearoa, the Maori cycle was a wheel going round until Pakeha came with guns and sickness, ripping the wheel to shreds, spokes strewn all over the beach, like driftwood after a storm. I could see the earlier ways of life – people living, working, tending animals, raising crops.

As I read, a strange echo filled the room, as if Wind had arrived with sounds from the sixteen hundreds, from Aotearoa and Essex. I could hear the slam, bang and shuttle of William Brewster's loom before the plague. I heard the suck and pull of the river when the ferryman's widow rowed Martha and Ruth across; the slap of water against the jetties; the low of oxen; the creak of a plough; scythes swishing at harvest, then the tread of animal feet as they were let into the Lammas fields to graze the stubble.

Outside, a sudden commotion told me Wren was back and Roof was annoying her again. I dashed downstairs.

'Just stop it. No more noise. Leave her alone.'

In the philadelphus, that was so tall it was almost a tree, the loudest song came from the smallest singer. She had a wonderful sense of humour. She sang, 'Oh for the wings for the wings of a dove far away far away would I rove.'

'Know how you feel.'

'The lake lay blue beneath the hill, blue,' she sang.

'You mean reservoir round here,' I said, thinking of the flooded marshes.

'The reservoir lay blue beneath the hill, blue,' tried Wren, but it didn't scan so she put her head on one side again: 'Oh for the wings for the wings of a dove.'

The afternoon was warm for the time of year so I made tea and sat with it under Wren's tree, while Roof, who hated to be *too* hot, sulked on the concrete bit you couldn't call a patio; and I missed and missed Maria.

Graham rang and we talked about the Gulf. We'd both been following developments there by reading the papers and listening to the news.

Shipping sources had confirmed that at least three vessels had been hit off the Iranian coast: the *Coral Cape*, the *Shirvan*, and the *Merlin*. There were no reports of casualties.

The Iranians were saying that the Gulf conflict could only be ended if the Iraqi president, Saddam Hussein, was overthrown. Iran was pledged to continue a Holy War against Iraq until the Iraqi people were delivered from Saddam Hussein.

Tension in the Gulf was rising sharply. Iraq seemed to have decided to carry on attacking commercial vessels – this was happening after the sinking of several Iranian minelayers by the Americans.

Meanwhile tanker captains in the Gulf were becoming nervous; had taken to tagging on for safety behind navy ships; and there was more reflagging of ships by Britain and the US.

Graham said, 'Phil's a sod, always was, but he's a damn lovable sod and I can't help caring.'

'I know. You're superglued.'

'I'm certain if he was in trouble he'd get in touch with me or you or both of us. Dead certain.'

'Not dead.'

'Freudian slip, sorry.'

'Why so sure?'

'I'm sure. That's all. I talked to Jeff our tutor who does International Relations . . .'

'An expert,' I said, coldly. 'Better than a mother or brother.'

'No. But he knows a bit about the Gulf. A cowboy like Phil's likely to be on one of the one-man jobs. Little vessels trundling about, not unionised. Nipping in and out. I reckon he's on one of them.'

'Makes sense to me,' I said. 'Phil would hate yes sir no sir on a super-tanker.'

'He assuredly would. He's the original anarchist.'

I didn't reply to Graham, resisting the temptation to laugh at his university-speak. Intuition told him so. His voice changed: 'What about you, Mum? How're the old maps?'

'Love them. They take my mind off things. I mean the Gulf. But not for long. The news jolts me. Like: they hit the Indian Tanker . . .'

'The *Spic Emerald*. Yes, I know.'

'In international waters . . .' I said, pausing for effect, 'off the United Arab Emirates. I can reel the names off now, but I still don't know where Phil is . . . I go about my business . . . I might get myself to classes. Taken me long enough.'

'You're too hard on yourself. It's a most significant step,' he said. I giggled, despite myself.

'What's funny?'

'You talk different.'

'Yeah. I'm starting to talk like I have to write. I swore I wouldn't. But I am. I catch myself out – intoning on a bloody podium: so and so's recent study shows that . . . It has been argued that . . . So and so claims that . . . According to so and so . . .'

'So and so's got a lot to answer for,' I said, laughing.

'So's our other so and so on a boat.'

'Anyway, love, thanks for phoning . . .'

'OK, Mum. Talk to you soon. Love you lots.'

'You too. Bye now.'

The newspapers reported that England, that is to say the government, had asked the Iranians to leave, and closed the possibility for further arms deals.

I didn't trust the government, the papers, or the arms dealers. There would surely be undercover promises, higher prices. Thank heavens Phil wasn't in the navy. At least I knew he didn't work on a minesweeper or a warship. The Belgians and the French were steaming towards the Gulf. The USA said it was increasing its presence daily.

I missed having Maria, Daphne and Bronwyn to talk it over with. Sorting out the issues. Will there be a full-scale war? If so, what will happen to Phil?

I went to bed but couldn't sleep. Where was Phil? Why didn't he let us know?

Lying awake in the dark, I seemed to hear two voices, in stereo. I'd heard them before and was extremely frightened.

They were the voices of the twin sisters: Fire and Burn.

'There will be a war, Denny.'

'She's right, there will be. Reagan wants it, and Thatcher for all her assertion to the opposite, loves a good and fearsome fight. Witness the Falklands.'

'Stop it. Please stop it. Leave me alone.'

'The purifying flames of violence, Denny.'

'So we can't think why you're bothering with all this Speaking Paper. Cutting things out of the newspaper about the Gulf. Paper will burn. Whoosh. High into the air when the fuse goes up. World War Three was destined to begin in the Middle East.'

'Yes, Denny, the great philosopher Nostradamus himself said so. You know that's true. You heard that on telly.'

'London's burning, London's burning, fetch the engine, fetch the engine.'

'Stop it. People have learned since those times. No more war.'

'War is the wrong word, Denny. We are the forces of right and wrong. There will be Fire. All that oil. The flames burn higher.'

'No. No.' I was shouting into the night. I couldn't help myself. 'No more fires. There've been too many. We'll stop it. Women will stop it. We won't let any more sons and daughters burn. Somehow we'll find a way. People will come to their senses.'

'Ha, Denny, you're so naive.' The laughter of Fire and Burn echoed unkindly: 'Such a simple view, ha ha ha ha.'

I sat up in bed crying, rocking to and fro, my hands over my ears. Roof nudged me, licked my hands, offering me comfort.

I slept with the light on.

Next night, I was afraid to go to sleep. I sat in bed reading a gardening book as usual, with the window open a little. Presently I shut the book with a snap and put out the light. The open window rattled as Wind came in.

'Tell me there won't be a full-scale war in the Gulf,' I demanded.

'I can't. It's not for me to say.'

'I wish I'd never done that dare. The first time in my life I've *really* wished such a thing. Never before did I truly wish I didn't have my sons.'

'Both lads?'

'Yes. It's all too much. Graham's needs. Phil's needs. I'm so fed up with juggling. But I know the answer's not just to wish them away. And it wouldn't be any easier if they were daughters; only different. I mean, they might be so straight,

72

and their lives full of men, like Cheryl. At least I can be clear what I'm juggling. Are you a mother?'

'No, a facilitator. All those gorgeous flowers. Beautiful and oh so sexual.'

'Yes, I've often thought as a dyke it would be nice to be a bee.'

'Shakes-spoke thought so. Where the bee sucks there suck I. In a cow-owslip's be-ell I lie. And all that.'

'Can I ask you something very personal?'

'Try me. I want to be your friend.'

'Have you ever regretted your actions? Really regretted?'

'I have. It isn't easy to live with some of the things I've done.'

A chill changed the air around me. There was a long silence. Gone was the light, erotic sense of a moment ago. Now I waited, and waited. I had a dull foreboding, as the minutes cooled and a frost of time-ice replaced my picture of time as a sheet of flame.

Wind said: 'It isn't easy to risk telling you. I have done evil things, which I find hard to face up to. There was a sudden flash of light. I was forced to move, to take up speed. I've never before been forced to move so fast. Oh I've been an unwitting accomplice of Water, on several occasions – tempests, hurricanes, flash floods. Water and I can be terrible partners in crime. But this flash of light was of a different order. Something new and atrocious. For this was instigated by Fire.' Wind paused, then continued: 'Sudden. Violent. I was caught unawares. Caught up. Three hundred miles an hour; five hundred. Myself part of it – total destruction. People turned to shadow. Vaporised. Hundreds of thousands of people.'

'You did that? Death by your hand?'

'Do you hate me – now you know what I was part of?'

'No. But I'm frightened.'

'I wouldn't have gone there if I'd known what I'd be drawn into.'

'I don't understand.'

'They have ways of making me change.'

'They?'

73

'I'm terrified of Them. That they might pull me in again.'

'They are coming to get me – I'm terrified of Them too.'

'With good reason,' said Wind.

'You're so elemental – you scare me. I need a rest.'

'But I need your help.'

'Because of August 6th 1945? I wasn't even born.'

'But you are Earth, not Fire. You *can* help me.'

'No. You're elemental, I'm not. Besides, you risk my son . . . he's not safe.' I began to shout, 'Go away. I'm very frightened. Frightened for my son. D'you hear me? You stay away from the Gulf.'

Wind whistled, long and low at the depth of my fear. Then, hurt by my rejection, she left by the open window.

It was difficult to work the bedside light switch because my hands were shaking. The room now seemed a timeless void. I put my hands to my temples, rubbing round and round.

With the light on, I took up my well-loved copy of *The Common Woman*, turning the pages slowly until I came to 'Vera – From My Childhood'. I read aloud: 'The Common Woman is like good bread and will rise.' Then with a rising sense of panic I followed the words on another page: 'A Woman is Talking to Death.' After a while, I returned to Vera, comforted by the rhythms and the life there, the future there.

I rose from the bed, deliberately pushed up the top sash of the window against Wind, and pulled the latch to click the bottom and top sashes together. I found the old-fashioned window-lock and screwed it into place. I shut the curtains, folding the free edges until I was sure there was no gap.

With Vera beside me and Roof at my feet, I slept. With the light on.

Next day it rained heavily. I drew maps, kept making errors, and rubbed them out carefully, glad I wasn't learning the piano. Imagine playing the same scale over and over, knowing the neighbours could hear each mistake.

I must have mumbled aloud, because Roof, who hated rainy days, said: 'Never mind the neighbours, what about *my* ears?'

'Don't whinge, old dog.'

'Bitch.'

'I beg your pardon?'

'You coming out?'

'No. Wait till it stops.'

'I'm desperate.'

'Dog-flap's open. Use the garden.'

'I don't shit on my own doorstep.'

'Then go down the end. I'll clear it up later. I'm busy.'

'It's a dog's life.'

'It's almost stopped raining. Use the garden for now. Give me half an hour.'

'Huh.' She put on her most resentful air, and gave me a filthy look, before going downstairs and out through the flap, making fuss and noise all the way. Then she set off to the rockery to annoy Wren.

I worked on, trying to ignore her. I daren't pick up a pen because I couldn't bear any more horrors from Chingford Meade. I didn't know what was happening to me, but the maps were lovely and one was almost good enough to frame.

The rain stopped. The housemartins, who lived under the eaves outside the small bedroom window, exited one by one, flying off, over the recreation ground.

At the far end of the garden, Wren took up position about three feet above Roof's head, as if fully aware that Roof couldn't jump that high. Miffed, Roof barked continuously. The neighbours both sides were out at work. No one was home to shout at Roof.

It was easy to enter their world, imagine their humour.

'How much is that doggy in the window, the one with the waggly tail? How much is that doggy in the window, I do hope that doggy's for sale.'

'Stop it. Stop it. Stop it. Stop it.'

'Troglodytes, troglodytes, flying through the glen. Troglodytes, troglodytes, known as Jenny Wren. Feared by the bad, loved by the good . . . We are the greatest, we are the greatest.'

Wren sang. Roof frothed and barked to no avail. Wren, bored, flew off. Roof, abandoned, furious, chased her tail around the garden.

The lovely sketchmap on my table mocked me. Agitated now, like Roof, I turned the map over and began covering the clean side with circles of questions, none in straight lines, all curves and swirls in a doodle:

Why Maria? Why at her age? Where has she flown to? How could love mock me then fly away?

Where is Maria now? Where has she flown *to*? Is she safe? Is she happy? Is she peaceful, not like me? Is she at rest?

How can I fly away? Where to? What jobs could I do and find? Where to live? Could I go, like a housemartin, somewhere else? Settle under a new roof? Make a new life?

Could *I* walk a roof ridge, learn to fly? How far? How high? Could *I* look across the world from a *new* roof-top?

What am I? A wren? A housemartin? A mad woman in a back bedroom with a list of silly questions? Will They come for me after all?

With sudden anger at myself, I snatched the lovely map with its swirls of questions and crumpled it into a tight ball.

I slung it into the waste basket.

I slammed downstairs, grabbed Roof's collar and lead and my anorak, yelled out of the louvre in the bathroom for her to go walkies; and, not forgetting my keys, let myself and my dog out of the madhouse.

From the ridge on the top of the roof Wind moved fast, taking me by surprise, almost leaving me behind. I had to open my wings, my Eagle wings, on full span before I leaned forward grasping the edge of cloud as tightly as possible.

I hadn't expected England to be so green. My body was streamlined, my thoughts sorting themselves behind me.

For the sky was a high, wide, open field now that the rain had gone, and rabbit clouds scurried fast ahead of me, tails bobbing. Then I saw them, the wild horses, galloping fast, their manes streaming in the wind. Neck and neck I flew across with the leading filly. She was fast and I was also. Across the plains we sped, her below, myself high above. Eagle, full wing stretch, enjoying the freedom, the pace, the open blueness. To the distant hills we raced, where we parted as I soared, clean and knife-like across the sky, but hurting no one. Too much death had gone before me. Today was life. Up there I could scream and cry, full-throated cries across vast spaces. Letting it out – the anger, the fear, the fire inside, in streamers of blue-red-gold and orange, flying nearer to the sun. So much was opening up ahead.

Abruptly, the sky-land ended. Suddenly there was only sky-sea. The drop to the waves was alluring, beckoning.

But on I flew, across seas, across oceans, estuaries and rivers. Seas again and islands.

I followed Wind. I had come too far from home to let go now; and I was used to hanging on when things were dangerous.

Polynesian islands loomed up in a glittering sea. I heard Wind calling to land, heard the reply, felt the tug as Wind veered off, passing down the coastline of Aotearoa. Voices clamoured at Wind. Wind, restless, surged, spiralled, turned, dragging me mile after mile. Nothing gentle. Venturing, changing direction.

Eventually, I was exhausted, pleaded for home. Wind accused me of cowardice – I begged for peace: 'I'm afraid of leaving home, starting again. Besides, I haven't the money for travel. I can barely afford the bus fare to the job centre, let alone flights with you to the South Pacific.'

'Not Polynesia then, nor Aotearoa. You're tired of aloneness. I'm offering a way out, a way up.'

'I can't go at your pace. You're too fast for me.'

'I thought you were Eagle. I find you're merely Rabbit. No match for me. Stay indoors and grieve then. I'll be back.'

'Please yourself. I don't need this. Not now. I've enough to cope with.'

'For today maybe. But I beckon you, Denny. You can't resist me for ever. You'll be bored when I'm gone. Here's your own doorstep again. Your dog will keep you company.'

With that final remark, Wind moved on.

I half feared her return, which was usually unpredictable, and half longed for her.

She fulfilled a need in me: for excitement and glimpses of other worlds, far from the few square miles I knew of – the London of unemployment, television and Thatcher's lies.

Ten

Two weeks on Sunday, I met Freyja as we'd planned, at the corner of Shernall Street, to take the long walk to the woods.

My reserve was gone. I needed her. As Roof and I approached, I recognised her, leaning against a lamp-post, hands deep in her jacket pockets. She had a new hat, a fantastic thing, a sort of trilby.

'Hi, Radclyffe.'

'Hello, Denny. Like it?'

'It's wonderful. Wish I had the bottle.'

She saw that my defences were down and she held her arms wide open and we hugged. I was shaking, short on hugs. She took over, strong. Not coming-on-strong, but friendship-strong.

'Walk or talk?' she asked, bending to pat Roof.

'Walk and talk, but I want to talk in the woods, not here. I have to watch the roads here, for Roof. How are you, under the hat?'

'I'm good. Yeah. I'm OK. It's you that's done that. How 'bout you?'

'I want to tell you about Maria. I want to sit on the log seat, where we used to sit. Hang on a minute, this crossing's lethal. Roof, sit. Good girl. Wait. OK, cross. There's a good girl.' I patted Roof then continued to walk.

Eventually we reached the forest, and the clearing. After some forays in and out of the streams, Roof ran off. I had Freyja to myself.

'I was worried after I dumped all that stuff on you about the fire,' she began. 'I didn't mean it as a dump. I'm sorry.'

'I know.'

'Were you angry with me?'

'Yes and no. I'm having some trouble sleeping, but it's been better the last couple of nights. Hopefully that'll carry on.'

'Back home, I lost some friends over it, Denny. I told myself there that if they couldn't take the real me, they weren't true friends. But I hardly knew you at all. So it was a dump and I'm very sorry.'

'You must have known you could tell me, or you'd not have taken the risk, would you? Not with a stranger, somebody you wanted to become friends with. And you do need a friend, don't you, like I do?'

Freyja nodded and put her arm through mine as we sat. It was deep autumn, one of those mild days, not cold. In the distance were a few people and a couple of dogs. Roof played by the stream, utterly happy.

'Aren't the colours lovely? The forest wears a magic necklace, and it's amber, look around.' Relaxing and feeling very glad to be with Freyja, I asked, 'What was it like in York? Did you enjoy it?'

'Wonderful, but we'll talk about me another time, another place.' Freyja looked around the clearing. 'I can understand why you and Maria loved this place. It's almost rural even now. Hard to believe it's the suburbs.'

'We used to bring picnics here. Sometimes with Bron and Daphne as well. And if Maria and Bron were working weekends, which they did sometimes, then Daphne and I spent a lot of time together.'

'You're sparkling Denny, did you know?'

'Am I? No, I didn't know. There was a lot of sparkle, Daph and me.'

'Were you . . . ?' she hesitated.

'Confessions?' We both laughed. Silly ass. Why couldn't she come straight out with it? 'No, we weren't lovers, but we were in love for a while. We really fancied each other and neither of us had perfect partners, and we weren't perfect either. I don't believe in perfect women, do you?'

'No. Nor perfect relationships, either. Go on, what happened?'

'Nothing. We both had too much to lose. We couldn't cope. Actually, it was Bronwyn and Maria that had been lovers, years and years before. Long before I met Maria. They stayed best friends, like some do, gawd knows how. Then Maria met me; and Bron met Daphne. Hey presto a foursome. We had some wonderful times. Complicated though. Daphne and me really did sparkle and we all had to sort it out. Took some doing. When I was thirty, Maria gave me a small silver chain with my birthstone. It's magic . . .'

'The magic necklace.'

'S'pose so. Emerald though, not amber. Later, for another birthday, Daphne made me a box of soft padded satin, to keep it in. Her way of saying that we sparkled but we'd leave things as they were. Making covered boxes was her hobby. I miss her. And I treasure that box.' I paused, then, 'Sometimes the memories make me feel guilty.'

Freyja said: 'Not only love that's unfinished? Guilt as well?'

I laughed. 'Tell me about it.'

'You've been carrying this alone. What a weight.'

'I miss Daph terribly. But I really loved Maria, and Daphne really loved Bronwyn. Daph and I could never have lived together, lived our lives side by side. We knew that. There'd have been no peace, and we both needed peace in our home lives. You do, don't you, when the world around is in such a turmoil?'

'What did she do for a living?'

'Sports teacher. Brilliant hurdler, and loved climbing. That's how she met Bronwyn, climbing. It's all part of the story. And I want to tell you about Bronwyn as well, because she was an amazing woman – they both were.'

The story I told Freyja went like this:

Bronwyn grew up in North Wales. As a child she felt isolated, because she knew she was different. Was always in love with girls, women teachers. Never interested in boys at

80

all. She used to say she was born a lesbian.

She didn't have an easy life because of that. Her family were comfortable, ran a successful boarding-house in Llandudno. She grew up very secure, but lonely.

She went to London to train as a nurse – a way of getting away from home, working with women, putting a roof over her head. She lived in, and she liked the life. She went into Aids nursing and became one of the pioneers. In her time off she did a lot of sports and that's how she met most of her lovers, including Daphne.

Bron was involved in the campaigning as well – trying to get rid of the myths about Aids; challenging the stereotypes. She was tired. All the workers and carers were.

A natural break in the story. I watched the forest for a while, gathering strength for the next part. Freyja waited.

I said: 'So one weekend we sat her down and we said in no uncertain terms that she must take a break. A short holiday and then a long break, maybe a year or two. Then she would be able to return to the work refreshed and able to give more. They call it burn out over here, do they back home?'

'Yes. It can kill you.'

'That's what we said. You should have seen her – she was grey, utterly exhausted.'

'Did she listen?'

'Not at first. Daphne was a catalyst: she deliberately resigned her job and then worked as a supply teacher, so she could plan when to take time off. Meanwhile, Bron's granny had gone to live with Bron's aunt, and she asked the family to sell her terraced house and split the money between her two grandchildren, while they were young enough to enjoy it, rather than wait for her to die. So Bronwyn had ten thousand.

'Bron said she wasn't ready to resign her job but she would go on holiday with Daphne and have a general look at the housing market in North Wales.'

'What was Daphne going to do in North Wales?' asked Freyja.

'She wanted to run climbing courses for women and make

81

the facilities available especially to Black women, because there tends to be a monopoly by rich whites on the most beautiful areas. In climbing, well sports generally, it's still male dominated. In this country it is, anyway.

'Courses on outdoor pursuits, climbing, abseiling and so on tend to be run by men and to be mixed. Then you get not only the usual sexist stuff, but also you get het couples and it makes it hard for women who're on their own, and for lesbians.

'Daphne wanted a cheap place, run down, that we could all do up together. I'm pretty good at DIY and I like it, and Maria would do the electrics. I had time on my hands after I was made redundant so it appealed to me. Gave me an aim, a purpose.'

I stopped.

I couldn't go on. I wanted to, but it was so painful.

Freyja said: 'Take your time. There's plenty.'

'All right.' I took a deep breath. I noticed Roof was by the stream. 'It'll sound like a soap opera to begin with – though it's really a Greek tragedy: *Antigone* – saw it on telly. I'll have to start with where everyone was or it won't make sense. Where to start? Cheryl first. Her firm was about to change their computers. They sent the whole workforce on a grand retraining week to Brighton. So that's where Cheryl was.

'Phil was away. He was always off somewhere. At that time he was labouring on a site up north.

'Meanwhile, Wendy, who was Graham's fiancée, broke off their engagement for the second time. Graham was working in a bank, which he'd gone into hoping for a low mortgage. He was all for settling down, getting married young, the whole bit. I liked Wendy, but I couldn't believe Graham would be happy in banking. Anyway, Wendy had just left him, and said it was final, and he was in an awful state so he came home. So he was in the house.

'Maria and I had a phone call from Bronwyn and Daphne, in North Wales. They rang to say they'd found a wonderful old place to buy, would we go up for a long weekend, tell them what we thought, and could Maria give them an estimate for rewiring.

'After their phone call I was in a quandary. I felt I couldn't go, not right then. You see, Graham never asks for anything. He always takes second place to Phil. I've tried to change that but Phil makes such demands, even when he's not around. I get angry with Phil, over and over, and Maria used to call him an "arrogant young turd". But not Graham, except for this particular time. His world had fallen apart; he was thinking of leaving banking, getting more A-levels, going to college. He was changing his whole life.

'So were Bronwyn and Daphne – my very best friends. I was torn in two. Maria was furious. How could I put a man before two dyke friends? What were my politics, what did I really care about women's lives, and what about Daph's vision of a centre where Black tutors could be working? Accusations were flying.

'I said: "Look, you're the electrician, you go. And why not get in some climbing while you're there? Give me a week, and I'll come and join you all. I'll be there. I just can't come this weekend. I need to talk to my son."

'Eventually Maria calmed down, and I helped her pack. And I thought about that when you told me about Gemma and your plans, that at least you'd parted happy. But we didn't – I put Graham first. If I'd only known – life is full of if onlys, isn't it?'

'Yes.'

'I chose my son. I didn't know what I was *really* choosing. Anyway, we packed Maria's things, sorted out her climbing gear. She was meticulous about everything. That was Maria. Safety first every time. When she was climbing, or on the motorbike, or working on dodgy electrics, she never cut corners.

'She'd been a diabetic since she was young, quite a rare form. She had a kit for monitoring it and she always had her insulin with her. She wore a bracelet on her right wrist – the word DIABETIC in block capitals and her name underneath and our phone number. She never took off that bracelet. "Just in case," she told me, "in case I'm ever found anywhere, for any reason, unconscious."

'So off she went. There they were in North Wales. The house was worth buying, according to Maria, and all was set in motion. They then had time to do some climbing.

'They must have set off just after daybreak. You could only get to the climb after a couple of hours' trek. The last half an hour to the foot of the climb would have been hard.

'The other side of the valley were a woman called Josie and her boyfriend, George. They were watching the three women through binoculars.

'It was perfect weather for the climb. The forecast was good, and other climbers in the area said later that conditions on the mountain were good. It was a very hard route, the climb itself, but well within their abilities and experience. Besides, they'd done that very climb before.

'But the face they fell on to was slate and shale, and was unstable. They fell roped together down the scree, rolling over down the slur, causing a horrible rock-slide. It gathered speed.

'The three would have been buried for hours but for Josie and George. They dashed for the mountain rescue.

'The phone call came to me Monday about half-past three. Bangor. The other hospitals don't deal with such major emergencies. Bron and Daph had died in the fall. Maria was in intensive care with multiple injuries. She was conscious, asking for someone called Denny.

'I phoned Brighton, couldn't get Cheryl. Left a message. Phoned the station and explained. They were wonderful, reserved me a seat.

'I snatched a bag, spare knickers, toothbrush. Graham lent me cash, drove me to the station. I was with Maria in hours.

'Before they let me see her, they talked to me. They wanted to prepare me. They said she was heavily medicated, but conscious. In severe pain. Impossible to tell the full extent of all the internal injuries. So I expected her to look terrible, and she did – a high-tech Egyptian mummy, all tubes and drips.

'Mercifully, her nose and mouth, though bruised, weren't bandaged, but her forehead and eyes were. I sat there, leaning close. Daren't touch her in case I hurt her.

'I said, "It's me, Denny. Can you hear me?"

' "Denny, I knew you'd come."

' "I came as soon as they phoned. Cheryl will be on her way by now . . . I didn't stop for flowers or anything. I just brought me."

' "I knew you'd come," she said again.

' "I love you. I'm here. I love you so much."

' "I love you too," she said. It was very difficult for her to talk. She seemed exhausted by those few words. But she knew I was there and she did hear me. Her lips parted again. I leaned closer to hear. Again she said: "I love you." Then she said something else: "Pain . . . bones . . . on . . . fire."

'There was an awful sound when the air left her. My face was very near hers. I was listening intently. I knew she'd gone.

'After that I don't remember anything until I woke up not in hospital but in a hotel bed. The world was swaying quite far away but Cheryl was there, in the twin bed next to me. She'd arrived completely exhausted. Her boss had lent her his Jag. She'd driven through the night.

'The hotel didn't charge us. It was amazing, people were so kind. Bronwyn's parents came from Llandudno to see me. They were in a state of shock; we all were. We were distant, kind. My bone marrow was cold. That was a strange thing. Whatever people did for me, I couldn't get warm.

'When I got back to London, I saw Daphne's parents. I met her sisters and one brother, and some of her women friends that I knew but not closely.

'To this day no one knows how or why it occurred, nor what actually did happen.'

I stopped talking for a while. Watched some leaves fall. Beside me, Freyja waited. Her hand found mine and squeezed it. I met her eyes, deep, filled with her own memories.

Neither Freyja nor I were widows, with widow status. In the wider world, our grief wasn't known as real grief. She would have understood if I'd tried to explain it. So Freyja was the most important person I'd met since Maria died, because I didn't *have* to explain.

'We had the funeral back in London. Maria was cremated. Cheryl told me that's what she'd once said she wanted. I didn't know. Maria and I never talked about death. Too busy living.

'Graham stayed a while then went back to his flat. Cheryl had a fortnight off work.

'The circle of friends we'd gone round with – to discos, theatre, demos, parties – they were all kind. For the first two or three months they wrote and phoned, called in, invited me round. But close friends are different, aren't they? You can't make close friends happen, if they weren't close before.

'My close friends, lesbians, had been Daphne and Bronwyn. I'd have turned to them if Maria was ill, or if there was some terrible accident. They were gone. So was Beatrice, back in Aotearoa. Anyway the others of our circle had their own lives to lead. I wasn't the centre of the universe. Not their universe. So I turned down some of the invitations, then the rest.

'One or two of them said to me, "Join things, Denny. Go to classes." I know they meant well but there are women in those classes that have been to college, got degrees. They don't mean to be snooty, but I feel outside. There are things they know, take for granted. Things they've already learned. Now, I feel a bit differently, but then it was too soon.

'So I was on my own. Just me and Roof. I had to see if I was made of grit. A day at a time. And if not a day at a time, then I'd try hour at a time. Then I walked into the library and met you – and now things are changing.'

'For me, too, since I met you, Denny.'

As we sat in the forest – Freyja and I – hugging, and crying, I felt as if my skin was being put back on, over all the rubbed raw places.

Eleven

Next morning I woke up strangely curious about Roarie. What was happening to Candace, Bess, Mary, Martha and Ruth?

As soon as I put pen to paper, Roarie arrived.

'I'm so glad you're there again,' I said.

''Tis you hides away, Denny. But I know why. You're feared of the fires, too many, too fast.'

'I've been avoiding you, and I'm sorry. I lost courage. Maybe I am going crazy, but now Freyja's back I can talk to her about things, and I can cope better with the voices.'

'I shall not hurt you, Denny. I am your friend. I plead with you to trust me. 'Twas heartache for me these days past, waiting for you. My voice calling, calling you, to no avail.'

'I sound heartless, Roarie, but I was going crazy and I couldn't stand it. A day at a time, that's all I can promise.'

'Shut your heart to my call?'

'Yes. Or my head'll blow off. Please don't recriminate. It makes it much harder for me.'

'All right. 'Tis cold here, winter is on the way. We have work to do.'

'I'm so curious. Tell me about Candace. I'll read again what you said already, then I want you to meet me on south bank.'

''Tis a turnabout. That you shouldst demand a place, a person.'

'That's right. I'm a toughie like you and I'm not the sort to follow quietly. I want some say in the journey. I want to arrange it with you, not sit around waiting for you to make all the first moves. If we're going to be friends, real friends, I'll be more active, lively. Not be told where and when to meet. I mean, not every time. I'm nobody's yes woman, I never was. Crazy, maybe. But not passive!!'

'I like you, Denny. 'Tis well I chose you.'

'Good. I'll meet you on south bank, about noon.'

Candace Barton lives alone in one room. Hers is the attic, seven feet wide, freezing in winter, stifling in summer. Below her live the Harrisons, below them the Woolleys. On the ground floor is the landlord, his wife, and six surviving children.

The house, fourth along from the sign of the Green Dolphin, third alley east off Long Southwark, is one room wide, each floor opening straight in off the two-feet-wide stairs. They can't get a table up the stairs, but if they juggle at the turns, they can just manage a wooden chair, round and up, and a bedding roll. If they want a table, like Candace, then they carry up each narrow piece of wood, and nail it together in the room.

No one has a bed, not the Harrisons, nor the Woolleys, nor the landlord and his wife. They all sleep on the floors, rolling up the bedding each day and sitting on top of the lot.

To the others, Candace lives in the height of luxury. She appreciates the room herself.

Back in Ibadan there is always an aunt or grandmother to stay with for a few nights if too much is going on at home. And there is so much outdoor space, the courtyards outside the family home, and the warmth of the sun, not this extreme London weather. But Africa is now another time, another world.

They aren't many days into the voyage after being forced aboard. She is sixteen. On deck. She and ten other girls, young and beautiful.

The moon is new, she will remember. However hard she will try to forget the scenes they will remain vivid . . .

The moon is new. They dance there, almost unable to

stand from hunger and terror, wanting to vomit, made to dance round a pile of chains and shackles.

She plans to leap overboard. The white crew, though drunk, watch closely. There are two men between herself and the edge.

The ship suddenly lurches. The drunken crew are thrown. Some sort of explosion. The entire ship shudders, the deck tilts, the masts crack with a sound like heavy gunfire.

Screams split the groans from the hold: others are trapped, chained. Suddenly, they are all in the water. She swims . . . swimming without shackles. Stroke on stroke cutting water fast, like in the river at home.

But this water is very cold.

Later she learns that some London broadsheets carry news of a ship. It should be en route to Bristol, perhaps detouring for an illicit docking in London.

The owners claim they know nothing of the human cargo; or the contraband that washes ashore.

At dawn, fishermen find her clinging to a floating mast, drifting towards the Sussex coast. The fishing boat is from the twin villages of East and West Warren, where a river flows through a wide flat estuary over a shingle beach. Either side of the beach, high cliffs rise and fall to the west and east.

Fishermen carry her to the house of Harold Barton, a Quaker farmer who owns most of the land around the two villages, and whose brother, Francis, is an elder of the local meeting.

When Francis sees her, he immediately thinks of the Acts of the Apostles. To him, Africa is all one place. To her, all is confusion around one clear intent: to survive. She isn't in a position to insist on her own name, and hasn't any knowledge of the new language.

Later, fluent in English, she thinks how easy it is for the Bartons to confuse the queens of Ethiopia with the queens of her own country. So for want of any power, she answers to the Bartons' name for her, Candace.

From East and West Warren, Candace is taken to the London home of the third brother, Henry Barton, in Long Southwark.

Much of the area from the Barton household eastwards along south bank has, in one way or another, something to do with leather. Some of the firms are tiny, perhaps two brothers, occasionally a brother and sister, or father and son. Exceptions are the tanneries, but even they aren't large. They're small concerns, maintained by family networks.

The Bartons are such a network, very prosperous by the yardsticks of the era.

For the first time since capture and shipwreck, Candace finds something familiar. Leather. Her people, she knows, have been town dwellers and leather workers throughout family history. Some of her family leave her town each day for work in the surrounding fields; others make things; others are traders.

By comparison, London is backward and uncultured. People stink, being dirty in their habits. They don't keep themselves bathed, nor clean their clothes, and most have fleas, which horrify Candace.

She keeps her disgust to herself. She has survived her uprooting, the fire of the white men's guns, and intends to go on surviving. She is not the only African woman in her part of London, but she has yet to meet anyone who speaks the same language, let alone dialect. She searches constantly, will not give up searching, but doesn't have much hope.

She desires a trade, to work in leather, as she did before. Hannah Barton, Henry's wife, suggests she specialise in riding boots, and makes some introductions.

The Bartons don't think of Candace as property, nor as their servant. This sets them apart from those people who find it amusing to keep Black children as pets, and gain status from having Black servants.

Once, she is fitting boots in a large mansion by Hampton Court, when through an open door, she sees a Black butler, passing across a huge dining hall, finely dressed. Around his neck is bolted a thin silver collar. He cannot take it off.

Candace runs to the outside privy where she is violently sick. On her return to the fitting parlour she hurriedly makes an excuse about something she's eaten. She struggles to finish the fitting. She leaves, in the carriage provided, without challenging. For nights after, she dreams of the collar, and swears that she will never wear any necklace. No matter how fine the craftsmanship, she will always picture the servant and his neck, with the band around it.

Papers are drawn up by the Bartons for Candace to be legally adopted into their kindred. She's given the papers formally on Monday, mid-morning, in a quiet ceremony in the house in Long Southwark.

Legally, she cannot be sent back to Africa where she would risk recapture and enslavement; cannot be sent to the West Indies to be enslaved on a plantation or in a household there; nor likewise to the southern states of America.

In England, she has the right of free employment; and the right to reside. In the event of the deaths of the entire Barton family those rights remain hers. She has the papers signed by all three Barton brothers, to prove it. Hannah Barton tells Candace that the law is ambiguous. Some say that no Englishman or woman can own a slave on English soil; others say this refers only to white slaves; yet others by-pass the law – and in practice they flaunt their unfree Black servants as a sign of wealth.

Candace sees a notice in a street: Black children for sale. Such notices may be few and far between, and Hannah Barton says a time will come when such sales will be openly challenged, but meanwhile in the 1660s, there are few who would speak against the great slave-owning families.

Baptism is no protection for runaway slaves. Recapture notices appear often in broadsheets. But some runaways are never found. Candace begins to piece the puzzle together. She reasons to herself that people somewhere, Black or white, must be hiding and helping runaways. No one on the run is pursued for ever. At some point, fugitives are presumed dead. Masters and mistresses stop advertising for their recapture.

Candace trusts no one, including the Bartons, though they are not bad people. But they are using her, she feels, in their own way. Helping her makes them feel good and righteous. They have power and money, tanneries on the south bank opposite the Tower, and houses by a lovely estuary, near a shingle beach on the Sussex coast. Good deeds stop them from feeling guilty about their riches.

At night, lying alone and awake, longings set her on fire; longings for the gods and goddesses, ceremonies and rituals of her own beliefs and ancestors. But by day she needs the Bartons if she is going to survive. She wants their knowledge of law and lawyers, of books and the ways of the new country.

For three years until the outbreak of plague Candace lives mainly in London, rarely travelling with Hannah and Henry by carriage to their family in East and West Warren.

She respects Hannah Barton, who works extremely hard, running the Barton household meticulously, supervising servants; teaching them all to read; keeping books, diaries and household accounts; teaching her sons and daughters the Bible and family prayers; keeping up to date with the news and the guilds, and changes in the outside world of finance and ideas. The Barton women are all well read, some of the girls equally with the boys, though the girls are being trained to run their own houses after marriage, not to become employers organising tanneries and farms.

The women keep still rooms and store rooms; they treat ailments and create recipes. They are extremely capable and work from dawn until late evening, as does Candace herself.

She builds up regular orders for expertly made riding boots for wealthy women and men, and even makes small boots for their children, who ride almost as soon as they can walk.

Her appearance must be impeccable at all times; her manners perfect. It is a strain in London, where everything is done by strange rules and customs. In England, Candace observes how the Barton children learn from the cradle by copying the adults, just as she did herself back home – from her mother and older sisters, her aunts and her grandmother – but *what* they learn is different.

So, as a free Black woman surviving in a new rigid country, where Black people are advertised for sale, Candace learns a lonely, difficult path.

Everything changes in summer 1665 when plague hits the household in Long Southwark, before Henry and Hannah can flee to West Warren. The heat in June and July is intense. It builds up each day. Whenever the wind changes, it brings towards the rich the flies and stench from poor areas.

Henry and Hannah are victims, as are several of their children and some of their servants. Candace and the surviving servants do not inherit the house, nor any money. Candace has her papers. It seems that Henry, Francis and Harold Barton felt their duty was done by those papers alone.

By the end of the plague year, as people pass on the count of the dead by word of mouth, estimates of the total increase weekly. News comes into London of the victims from villages around. Even if people take off several thousand for exaggerations, it's difficult to get the figure below sixty thousand by Christmas.

Knowing that Candace is desperate for lodgings, the new landlord overcharges her. She accepts his price. The house is crowded but clean, in the area she wants, and she has a room to herself. Since it's at the top of the house, no one tramps to and fro past her door. She has a trade, so the landlord knows he'll get his rent.

Candace decides to turn the disaster into one of life's chances. She has her work tools with her. Some of her wealthy contacts are still alive.

She becomes one of the working poor, in the area called south bank, where rich people seek adventure and then leave, and poor people seek each other because they cannot leave.

This is a place of pickpockets and card sharks, where newcomers mutter prayers and spells; of beggars, and brothels, where rich men sneak for pleasure, but pay meanly.

It is to this area that runaways like Bess and Gabriell come, to hide and start again. Here Candace finds an unexpected customer – John Wild; and a few people she dare trust and then a sense of belonging while in exile. In later years, one of those whom she trusts is a white weaver's daughter, a healer's apprentice, from miles to the north east.

Twelve

There was a wide circle of fire, from the Australian bush to the shores of Aotearoa, Hawaii, and back again, circling the Pacific island of Mururoa.

I was with Freyja, in a vast underground cave on Mururoa. It was the size of several football pitches. There was a roaring noise – the sound of Wind bellowing through underground tunnels. We ran but found the tunnels blocked: Wind and Fire had an assignation. We were trapped, in the middle. The heat was intense – the hottest place I'd ever been.

I grabbed Freyja, shouting: 'It's a war. They're starting a war.' There was an almighty bang, a bright flash.

I woke up.

Time and place were moving as the room spun around. I put my hands over my eyes, looking into the darkness in my palms. I didn't know what was dream, what was real.

The walls of my bedroom turned round like Roof when she chases her own tail. I fumbled for my dressing-gown, shrugged into it, held on to the walls, then the bannister.

Downstairs, the air was crowded with voices, like a railway tannoy. I jumped when the kettle whistled loud as an old steam train.

I made tea, let Roof into the garden and prepared her vegetarian dog food. Then I took the tea up to the small back bedroom, and picked up some felt pens and drew the pictures of the dream. I'd never bothered to do that before.

The worst thing about all the people in the dream was they all had paper cups instead of heads. Disposable people.

Throw-away heads.

In a panic, I phoned Freyja, early, before she left for work. We arranged a time to meet, then I spent the morning with Maria's books on Pacific peoples, nuclear issues, and land rights. I didn't pick up a pen in case Roarie spoke to me from the paper.

It was too chilly to sit out at lunchtime, so Freyja and I walked about, eating chips and keeping Roof on the lead.

'I'm getting voices,' I said. She listened as I babbled my words fast, running sentences together: 'Voices, from the past – I'm tapping into something I don't understand, but I can't stop it and it's all around the time of the Great Fire of London, and I've written some of it down, and I'm very frightened, and I'm having terrible dreams about fires and it's all tied up with nuclear things, like nuclear subs in Scotland; Sellafield and leukaemia; and Pacific peoples being used as guinea pigs and how humans live with radiation – things like that, and I'm frantic for it to stop but I want to know what happens, and now you're in my dreams too and it's all going round in circles.'

'Tell me the whole dream, will you?'

I told her the dream and that I'd drawn the pictures of it. She nodded, then said: 'Seventeenth-century voices, did you say? Tell me about them.'

'Yes. The plague was 1665 and the Fire of London was 1666, and I think I'm going crackers. If I don't talk to somebody about it and get it sorted out, I really will be out to lunch.'

'And you've got pictures with the voices?'

'Yes. I can hear them and see them like a film in my head. It's so vivid it's like I'm there with a camera and a sound track. It's really driving me crazy. It's so clear, that's what so frightening. When they're talking I can hear their actual voices. But when it's just the story, unfolding, it's like a sort of filter, in my own words, in my language now, not all this "'tis" and "'twas" and "is it not" sort of stuff.'

Freyja linked her arm though mine as we walked. 'Telly documentaries? Some of the history programmes? Reconstructions? Theatre?'

95

'Dunno, s'pose so. Come to think of it, yes, I've seen plays, the odd film. Why?'

'Time's running on, Denny, and I've got to get back, but I'll come straight round when I've finished, and so I'll see you as soon as I can get to you, after work. I promise. Now, listen, I want you to go home, and catch up on some sleep. You look absolutely knackered and it's no wonder with dreams like those and all that head stuff. Get into bed, right under the duvet, and zonk out for the afternoon. You can get up when you hear Roof barking; that'll be me arriving. Promise?'

She put her hands on my shoulders and turned me to face her square on, leaned forward and kissed me on the cheek.

Taken aback, I promised. She left and I went home and surprised myself; did as I was told. I woke, as she said, when Roof barked.

In the small back bedroom Freyja wandered around with her mug of tea, unwinding after her day's work, and peering again at the pictures and photos on the walls. She stopped in front of a collage of old photos of Epping and Walthamstow in a clipframe. I watched her from the single bed, where I sat leaning back against a cushion, knees tucked under me.

'A lovely room, this,' she began. 'I like these shots of old Walthamstow. But I love the new design, and being in the library right there in the middle of the market. Not that I had my mind on work this afternoon.' She sat the other end of the single bed and leaned against the wall. 'I shelved books like a dingbat to make the time pass, wondering how you were. No point in asking if you're OK; where do you want to start?'

In reply I passed her my writing pads, covered in lines and lines of handwriting. Then I closed my eyes and leaned back, thinking of Roarie, Candace and Bess, Mary, Martha and Ruth, as I heard Freyja turning the pages, reading quickly. She must have done a course in speed reading. I envied her, as it took me much longer to absorb anything.

As she came to the end, she said: 'This is fascinating. Is there any more?'

'Yes, but it isn't written yet. I'm avoiding some of it.'

Her voice was gentle as she asked: 'At lunchtime you said you were frightened. What is it that scares you?'

'It's easier to say what I'm not scared of.'

'All right. Whatever you want.'

'It's not the women themselves, the people. I love Roarie and she intrigues me. Candace and Bess, and Martha and Ruth love one another – how could I be scared of them? Mary By-the-Well is a healer, and I don't know that much about healing, though I've gleaned bits and pieces from friends.

'So it's not the women you're frightened of?'

'No. It's not. It's how they come to me. Getting the voices, seeing and hearing them going about their lives. Their lives were then and mine's now and I don't know what's going on. Then in last night's dream it's like I was there, watching Mururoa die. Being bashed to bits by nuclear tests. I mean, with Maria being from Aotearoa we talked about all those things, and I read what she read and she was usually up to date. She used Rosalie Bertell's book like a bible; chapter and verse. She could quote bits, and she was angry. So was I.

'Nothing like this has happened to me before. The dream was so real and so are the voices. So real. It's weird. It's all linked up, I know it is. But I don't know how. My head's so full of voices I'm scared to be quiet. I turn on the telly or radio to crowd them out. Even thought of borrowing Graham's walkman. But I don't think I'd feel safe outside with a walkman on. Might miss the traffic, or somebody creeping up on me. My nerves are in a mess. I need some help.'

'I can only talk as a friend,' said Freyja. 'I'm getting really fond of you, and I want to help but I'm a bit out of my depth as well; and I'm a little jealous too, so it's confusing.'

'Jealous? Jealous of me? I don't understand.'

'I'll try to be honest, but it's not simple . . .'

'Life never is, is it! Sorry, go on, I interrupted . . .'

'The thing is, I've always wanted to get voices.'

I laughed. It sounded so funny, and she looked so sad, but she laughed when I did.

'I know it sounds funny. Like I want to be a professional schizophrenic or something . . .'

'It does, you're right.'

'It happened through my job. I'm the link person for organising writers to come and give talks. Their life, their work, their creativity, early influences, everything. I love that part of my job, and I go along to the talks because I have to. I do the introductions and make the coffee, hand around the biscuits and all that. I get to hear some wonderful people. I listen and take it all in, and go home and try to write and . . . nothing. I dabble in my diary and come up with quite good bits sometimes, but no voices. How I've tried to get voices!!'

Roof went to Freyja and watched her, wagging her tail slowly from side to side as if to say that she trusted Freyja and why didn't I read Freyja's body language properly and trust her too?

Freyja patted Roof and said to me: 'What if I called you a writer, Denny?'

I started to laugh. High freaking laughter, tin can on a cat's tail, cemetery shriekings. Roof, hating it, sat on her haunches, howling, calling up wolves from Siberia, ancestors; bats flew from old belfries; the moon was blood green, tarnished metal; and maybe there were goblins in the garden.

Freyja shushed Roof. Roof nudged me. Presently, I stopped.

I spoke to Roof: 'She's calling me a writer. She says I'm a writer. I'm not crazy, I'm a writer. Or maybe that is crazy, huh?'

'Denny, can I ask you something?'

'Fire away,' I said flippantly.

'What would be the worst thing that could happen to you and Roarie?'

'Me and Roarie?' I screwed up my face, thinking hard. 'I'd go mad and Roarie would disappear into thin air and never come back.'

'So that's two worst things?'

'Suppose so. I might go mad anyway if all this voice stuff doesn't let up. Even if Roarie came back, that's no insurance.

I mean, she wasn't in my fire dream last night, but I still woke up crazy.' Pause. 'It's more than just me and Roarie.'

'But you don't want her to go away?'

'No, I don't. That's the trouble. I want to go on talking to her; I want to know what happens to her.'

'So do I, that's why I asked if there was any more.'

'But I didn't write that stuff. Not by myself.'

Freyja looked at me quizzically, a small smile catching the edge of her mouth.

'Roarie and I wrote it together. It came out of my pen after we talked about it. She can't write it without me. I mean, if I left my pen on the paper and went out, it wouldn't be written when I got back, nothing like that. It's the two of us together. I didn't write it by myself.'

Freyja rubbed her chin. She had a habit of doing that when she was thinking. After a little while she said: 'I've heard more than one woman writer describing her process like that. Couldn't your interest in old maps have brought it on? So that fictional characters came through?'

'Still wouldn't make me feel sane. Doesn't mean I'm not mad, not at all. One night I'm dreaming of Fire and Wind as people, I mean women, warring and destroying an island. Next day I pick up my fountain pen to write to my oldest, dearest friend, Beatrice, and out pops a weaver's daughter in the 1600s!'

'You're not making this easy are you?'

'Who said it had to be easy?'

But her tone was bantering and my reply swift. It made us laugh; a small piece of fear broke off and dropped down behind the table.

Freyja said: 'I don't think you're crazy. It's not crazy to care about global issues, nuclear power, other people's lives, *where*ver they live, *when*ever they live.' She put the emphasis on where and when. I liked Freyja's voice. I could listen to her for hours. 'I think the whole world's going crazy, not you. Uranium, wars, refugees. Gluts and famines, people being driven off their land. Modern slavery, camps, reservations . . . I came along and reinforced your cares and fears, unwittingly; all my talk of fire.'

'Put like that, it makes sense.'

'Work was the vital thing for me when Estelle and Gemma died. It was my structure. I had to get up, get dressed, go to work. I admire you for going through it alone, like you did.'

'I couldn't have gone half-way across the world, like you. That's a strong thing to do.'

Freyja put her hand on her chest, mocking Sinatra – I did it my way. I laughed at her macabre humour till I ached. She had a very funny body language, given to clowning. It often lightened her words when she talked, even the most serious things. I found it endearing. Just as well; could have been infuriating.

Things were starting to fit into place. I found myself blurting words, chasing ideas. 'Going mad's not the worst thing, no, it's not. The worst thing would be to not know what happens to Roarie. She's part of me now and I don't want to stay sane if I have to lose her. I'd rather let Them come and get me, take me away, than lose her. She could come with me. So long as They let me have my own pen and some paper, she'd be there.'

Freyja regarded me strangely for a few moments, trying to get the measure of what she dare say and I dare hear.

'You want me to be honest, don't you?'

'I know it's risky, but yes, I do.'

'I think to be creative you have to walk along the very edge of your mind. Sometimes you have to walk at night, without any moonlight. It's slippery underfoot. It's dangerous but it's exciting. You look into the night-darkness, it's warm and you feel sound like vibrations on your body. You can walk at night like that, back home in some places. You could fall, stumble over the edge, only thin grass for handholds. Or you could stay still, not daring to move.'

'You want me to go on writing?'

'It's what you want that matters, what it means to you. I don't know the edge between creativity and madness. I know it's hard to hold on to thin grass, when both feet are already over the cliff and your whole body's in mid-air. But where the edge is to fall over, that's a different question.'

'And there's no one to catch me.'

'There never is. Not in that actual moment. Maybe someone will come along and find you, and maybe not. That's why it's got to be your needs, what you want that makes you decide to keep writing, keep painting, keep composing, whatever your creativity is. It's the edge of your mind, not anyone else's. The only one who can go to that place is you.'

'So Roarie is mine because we had that conversation, her and me? Whether she's real or fiction?'

'We agreed it was risky. I know what *I* think you're dealing with, but I could be wrong. What I do know about is fiction writing. I'm a librarian. I don't *know* if Roarie's real or not. If she is, then she might be a ghost, if you believe in ghosts; or you might be time travelling, if you hold with that; or she might be time travelling, if that's possible. It's called channelling, if she is real. It would make you a medium, and I've never met a medium and I don't know anything about it.'

'I don't want to be a medium. It terrifies the pants off me. But to me, Roarie is real – they all are.'

'So you will go on "Speaking Paper?" '

I agreed. I just wanted to 'be' and Roarie was part of that. So was Freyja. I realised with a jolt she must be hungry.

After a meal, she stayed over, sleeping in the twins' old room. I slept in my room, restfully, without dreaming.

Thirteen

I didn't see Freyja for a few days, then one evening there was an unexpected ring on the front bell, and I thought it was her. I shushed Roof and opened the door.

A Black woman, my height, stood there, carrying a large plain cardboard box.

I gasped: 'Rosa?' She had her hair in braids, a new style. It suited her.

'Hello, Denny.' She wasn't smiling. Neither was I.

'Be quiet, Roof. Rosa, this is Roof, my dog. She'll settle in a minute.'

'We have unfinished business, don't we, Denny?'

'Yes. You'll come in, will you?'

'Thanks.' She stepped into the narrow hall.

I stood, as Rosa leaned back against the door to close it; then, carrying the heavy box, she followed me into the small front room, juggling with some difficulty around the door-frame.

Why Rosa? Why the box? And how could we begin?

We sat opposite one another, with the box unopened on the floor between us. What was in it? I wanted to open it. I waited. Rosa and I seemed far apart either side of the room; two sides of a gaping wound.

She was agitated. Her eyes dropped to the cardboard box then she raised them to me as she said: 'Daphne is haunting me. All around me. Haunting me.' She regarded the box again for a moment, then said stonily: 'I didn't want to come here. I wouldn't have, but for Daphne.' We exchanged glances as I nodded.

She repeated: 'But for Daphne.' She sighed, 'All those years. We were together a long time. We knew each other in the sixth form . . .

'She's in the flat, in the wallpaper, the pictures, the plants. I took to sleeping at my lover's place. To be free a while. But I always went home. And there she was.'

Rosa seemed unhappy, uneasy, angry, as the unopened box loomed large, its presence huge.

She said: 'I don't know if I believe in ghosts. I just know Daphne was there. And while she was there, so was Bronwyn, and Maria . . . and you.'

'Me?' I stayed as calm as I could.

Rosa's body went very tense, and her hands were jumpy now. 'When Daphne said she wanted to leave our flat, to move to Wales and live with Bronwyn, I thought that if I didn't die of pain, I'd die of anger.' Her mouth went tight, her voice now fighting for control. 'Not for me a foursome. Me and my lover, Daphne and hers . . . Four strong women all different, all linked, all Black women. Oh no . . .'

Then Rosa's voice softened, her shoulders dropping slightly, as she said: 'And now . . . Not for you a foursome with her, either. Not now. Me in one home grieving, for things that never were, and you, here, grieving for things that cannot be . . .'

She fell silent, looking at her hands, working out what to say. 'I think perhaps that for every moment you grieve Daphne, I hear you. And somehow, Daphne has stayed with me, long enough to get me to tonight.'

At these words, it seemed right for me to respond: 'I know you don't want to be here . . .' I glanced at the box. 'It's not easy, for you or me. It's important, for Daphne's sake. Would you like some tea?'

She had clasped her hands together in an unconscious action, almost wringing them, but not quite. She replied: 'That's kind. Thanks. Could I use your loo?'

'Yes, it's through the kitchen, this way.'

Back in the front room, tea and biscuits beside her, Rosa

said: 'I can't live there now. Not with her gone. She's never coming back. I'm moving out.'

Roof interrupted Rosa by sniffing at the box and watching it warily. By now I was so curious about it, I could barely stay calm.

Rosa said: 'There's a small loft. The landlord didn't want us to put stuff up there, but we did. I went up to clear it out. Ready to move. At the back, I couldn't see it from the hatch, I found this.'

She now pushed the large plain box towards me, indicating I should open the folded leaves at the top. I did so, and, as I saw inside, Rosa said: 'At first I thought it was just an empty large box one of us had shoved there ready for a move together. Then I opened the leaves and I saw what you can see.'

There was, inside the large plain box, loosely wrapped in fading tissue paper, a slightly smaller box with a fitted lid. On the lid was a note in familiar handwriting: 'For Denny.'

Carefully removing the tissue paper, I lifted out the inner box, placing it on the carpet, where it shone. It shone because it was entirely covered in patterned satins and brocades of every imaginable colour, and silver and gold lamé; it gleamed and caught the light. It was about a foot by a foot and a half, and about a foot deep. I didn't open it.

Rosa said: 'I didn't want to bring it. I wanted to throw it away, and I couldn't. How could I? I wanted to dispose of it, but where? I wanted it to say, "For Rosa", and it didn't. To burn it, but how, when *she* put so much exquisite work into it. She meant it for you. Not me.'

'For me, yes.'

'How do we do this?'

'I don't know. But you came here and I respect you for it. You did this for Daphne . . .'

'And myself. Rosa. For me. I thought if I just dumped it on your doorstep and went, maybe she'd stop haunting me. Maybe I'd have done what she needed. But no. She wanted me to ring your bloody door-bell, come and talk. Meet you . . .'

I said: 'I wanted to reach out to you. But I wouldn't. I

could. But I wouldn't. I didn't have anything to reach with, anything you wanted. The last woman in the world you wanted to hear from was me . . .' I paused, she listened. I carried on: 'I'll tell you what I know. But I don't know if it'll help, or make you more angry.'

We looked at each other, though neither of us smiled. She drank her tea and listened to me.

'I know that you loved Daphne deeply. It was mutual. Outsiders thought you were lovers still, though you hadn't been for years. But that kind of closeness, and sharing a home, and both being lesbians, some gave you both a hard time. I know that you both made a decision many years ago not to have relationships with white women for reasons about power. Later, Daphne changed. You didn't. It was hell.'

The room was silent for a moment. The gleaming box was very beautiful. Daphne had excelled herself.

I said: 'I respect your position. I respect it deeply, and that's why I never reached across.' I drank my tea hurriedly, and rushed on. 'I don't know much about you, because Daphne respected you too. She loved you so much, but she also loved us – the three of us – I knew you were angry and hurt; that originally Daphne made the same decision as you. She shifted her position. *I'm not saying she was right*. When I met her – when she was lovers with Bronwyn – I'd find myself thinking of you, what it would have meant to you if we'd been Black.'

Rosa listened, as if she truly wanted me to go on talking. I said: 'Daphne and I went to an art exhibition. I'm not the arty sort, but there was this series of huge paintings, by a Welsh woman. Daphne and I – we fell in love with each other and the paintings.'

I stopped, aware again of the wonderful covered box that Rosa had brought to me. I said: 'Daphne bought several sets of the cards, she said she was going to send them to me, now and then. So I knew, when she died, that this box, or something like it, existed. That was Daphne – always with a box project on the go – and there were cards she hadn't sent me, from the series.'

I paused, then I said: 'For you to bring this . . . It's hard to begin to say what it means to me.'

Eye contact. We smiled our first smile.

She said: 'I wasn't going to ring your bell. I didn't want to. You might have shut the door in my face; left me standing there; taken the box in. But I wanted to be released from haunting. How dare she stay in the flat when she was dead, if she wouldn't stay when she was alive?' Rosa put her face in her hands.

I left her and made her some more tea.

When I returned with it she was calm again.

She said: 'I've been supported – my lover's been there, there for me. I'm sorry about Maria, I really am.'

'I'm sorry for us all,' I said. 'I never dreamed you'd come. At first I wanted you to. But I knew you wouldn't. Couldn't.'

'And you knew why?'

'I knew your boundaries were not the same, yours and hers. We all have boundaries. I respected yours. That's why I didn't come to look for this.'

Eye contact. Our second smile.

I said: 'I was the final straw, for you.'

'You're not wrong, Denny. Daphne and I had a terrible confrontation concerning you. She wanted *me* to comfort *her*. She loved two women at the same time. But I longed for her to find a Black woman, so I could come back to the inside of her life. She turned the knife around and around. Though I can't and won't curse her. She waited for me. She waited in our flat for me. She knew the box was there, and that it was for you. She knew how nosy I'd be. That I'd open it; try to hear her speak to me; try to find her through it.'

I replied: 'She was no more a saint than me or you. She was real. She didn't always behave well. She sometimes behaved very badly. I loved her dearly but I couldn't live with her. That's why we didn't become lovers. I already had a lover; and so did she. But I loved her; and she loved you. She never once said anything private about you. She never told any of your stories – not if they were yours to tell. From that point of view Rosa, Daphne never let you down.'

'Yes. Yes I know. I hope she'll let me move now. I've

things to do with my life, besides deliver messages for my dead bosom friend.' Rosa took a deep breath, glanced at Roof spread on the hearthrug, then took a last look at the shining box. 'It's your box. I won't stay while you open it. I know what's in it, but it's yours and hers. I'm going to go soon . . . but . . . there's something else. On the back of the card there, that says "For Denny", she wrote my work number. Daphne wants you to have it,' said Rosa, meaning: I don't want you to have it and I don't want you to use it but I'm desperate to get rid of this haunting, to finish this business.

'I don't suppose I'd ever use it but thanks,' I said, meaning: don't worry, I know it's not the start of friendship, and I know how it is to feel haunted.

We didn't hug. We smiled for a third time, thinly.

'Will you have more tea before you go?'

'No thanks. But I'm glad I came here.'

'So am I, Rosa. Thank you.'

When she'd gone, I opened the box, found the sets of cards, and walked again through the gallery with Daphne.

I woke to the ringing of the phone. Morning sunshine streamed into the bedroom. Who could it possibly be at this hour? It was only eight-fifteen.

The voice was Freyja's: 'Denny, it's me. I'm sorry it's so early, but could I come round and see you?'

'Of course. What's wrong? What about work?'

'It's Wednesday. We're closed. Been up for hours, out for a paper already. Can't sleep. Really like to talk.'

'We'll have breakfast. Come now.'

Over tea and toast up in the back room, she told me: 'I'm in such a tizz. Last night I finally decided to go and find Estelle's sister. I'd tried phoning – kept getting unobtainable. So I went there.

'Well, what a shock. She's the image of Estelle. Older, of course. But I just shook on the doorstep. There was Estelle, in the flesh, a few years on, same eyes, figure. They all have very black eyes and very thick hair. Estelle's was black. Her sister's is grey now. She invited me in. She's a very warm person. I liked her. She said she'd been meaning to phone but there on the table was the reason she'd been preoccupied. Her passport and some plane tickets. Then another woman arrived. You could cut the air with a knife. Estelle's sister's called Lindsey Shepherd and the ex-lover – the woman who turned up – is Lerryn Trevonnian . . .'

I interrupted: 'I know those names. I don't know the women themselves. I didn't know they'd split. Lerryn works as an artist. I've got her cards. Cornwall mostly. Lovely. Lindsey works in a glove factory. I mean, she *did*. She has a daughter.'

'That's right. Rosie. Gone to university. It's all such a shock. I'd no idea Lindsey was a dyke. Is a dyke. It's so bloody ironic. Me flying here, her flying there. Just as I was hoping to meet up, make friends, a connection.'

'Where's she going?'

'Australia. To stay with my aunty – her mother. Longed to go for years and years. Says the timing's right now.' Pause. 'Lindsey's got a new lover . . . a woman from Sydney.'

'Oh, what?'

'No kidding. My home town. I can't stand it. My head's blown off.'

'Hey, you'll be OK.'

'Scattered. That's me. Bits everywhere. No continuity.'

I reached out and held her hand while she fought against tears. She said: 'I'm jealous of her being there. I'm jealous and selfish and I hate myself for it.' Then she grinned: 'I'm goin' down the garden eatin' worms.'

'Toast is better. You have a look at Lerryn's cards. They're from a women's bookshop. I'll go down and fix more food, what d'you say?'

'Please?' She smirked.

'Clown!! Here they are – I'll only be a sec.'

Later, Freyja said: 'Lerryn gave me a lift home. We talked half the night. I told her about you. She asked how you were. I said you were surviving, was that all right?'

'It's true. I am. Yes. That's all right.'

'She met Bronwyn once. She asked me to say how sorry she was.'

'Thanks.'

'This picture – it's her aunt's place in Cornwall,' began Freyja. 'Been rebuilt. Still a bungalow, but huge now. This picture's history, Denny. You're looking at history again.'

'I always am. I made a discovery. Here, look at this map.' I pointed with the sharp tip of a pencil at one of the maps I'd drawn: 'See this line?'

'Through the back garden here?' asked Freyja, closely scrutinising my map, then running her finger along the line.

I nodded. 'It's a footpath that Roarie, Martha and Ruth used, between the river and Chingford Meade Mill, when they went to the river to gather rushes.'

'Spooky.' Freyja shivered. 'Keep on writing, won't you?'

'Can't stop now,' I said, pleased at her response.

'No. You're on a journey. So am I.' She became thoughtful for a moment, then said: 'You can plan what you'd like to finish, but life doesn't always give you the chance. You can plan who you'd like your friends to be, where you'd like to find them, but life's not like that – they turn up in other places, when you least expect them and weren't looking. Like you and me. I don't know what I'd do without you. And last night, talking with Lerryn, I had the feeling that the future's here.'

'Lerryn?'

'Don't look at me like that.' Freyja laughed. 'It's not about lovers.'

'Oops.'

'I didn't mean it that way,' said Freyja. 'Not at all. I'm an emotional mess at the moment, and so is Lerryn. Neither of us is anybody's good luck at the moment. But I think we're going to be friends, and I want you to meet her. What's so strange is, the connection's with Lerryn, not Lindsey. I could never have predicted that. Anyway, I'm thinking of staying here.'

I said: 'I'd love you to stay in this country. Even if you went north, settled in Scotland or something, it's only a day away. Not like you going back to Auss.'

'Scotland's not very likely, with Gran in London. But I know what you mean.'

'Things are moving on, aren't they?'

'Yes, they are. But I really am in a mess.' She grinned again, with a rueful, lopsided smile: 'I'm a walking disaster area.'

Fourteen

I slept through the hurricane. The first I knew of it was a street strewn with branches of mountain ash, a dead phone and a dead electric clock. Every so often I dialled Freyja, to test the phone. Nothing.

On Tuesday 20 October I bought a paper and read: following Friday's attack on Silkworm missiles on the US flagged ship, the Kuwaiti-owned *Sea Isle City*, a twenty-minute warning was given to two Iranian oil platforms in international waters.

Four destroyers bombarded them.

Then I read: this had won support from the US Congress even though a Senate report warned that the administration's dangerously nebulous policy was leading to an escalating war, in order to save Iraq from defeat.

Iranian tugboats were reported to be rushing to the platforms, which were sending SOS messages.

I searched through my dictionary. *Nebulous*: cloudy turbid hazy vague indistinct obscure uncertain muddled bewildered; belonging to/resembling a nebula; *nebula*: a cloudy patch in the heavens produced by groups of stars or by a mass of gaseous or stellar matter.

Later, on telly, Sir Geoffrey Howe revealed that the British government and other allied countries had had advance notice that America wanted to retaliate for Friday's attack on the *Sea Isle City*. From America, reports showed politicians on both sides of the US Congress warning of the deepening danger, as they put it, and some of them wanted the War Powers Act invoked.

The hurricane. Wind's night out. Now, days later, I was hazy as to how I'd slept through it. I wished I understood how Wind took on moods like this. What had happened elsewhere to cause such fury? From outer space the earth was a marble – beautiful swirls of deep blue. Earth's atmosphere. Wind could be so gentle. Carrying hope, bringing warmth. And so terrible; carrying disease, doom, destruction.

Nebulous: a great word for my bewilderment.

And what about the word nebula? I liked it. It sounded biological: fibula/tibia/labia . . .

Nebula: Starry starry night; Van Gogh was a painter who went mad and cut off his ear, and there was a song of nebulas about him. Would America go mad and escalate the Gulf war, blow off everyone's ears? Next time? Another Hiroshima? Nagasaki? No one left, not even bewildered children? Nebulous policies?

I was thinking about war-mongers who wanted stardom, when the phone made me jump.

'Mum? It's on at last. I've tried every night since the storm.'

'Gray – hello love – how kind. I slept through it, don't laugh. Honestly. But you can tell its path by the slope of the torn trees, and you should see the poor old rec. All my lovely poplars, all torn and bleeding. It's awful, poor things . . . But listen, I'm more worried about Phil, it's hotting up out there.'

'He's OK, Mum. That's the news; why I've been going mad trying to get you. He phoned me.'

Pause.

'Mum? You there?'

'Yes, just a minute.' Pause. 'Silly me. That's better. Where is he?'

'Mauritius.'

'What the fuck's he doing in Mauritius?'

'Hated tankers. Jumped ship. Got a girlfriend and works for her dad in a bar. Been there less than a month. No bother finding a girl and a job, so he said. Full of it.'

'That leopard and his bloody spots,' I fumed. Less than a month was easily more than two weeks. So for more than a fortnight, Phil'd been on the end of a phone and only now he deigned to let us know where he was. I said as much to Gray, effing and sodding until I'd run out of words. Then we both started to laugh with relief, and it's strange to share hysterics down a phone line.

I said: 'Did he give you an address, silly question?'

'Nope. P'raps he'll write.'

We laughed, self-mocking.

Then he said: 'Right then, Mum, I'm off to the pub. No more tens. Love you lots.'

'You too. Thanks, love. Bye.'

On a biting cold evening, Lerryn Trevonnian and I met, as we waited, hands in coat pockets, in a large tiled Victorian porch, outside Freyja's grandmother's house.

'I was so sorry to hear about the tragedy, Denny. Did Freyja tell you I once heard your friend, Bronwyn, give a wonderful talk?'

'Yes. Thanks. You've not had it easy, either. I know your paintings – I've a lot of your postcards and I love them, but I didn't know about your, er, you and Lindsey. I'm sorry.'

Lerryn winced. She said: 'Thanks. I've some very good friends. I'm staying with Tessa – I helped her when she and Maureen broke up. And my Aunt Harry's a tower of strength. Oh, here's Freyja now.'

We saw Freyja's shape silhouetted by the hall lights behind her, through the lovely stained glass. The door opened and Freyja greeted us both warmly, giving each of us a hug. Over her shoulder I saw a hall like an art gallery, with a spotless white fitted carpet, fantastically expensive.

'You two go on,' I blurted, very embarrassed, shuffling to and fro on the doormat, making sure my trainers were immaculately clean. Ahead of me, a few feet along the hall, the others hadn't taken off their shoes, so I couldn't go over the top and do that, though I hardly dare step forward.

I held back.

What I saw in the entrance hall was evidence of monied socialism, something I'd heard of but never been part of, a class apart.

Nothing I saw as I began to walk forward was ostentatious. Nothing was out of place. That was the whole point. The hall was hung and decorated with original artwork with taken-for-granted confidence from generations back.

There were painted and embroidered pictures in exquisite frames; delicate watercolours; satin patchwork posters, some with a Greenham Common theme; and some with CND appliquéd on them. There were doves with peace symbols; and there were framed threadworks; Norwegian tapestries; and woven hangings.

It was beautiful – a blend and swirl and riot of colour off-set by the white carpet. I loved it, wanted it, was awestruck, and fascinated.

I wanted it all. The knowledge, of who, what and how. Worlds and worlds of something else, something other. I was pulled along by the beauty, the colours, the skill of the artists, weavers, needlewomen.

On thin-legged antique stands which probably had special names – that I didn't know, but they reminded me of antelope legs – were perfect, fresh flower arrangements.

I liked most of the framed things on the walls and they were in keeping with what I knew about Freyja's grandmother, whom I'd yet to meet on account of her busy schedule.

The others had gone. The hall was empty. As I turned through the door on my right, I entered a cavernous lounge, with a polished oak floor.

Wind arrived in the form of a draught, from a glass conservatory, through open french doors at the far end.

Maria seemed very near.

'Use your imagination,' said Wind.

Alone, I breathed inside a time-warp.

I wandered in time: a time-whirl of shining wood and glass and lights; of gleaming polished oak and glittering castle walls. I whirled inside the time-whirl, and I was alone.

Alone. A small being of insignificance. I knew things

others couldn't know; heard voices others didn't hear; in a myth I didn't write; in a place that wasn't mine; in a zone in distant time.

Then I saw her, with her back to me: a tall woman with short white hair, dressed in a long black skirt, over which hung a hip-length cloak.

The cloak. The magic cloak. The Queen of the Vanir.

The cavern spun slightly. The woman was regal, and from the nape of her upturned collar there flowed downward half a dozen falcon feathers. In full array the plumage shone.

Embroidered, not real, so finely needled I wanted to touch to make sure. Iridescent white and grey on black, luminous and shimmering: white and grey.

Sky-grey: storm cloud and rain cloud, thistle moon and gossamer. Strung on wings of night, from a fir tree in a snow-scoop forest, soft on soft, on long strong wings: not ground-grey heavy shining boulder-grey but airborne, high, from a ledge on a castle at an edge of a sky.

Near a cavern, on a mountain, shining.

From an ancient Scandinavian saga.

Then, behind the woman in the magic cloak, I saw on the wall one of the paintings I'd seen with Daphne. I heard Daphne's voice: 'I love you, woman.' It faded quickly.

I spun in a time-warp, surrounded by fire, as voices called and it seemed that people danced, arms held high, cloaks flying, whirling, dancing round fire.

Time was a sheet of red and orange flame.

Then, at my feet, Maria.

I saw her body, face down, dead, cold, shield maiden of the Vanir, warrior woman in a ring of fire.

Maria!!

Falling forward, I hit my head as I met the floor.

I came round in Freyja's bedroom, with Freyja beside me.

Many voices came in at different levels.

Freyja said, 'Gran and Duncan stayed as long as they could, but we persuaded them to go, or they'd be late for the Gala night.'

'Lie. 'Tis foolish to mention me.'

'I'm sorry. I don't know what happened.'
'You fainted, that's all. Duncan took your blood pressure but you're fine. He'll check you when he gets home.'

'I love you, woman. Woman.'

'I'm sorry.'
'Nothing to be sorry about.'

'My wish: 'tis to leave here.'

'I'll get up, come downstairs.'
'You're to stay put. Doctor's orders. We'll look after you. You've had a bit of a shock.'

''Tis winter. Much work to do.'

'Where's Lerryn? Is she OK?'
'She's seeing to dinner. Could you eat a little? Maybe some soup?'
'Nothing thanks. But I'd love a proper sleep. If you wouldn't mind?'

'Follow your feelings, woman.'

'Of course not. We won't disturb you.'
'Thanks. I do feel strange.'

'Volcano woman. I am Mahuea.'

'You'll be all right now. You couldn't faint in a better home than a doctor's, could you?'
'S'pose not, thanks.'

'Volcano woman with red hair.'

'And don't keep saying thanks. You'd do the same for me.

Sleep well. See you when you wake up.'

I was on a stony beach. It was Aotearoa. I'd been there before, many times.

It was a beautiful day. Inland from the beach I could see gardens, where sweet potatoes were growing. After that, quite far away, the land began to rise. First there was a small plantation of young trees, then lava fields, then a narrow path rising up, up high above the tree-line to a ring of volcanoes. They curved in a huge arc all around the beach.

Above the volcanoes the sky was blue, very sunny. Down the lava path a distant figure in a cloak was making her way towards me.

I walked slowly by the sea. The pebbles used to be lava. Now they were rounded by the rasping of the waves.

The colours of the area were marvellous. All kinds of different pebbles and rocks, the clear blue sky and blue and white sea, very bright, reflecting all the light.

I watched the spray. Sometimes it flew high, caught the white light and for a split second held – red orange yellow green indigo and violet. A moment later it dropped into the waves and dashed back to the ocean.

Turning back from the sea, I waited for the woman in the cloak to come through the plantation of young trees, towards, past the gardens, down towards me on the beach.

And, all the while that I waited, there in a hollow in the stones, face down, on the beach, as if asleep, there was Maria. But Maria was not asleep. Maria was dead. Face down on the warm, dry stones.

I heard the footsteps of the woman in the cloak approaching.

I thought: her cloak is of bantam feathers, soft and brown and white. In the past they'd have made it of kiwi feathers.

She was very old. She smiled at me as she took off her cloak, loaning it to me. I knelt on the ground and wrapped Maria very gently. When I picked her up, the cloak made her dead body as light as air.

I carried Maria's body in the cloak. I felt wonderful, very strong, like after making love, relaxed and happy. The body

117

in my arms wasn't just my friend. She was my lover. She knew every inch of my skin. And I knew hers. She would say she couldn't be a great lover if she wasn't a great friend too. She said to me: 'Love across years is an art – you have to discover it and keep it new. But you can't discover it every day, so being friends is the bridge over the off days, the bad times, the times between the new.'

I carried Maria's body towards the narrow path and started to follow it, walking up through the plantation of young trees, and further, higher, until I was moving, with Maria in my arms, up among the lava fields. The path was cindery underfoot, made of pounded lava, quite warm, but not too hot to walk on. It cut at my shoes, but not right through to my feet.

Beside the path the lava was sharp, frozen in huge, jagged clumps and clusters. On one side there was a new lava flow – red, orange, and moving.

At the rim of the volcano the air was full of sulphur, so my eyes streamed and breathing wasn't easy. Holding Maria safely, I looked over, down into the boiling mass below. The core was red, silver and swirling.

I unwrapped Maria and returned her body to the earth.

Then I retraced my steps, down the cinder path, towards the young trees, and past the gardens where the sweet potatoes grew.

Down on the beach I gave back the borrowed cloak to Mahuea.

Then I saw that Beattie had come to the beach to find me. She'd come by boat – a fishing boat belonging to her Maori relations. They took me to Beattie's home along the coast, for food and a long rest.

I woke up.

I was in Freyja's room, where she'd left me. I could hear Beattie's voice – Healing dreams, let them happen; and Freyja's voice – You'll be all right now.

Fifteen

I had the flu.

Days blurred, evenings faded, nights dissolved. Dawns were unnoticed. Dreams didn't surface.

Freyja and Lerryn brought food; walked with Roof; and slept by turns in the twins' old room.

Several days later, I woke, ready for action.

Lerryn invited me to a women's informal jazz night, to meet her close friend Tessa, and Tessa's new lover, Jules, whom Tessa had met through a Black women artists' group.

A room behind the pub was painted black, set out as a tiny theatre, with silver-legged chairs, small round tables and intimate lighting. Entering, I saw that Freyja, Lerryn and the others were seated, waiting. They all greeted me warmly, as Tessa and Jules introduced themselves. Tessa asked how I was, glad I was better now. Then Jules said: 'I hear we've the same birthday, you and me.'

'Twentieth of May?'

'To the day. Us Taureans must stick together.'

'Sounds good.'

So did the jazz. I listened, watching the players' hands, their bodies, the musical instruments, the lights on gleaming brass saxophones. The music took me miles high, remembering my eagle flight.

Next to me, I became aware of Lerryn's voice: 'All right, Denny?'

I smiled at her. 'Miles away, sorry. Thinking – couple of

weeks ago I'd hardly met you, now I'm here with you all – the music's wonderful.' I stood up. 'What d'y'all want to drink?'

Jules and I waited at the bar. We heard a tenor sax answered by a double bass: deep bass notes in syncopated rhythm resounded from the pub floor, the uneven walls. Then a clarinet was calling, echoes of Wind's voice, my night flights.

Down to earth, I said: 'What's your sort of work, Jules?'

'Residential care worker – but not for two weeks – between jobs.'

'D'you like it?'

'Mostly, yes. I'm lucky.' She paused, making eye contact. She had lovely unusual eyes, with dark lashes. She had very dark skin and a perfect complexion. Her face had an unsymmetrical beauty. She was mid-height between me and Tessa (who was tall, like Lerryn), and had masses of hair but it wasn't very long. She was dressed simply in jeans and a loud jumper in many reds. She said: 'Mega stress, now and then. We're often short staffed. They're mixed hostels – problems.'

'I'll bet. I couldn't do it.'

'Hey, Denny, I had a thought. Those three there (she nodded back to our table) are working next week, but we're not. Why don't we do the galleries? Haven't been for months.'

Embarrassed, not wanting to admit I could barely afford to buy a round of drinks, I said: 'It costs. I haven't got the fares, or the entrance.'

'Can you ride pillion?'

'Oh Jules, I'd *love* that! I haven't ridden since Maria; or done the galleries since Daphne.'

'We'll do the free ones. We'll have a great time.'

'No eating out?'

'None. We'll bring our own. Pick you up ten on Monday?'

'Sounds just right.'

It was.

But after that, the pace quickened again, late November,

when Lerryn's Aunt Harry arrived in London.

I'd never seen an older woman's face I could enjoy more than Harriet's. So full of lines and life I couldn't lose interest for a moment. She had grey hair, short, quite curly, and I could imagine her young, strong and wilful. I'd seen old photos: she'd been the stereotype wild flaming redhead.

At sixteen, she'd written from her home in Penzance to an antiques dealer in Chelsea, sending a photo, asking for a job. He was so impressed with her letter and her looks that he gave her the job and, later, his son Pierre's hand in marriage.

But now Harriet lived in Cornwall once more, alone, and in semi-retirement, thoughtful and rather reclusive. Intuitively, I knew she was lonely. I also knew (from Lerryn) that Harriet was not at all anti-gay or anti-lesbian, that she was sincere about her socialism, and was a serious patron of the arts.

On one of our outings during Harriet's visit to London, we went to Hampstead Heath: Lerryn, Freyja, Harriet, Roof and I.

No leaves left on the trees. No patched forest. No amber lights. The sky was wintry, set for afternoon tea with a deep pink cloth, white pleated serviettes, black and brown doylies.

Harriet wore posh cords, a soft felt hat pulled down over her ears, and a real waxed Barbour coat.

Freyja, in a quiet mood, scuffed along, winnowing dry leaves. She turned pale as Harriet suddenly, publicly, said to me: 'Denny, I would like to offer you a job.'

'Me?'

'Yes. I was going to advertise, but before I do, I'd like you to give it some thought. Would you like to work for me as secretary/companion?'

I gulped. Words fled. Harriet, looking towards Roof, who was dashing about, now said: 'She'd be welcome. I know you'd go nowhere without her. You'd be housed, employed, well paid, secure.'

'Lost for words, Denny?' asked Lerryn.

My face was zipped shut.

'That's my Harry,' said Lerryn.

Freyja was silent.

'I realise this must seem very sudden,' said Harriet.

'You're not wrong about that.' I linked an arm through Freyja's. 'I'm not the only one in a state of shock, look.'

'I'm all right,' Freyja lied.

'Harriet, thank you,' I began. 'What an honour. But I need time to think.' I met her eyes, as she smiled very assertively and said: 'Take your time, Denny. I want to talk you through the terms.'

Wind arrived, rustling some fallen leaves, and I thought: well now, Roarie Brewster, what do I do about this?

It was Harriet's sixty-fifth birthday, 10 December 1987, as we stood on the Cornish cliffs above Sennen. A steady sou'wester drove in from the Scillies on the horizon.

It was too cold to sit. As I bent down to examine the moss, I saw dozens of empty snail shells the size of a baby's thumbnail. Harriet's latest grandchild was ten weeks old. She had seven: four girls, three boys; they'd all be all right.

We crunched across the dunes, past Worzel Gummidge wigs – marram grass struggling to hold the sand; down past split logs, wired together, trying to be weather breaks; over boulders, smooth and rounded; to a long white beach.

Waves in ballet frocks, blue with cold.

In the wind, hugging herself, Harriet called to me: 'I'd rather be a woman than a dancing wave.'

'Too nippy for a tutu,' I yelled. But Wind snatched my words.

Harriet shouted: 'You like this place?'

'I love it here,' I replied.

We climbed back to the car via a steep valley where a stream ran and jumped, new lamb to its mother.

I thought: where Roarie is the sheep are pregnant, in the pen behind the empty manor house. The snow is deep now, but the end of winter's only a couple of months away, people will celebrate Candlemas, and lambs will be born.

Seasons will turn, and country people will work the land as old ways continue. It'll be many generations there before the Lammas fields are drained, but harvest will be Lammas for centuries yet – when animals are let into the fields to graze the stubble.

Lords of the manor will become squires, and villagers will doff their hats to the squire right up to the end of the Second World War there, in Essex. Squires will follow their old ways too: money and privilege; landowning and tithes; evictions and harassment; rent and bailiffs.

Roarie, this place is far from you. I miss you every day.

Back on the clifftop, Harriet turned the car round for me. I checked my L plates and drove to Hermit's Hut, on the north Cornish coast.

Harriet's unwelcome birthday present arrived a few days later – Clause 14 (later 27/28/29) of the Local Government Bill. This would make it illegal to fund, through local government, any venue or activity which was 'promoting' homosexuality.

So began six months' intensive work at Hermit's Hut, when Harriet threw herself into 'the arts lobby' – letter writing and campaigning with a vigour that surprised me.

In January, Lerryn phoned from London to tell me about the first demo. Harriet was at her friend JoAnne's, in Truro. 'It was a wonderful demo actually, though the end was awful.' Lerryn continued: 'There weren't any gates on the park. We could see mounted police, up a side street. We thought they'd charge. I was terrified. We were crammed tight in the park. I was next to a man in a wheelchair. How d'you challenge a police horse from a wheelchair?'

'You OK now?'

'I am now. But I wasn't. I've never been so afraid of horses. We had to leave in fives and tens. Two dykes with a megaphone, on a stand, telling us . . . telling us to leave in groups, arms linked.'

'Did you?'

'We had to. They were picking us off in twos and threes. Two women were arrested for kissing – near the gateposts.'

'For kissing?'

'That's what it's come to. Seven of us left together, arm in arm. In a chain. Jules' flat's nearby. We went there. Very shaken. It's the nastiest sneakiest attack. We expected it via an education bill didn't we, but no. They came from the back via local government. Clever. Where's the Labour front bench, bloody cowards?'

'Not the sort of campaign *they* want.'

'Homophobic bloody lot. They make me spit.'

'How's the gang?'

'OK, now. Freyja started writing. Since we got back from you, New Year. That's what did it she says. She sends love, so do Tessa and Jules.'

'Thanks.'

'How's the word processing?'

'Coming on like billy-oh. Speaking of which . . .'

'Yes. Got to go. Give my love to the mission lady, sounds like she loves the clause. Gives her a purpose, bless her. I need it like a hole in the head.'

'So do I, though the work's interesting. I'm learning fast. Love it. Love to everyone. Come and see us soon.'

'Bye, Denny.'

Weeks sped by, all of us busy with the dreaded clause. It was Easter before any of them could get to Hermit's Hut. They all arrived, thankful for a break by the sea, weary from demos and meetings.

I spent good hours with Tessa and Jules, walking and talking. They were very happy, enjoying the time together.

I also tried to make special time and space for Freyja, who seemed tense and unhappy.

'Are you still writing?' I asked, as we walked the coast path, with Roof. 'You were missing the sea, were you?'

'Very much. I was born and raised by it. Look, down there, however many times those waves break on the rocks, they can go back to the ocean and form again. Here, at New Year, I suddenly thought of my writing like that. I could make words, break them up, start all over again. That's what got me going, at last.'

'A good thing then? Part of the journey?'

'But . . . it's all so hard. I'm sorry. I don't mean to be heavy.'

124

Next day, when the others were out, Freyja and I took the chance to prepare a lovely meal for them. Right out of the blue, just as we'd finished, she said: 'Denny, do you miss sex?'

I looked at my watch, 'Let's go out and talk. Come on.'

Within minutes we were taking a high route on to the moors, with Roof.

It was windy. Beside me, Freyja strode on, her short hair tousled. She began: 'I'm coming awake again. Sexually, I mean. Are you?'

'Slowly. I'm thirty-six in May. Nearly two years ago Maria died, and I haven't had sex with anyone in that time. Not even with myself. I tried it but nothing happened. I've been so numb. I'm just beginning to wake up.'

Freyja replied: 'Strange thing is, I don't want a lover, not a one-night stand, not a fling, or anyone. I just want relief, now and then, from the need. You the same?'

I nodded, noticing she was a year ahead of me in her speed of waking up. It was just a year since Gemma died.

Freyja sighed. 'Bereavement – is an awesome thing. Didn't expect it. Wasn't prepared. Suddenly – nothing. I've not had times of nothing before. I've never been ill for more than a couple of days. And if I didn't have a lover I could always DIY.' She shrugged. 'Now I'm lost.'

We walked on, past Morvah Church along to Lanyon Quoit, one of my favourite routes near Hermit's Hut.

Presently I asked: 'Did you and Gemma do it often? Was it good?'

'Couple of times a week, I s'pose. I was trying to remember, but it wasn't easy. To remember, I mean. Sex was fairly easy, though we both got PMS, and I was uncomfortable. I couldn't do it. Too bloated. Memory plays tricks on me. Must be grief. Maybe anger. I think deep down I'm very angry. It's blocking me. It confuses me. My cycle's all over the place. Must be anger. I feel so cheated. Do you?'

'Not so much now,' I said gently. I didn't want to tell Freyja just how happy and contented I felt at Hermit's Hut. It seemed mean, while she was so lonely, raw and exiled.

'Your new life suits then?'

125

'Yes.'

'And what about sex?'

'Hard to remember. It blurs, as you say. We were a bit haphazard, I think. Now and then I'd take a morning off, and so would Maria. We'd have the place to ourselves. I loved doing it in the mornings. I make a lot of noise,' I said, grinning.

'So did we. And we laughed so much in bed, Gem and me. Now? No one to laugh in bed with. It's a special kind of laughter. It's good for you, you know?'

'I know.'

Ahead of us, Roof turned left, before we reached Lanyon Quoit and I let her 'choose' the route, leading us along a gently sloping rough track up towards Nine Maidens. When we arrived there, each of the stones had a circle of flowers.

'Ceremonies?' asked Freyja.

'Eoster, with an 'o'. Celtic.'

Freyja walked round and round the ring of stones, almost tiptoeing. I sat in the centre, hugging Roof.

Then Freyja sat beside me. She asked: 'Did you and Maria do it often? What was haphazard, actually?'

'If we were on holiday we did it all the time. Lived for it. But generally? I should think we'd go a week or so. Ten days, rarely any longer. All depended. It waited for us. It was there, when we were.'

'Tell you something, Denny. I almost panicked in the hut when you looked at your watch. For one awful moment, I thought you were going to offer me a quickie.'

'Freyja love, if you were the last woman on a deserted moor, I don't think I'd do it with you.'

She laughed. 'Thanks very much, Denny. I fancy you too.'

'No you don't you fibber, and it shows. You don't fancy me any more'n I fancy you, but you do love me. Besides, we've a dazzling dinner to serve.'

She stood, pulled me up to my feet, and tugging me, running to the path home, she spoke over her shoulder: 'Come on then, just good friend.'

Freyja stayed only another day as she was saving her annual

leave for a trip to Norway with her gran.

After she'd gone, Lerryn said: 'It's hard to know how to help her.'

'You can't,' said Tessa. 'Except to listen when she wants to talk. And you already do a lot of that.'

Without Freyja, the mood lightened considerably. At evening meal, sitting next to Harriet, Jules said, 'Well I think us all here need to play.'

'The New Famous Five?' quipped Lerryn.

'We've got a mongrel. She's game,' I said, affectionately.

'There we are then,' said Jules, 'Move over, Enid.' Quick-witted and acidly funny, amidst much laughter, she launched into a scathing skit, exposing the old white Famous Five, the Secret Seven and 'a racist little yuppy, called Noddy.'

On our day trips that week, Jules and I would find ourselves walking along together. An easy chemistry arose between us. Partly it was that we were the two relative newcomers to Hermit's Hut; partly our deep shared interest in music, especially jazz; and the rest we put down to personalities.

We also had the same birthday.

I had potted up some plants for Jules to take back to her London flat. She and Tessa handed me an early birthday present, long and thin, wrapped in red shiny paper. 'Open it now,' they insisted. 'We're itching to try it out.'

It was a bright red kite with a thirty-foot tail and double strings wrapped around plastic hand-holds.

On a clear April day, just before they returned home, we all went to some high flat grass above Zennor Quoit.

Wind, in a birthday mood, kept the kites aloft.

Harriet's kite was a large yellow bird, with bright blue wings. Tessa and Jules had a stunt kite – several shades of blue, with two tails. It whooped and dived – they took it to Blackheath near Greenwich Park, they told me, a favourite site for kites, in London. Meanwhile, Lerryn took photos of us in Cornwall.

Later, for my birthday, Lerryn sent me a beautifully framed enlargement. It captured one moment when time wasn't blurred, wasn't a swirl or blend of light, nor a mix of paints – one second when time posed for us, when light was held there in our hands, as clear as a primary colour, sharp as a kite, blue or yellow or red.

In June, despite all our work against the clause, it became law. Part of the statute books. Straight lines of ugly words. Parallel lines, like spiked railings – closing us out. Fences. Stay on your side. Outside. We don't want you. We don't like you. You aren't real.

It hurt.

It made us angry.

After the passing of the law, Freyja went to Norway.

Lerryn, Tessa and Jules came to Hermit's Hut. There, we put our heads in paper bags; wrapped our brains in thick paper; left our memories in a filing cabinet; and played, mindlessly, for a little while, beyond demos, or meetings, or lobbies.

We played: shutting off our minds that knew perfectly well that the world didn't love us.

Sixteen

In the two-foot thick granite wall of old Hermit's Hut, opposite the wide windows, a door led to a sheltered courtyard, given a horse-shoe shape by the new wings, and edged with tubs of bright petunias, fuchsias, geraniums, lobelia and busy lizzies.

There, surrounded by climbing honeysuckle, doing its best to disguise the new buildings, I'd persuaded Harriet to install a beer-garden table, for potting up seedlings, cleaning shoes, and when cleared and scrubbed, for eating outside on warm evenings.

On a mid-week August evening, 1988, just a couple of days before Freyja was due to visit, our courtyard meal was interrupted by the phone ringing. I dashed in to answer it.

'Denny, it's me, Freyja, thank heavens. I dreaded the ansa-thing.'

'Whatever's the matter, Frey?'

'It's a mess. I've blown it. Blown my lid off. I've been boiling up for weeks. Blown my top at one of Gran's dinners. Some silly woman wound me up. I went right over the top.' Freyja accelerated, nought to sixty in ten seconds: 'Not her fault, not really. Silly cow happened in on my stuff.' As Freyja sped on, Harriet put her head around the door. I mouthed, 'Freyja, in a state.' Harriet mouthed back, 'Bring her visit forward – it's only a couple of days – could she get the night train?'

I nodded. Harriet left. Freyja raced on.

'Listen to me,' I said. She didn't, so I shouted: 'Listen,

listen, Frey. Listen to me.'

She stopped hurtling words.

'Pack a travel bag, you only need knickers and socks. We've loads of spare clothes here. You could reach Paddington for the night train. It gets into Truro about half-seven. I'll meet you, with the car. Pack your things, be on the train. Yes?'

'Oh thank you.'

'Just be on the train. Love you lots, Frey.'

'Love you too, what a mess.'

Truro, seven-thirty a.m. She hadn't slept. I brought her to Hermit's Hut; we put her in the spare room; fed her camomile tea. She slept . . . all day.

While Freyja slept, Harriet's friend JoAnne came for supper, which we ate outside.

'The trick here at the hut,' quipped Harriet, as we scoffed salad and homemade bread, 'is to catch the most amount of sun and the least amount of breeze. We did think, Denny and I, of placing the table in front of the seaward windows . . .'

'So you could get blown from here to my place without driving,' joked JoAnne. They began to bat words to and fro, veterans at badminton-scrabble, but I barely listened.

Harriet had said 'we'.

The last time anyone said 'we' with that easy manner, I'd been lovers with Maria, sharing a bed and making a home. Harriet and JoAnne were now well away with racquets and shuttle-words. They didn't notice my confusion so I set about clearing the table, reckoning less than half an hour before the temperature plummeted. Out to sea the sky was a pinky blur, with apricot and orange clouds.

I washed the dishes and left them to drain. Not many – didn't take long. Long enough to realise I was in big trouble.

On the way to my room, I looked in on Freyja. She was snoring slightly, sleeping soundly. I fled to my own room.

Beyond my windows, heather and gorse bloomed, brambles fruited abundantly, and wild orange montbretia flamed with smokeless fire.

I lay on my bed, thinking of all the hours I'd been with Harriet, as I mentally counted the months from last December to this August.

Learning to drive, walking, listening to our favourite music – Roberta Flack, Aretha Franklin, and we both shared a passion for Joan Baez's voice – shopping, choosing colours for the spare room, laughing over grotty wallpaper patterns in DIY stores, working closely on the clause, potting up seedlings, watching them grow, and talking, often seated at the beer-garden table, talking about everything.

Ingredients for a life together. We'd become such good friends.

It wasn't her word 'we', so much as my surge of feelings about it. It wasn't nostalgia, longing for Maria. It was new. This was trouble, because this was about Harriet.

I dozed off, waking after nightfall to find a mug of tea at my side and Harriet perched on the edge of my bed, looking at me kindly. 'You had a sleep, good. Freyja's still out for the count. JoAnne's gone home. Would you mind if I took Roof out for a couple of hours?'

'No, 'course not. She loves a night stroll. I'd better stay. Wouldn't like Freyja to wake and find me gone.'

'My thoughts exactly. Good, that's fine then. I need some time, some thinking time. Later there'll be a mist rolling in, but it'll hold off a while. It's clear moonlight, surprisingly. All right, Denny?'

'Fine, yes. Thanks for the tea. See you later.'

Freyja didn't wake. My feelings were in a dance, over Harriet. I decided to write to Beatrice. So I made some more tea, sat at my small table in my room, and picked up my pen.

To my astonishment a familiar voice came on to the paper.

''Tis a long, long way to meet you, Denny.'

'Roarie? What a surprise. How are you?'

'Weary from searching for you. 'Tis so many miles across this bridge.'

'I'm sorry. I was suddenly offered this job and a place to live. I'm so sorry it was abrupt. I didn't want to abandon you.'

'Healer's apprentice, 'tis my trade. Was my desire to

131

comfort, ne'er to scold. Did you fear a scolding, from a healer?'

'No. But I knew I was letting you down badly. It was an awful time to leave you just when we were Speaking Paper so well, the two of us.'

''Tis fools who dwell on guilt. We shall talk of joy, you and me. 'Tis joy to speak with you this night.'

'It is. It is. I've missed you, Roarie.'

The words stopped abruptly. I waited, pen poised, trying to hear Roarie's voice.

'You are my true friend. I shall return to you. In a while. Shall not be soon. Is too far. So far . . .'

The words trailed off. I closed my eyes, willing her back.

'Bridge . . . Trust me . . . Fading . . .'

The words stopped completely.

I put my face in my hands: Roarie on the manor, rather blurred, like a soft focus ad on telly. Martha and Ruth near a corner of a farm building calling to Roarie, at twilight.

I couldn't hold the images and they faded, until the palms of my hands were empty.

I went into the shower room; ran the water tingling hot. Naked, I looked up, letting the spray fall full on my face, making me laugh and gasp.

To play with water. Memories – playing in the shower with Maria. Gleefully laughing. White blue gold high laughter, and dark red earth deep laughter; sounds of lust echoing through the house.

Now I showered but the memories weren't painful. I was waking up, moving on. Perhaps Roarie knew it too; perhaps she could hear me, playing with water, tonight. Roarie who are you? If you're real how do you reach me across the bridge? If you're not real, who are you? What are you? How will you feel about my new love? Will you be glad for me? You will, won't you?

I stayed in the shower, my arms high above my head. The water cascaded over my shoulders and down my breasts: my nipples responded willingly . . . I let the water be Harriet, making love to my breasts, my arms, my neck.

Then I showered my back, butt and hips, leaning my hands

on the shower-room wall: droplets splashed and danced on my skin. Water wonderfully hot slid against my thighs and down my legs.

Me with a new lover in the shower, not Maria, though I loved to make love in the shower with her. Now the shower and I played, perfectly comfortable, perfectly hot, perfectly exciting.

I let my need flow from inside me, my own wetness blending, responding. I was in love again, alive and wanting again. Strong waves of hope and desire trembled through me; sounds rose from deep colour: red and orange, the colours of want.

Hermit's Hut was safe: no one but me and the water to share the truth. Water and Fire, body need and body heat, me, myself.

After the shower I went to bed, and made love to my body, low tech, not high tech, just my own hands, my own fingers, imagining Harriet, until I fell asleep satisfied and glad. I surfaced slightly when she and Roof arrived home. Roof settled on my bed, and I slept soundly until morning.

After a twenty-four-hour sleep, Freyja woke refreshed. Breakfast over, I set off with Freyja and Roof along the coast path, so we could talk freely.

Freyja said: 'I shouldn't have stayed for dinner with Gran's guests. I might have known I'd do something awful. I wanted to please Gran, that's the irony. What a mess!'

'What happened?'

'There was an awful woman there. A real cow, scuse the right-off-ness.'

'You don't have to love 'em all. This is the eighties.'

'Thank the Goddess.'

'She's not all love and smiles. Think of Kali.'

Freyja laughed. 'You're quite a cynic,' she said.

'What did she say? Who was she?' I said, ignoring her remark.

Freyja watched the sea far below. Then she replied: 'She was there on her own – her husband's in the States. Big wig, something. She went on about having two houses: the upkeep was a problem, poor darling. At first as she talked I watched her coldly. Frozen watchfulness, like babies who're being abused are said to. They lie still in their cots frozen like ice, only their eyes moving, waiting in anticipation. I was like that. Cold as ice, at first. I don't know why. It was that specific alertness.

'I couldn't get the image of the baby out of my mind. But then as she droned on, centre stage, and everyone bored as hell, I thought, I'm not a child in a cot, I'm an adult and I don't have to listen. She was crass, really crass. She said when she was apart from her husband, she felt bereaved!!'

'No wonder you blew up.'

'It was awful. I could feel the ice begin to move. I knew it might be destructive, but I liked the cold, after the heat of the previous weeks. I tried to hang on to it, tried to be a glacier.' She sighed with a typical rueful smile, and said: 'Slow and heavy and silent.'

I commented: 'The films I've seen, glaciers aren't silent. They creak and groan and rumble.'

'That's the trouble. I couldn't hang on to the silence; and I couldn't hang on to the cold. The image inside began to change. It was awful. I knew I should leave. But how could I just get up and go from the table? My anger began to build. I thought – Oh Goddess, I'm boiling up again, I'm going to explode.'

'And you did. You said your gran foresaw it, so won't she understand?'

'I hope so. After a time.'

'I'm sure she will. She loves you, doesn't she, Frey?'

Freyja nodded and I, quite wrongly as it turned out, thought the rest of the holiday would be a healing time for her. It was, at first. We spent days just ambling about in the sunshine, blackberrying, never getting enough home to make a pie, too busy eating as we went.

But between the easy times, Freyja was tense and edgy. I put it down to her not wanting to return to work nor to face her gran.

One morning, we walked along the coast path with Roof, in

warm sunshine, stopping now and then as Freyja asked the names of the wild flowers.

Suddenly she changed tone and asked: 'Do you remember our conversation at Easter, about sex?'

'Yes of course I do.'

'Are you still waking up sexually?' she asked.

Something about the way Freyja spoke made me not mention Harriet. I don't know exactly what or why. I thought about it often, afterwards. So I replied: 'Yes, I think so . . . are you?'

Although Freyja had introduced the subject, she didn't answer straight away. We stepped across a small wooden stile and picked our way carefully along the path, which became quite rocky at this point, leading slowly downwards. Roof looked back at us every now and then to make sure we were still following. Far below, on low rocks exposed by the tide, I glimpsed a black, red and white splash of oyster catchers. I was delighted to see them, and show them off to Freyja. They didn't always appear at this headland. So the day seemed lovely, our friendship safe and warm.

Instead of continuing, she changed the subject: 'Oh look, here's a tiny ravine, look at the flowers by this stream. Oh I love this coast. Look at the stream bouncing down, so clear. I bet you could drink from it.'

'I wouldn't, Frey. It might be coming from an old mine; there might be traces of lead. Don't risk it.'

'Lead?'

'Yes. They don't use the mine-water even during drought.'

'Really? Water water everywhere and not a drop to drink.'

Above the beach we came to a red notice that warned us to keep our shoes on. I relayed the story to Freyja as we clambered across rocks to the sand: the beach was a struggle between nature and man. A huge wreck that could not be salvaged had blocked the cove, so in their wisdom the army came and blew it up, into hundreds of pieces of lethal, twisted metal now rusting away slowly. The sea corroded and pounded them, covered them with fabulous drifting sand and did her best to heal the scars.

'I suppose you couldn't bring children here, stuff like that.'

Freyja paused then added quietly: 'Nonie loved to go to the beach.'

We sat on some rocks as Roof chased along the beach. I relaxed. She knew exactly where to go and how to look after herself. She could smell any sharp metal pieces at a safe distance. I didn't have to worry about her.

'Denny, I want to ask you something.'

'What's the matter, Frey?'

'Nothing's the matter. I, er, would you have sex with me?'

'Me?'

'Don't look at me like that. It's a lovely idea. We're friends. We trust each other. We've both been celibate too long. It'd be lovely.'

'I can't.'

'Look you don't have to swear undying love, or anything. None of that rubbish. I fancy you and I fancy the idea of making love with you.'

'I thought you loved me as a friend.'

'I do. I do love you as a friend. That's what makes it all right. Don't you fancy me at all?'

'It's not that.'

'What then? You fancy me and I fancy you and we're good friends; and we have needs. Waking up to sex again.'

'I don't want to change things between us. I like things as they are.'

'Things don't stay just as they are. They never do. Everything changes.'

'I know, but not this change. It makes me feel unstable just to think of it. I need our friendship as a rock, not shifting sand.'

We were silent for a moment. I thought of Bronwyn and Daphne and Maria. How hard it was for Maria and Bronwyn when Daph and I fell in love. What a struggle Daph and I had to stay out of bed. What was the point of breaking up a foursome for a short passionate fling?

Then I thought of Harriet. How with her I was sure it wouldn't be short, but it would be passionate. If ever . . .

Freyja said: 'I remember when you first told me about Daphne, when we first met. I'll never forget the look on your

136

face as you spoke about her. You've got that particular look about you today. It's Daphne who's on your mind, isn't it?'

'You take a very accurate aim sometimes, Frey.'

'You've got unfinished business with Daphne, you always have had. Now that you're waking up it'll surface from time to time. But I don't see why it stops you having sex with me.'

'It doesn't. I don't want to hurt you, Frey, but I really don't want to change our friendship. *We* could end up with unfinished business.'

With awful dread, I watched her frame the next question: 'If we're friends, and you fancy me a bit, and there's love and trust and two lonely dykey bodies wanting it, then something else is going on. I hear what you're saying Denny, but there's metal under your sand.'

'You're pressurising me. I wish you wouldn't. It's *you* that's introducing a sharp knife-edge. *You're* the one with metal in the sand.'

'You're rejecting me and hedging about why. I want to know. Tell me.' She sounded like cold stone on a winter day.

'I've fallen in love . . .' I began, but she shouted before I could finish.

'What? Well if it's not with me, and that's crystal bloody clear, who the fuck is it with?'

'Don't you take that tone with me. What right have you to shout at me?'

'One of the dykes up at Exeter? Who?'

'I'm in love with Harriet.'

'Harriet? Don't be stupid – she's older than my mum.'

'That has nothing to do with it.'

'It has everything to do with it. You reject me and fall in love with that rich old bitch. Do me a favour.'

'Take that back, Freyja.'

'No. Because she is rich and she is old and you've no business rejecting me and falling for her. She's a rich old bitch. I don't take it back.'

'Just go away. Leave Hermit's Hut today. Go away, Freyja.' I was cold as a glacier, though I'd never seen myself as one before. It was usually an image I kept for Freyja and Scandinavia.

Freyja was not cold stone now. She was standing shouting at the sea, pouring forth words like a volcano, torrents of abuse and fire, and sulphur gases flung into the air. The breeze and the sounds of the sea crashing on the beach carried most of her words away from me, and the rest I tried to shut my mind to.

Roof returned and stood on guard, her tail held still, aloft, not wagging, as she summed up the situation. I went to her and whispered: 'Come on, we're going home,' and we left.

Freyja stood with her back to us, shouting, effing and cursing like a woman demented, which she was in that moment. I didn't know or care just then if it was irretrievable breakdown. I'd care later, but right then I wanted her to boil and fume and smoulder and blaze until she was burned out, like Krakatoa, the volcano that rose from under the sea and blew itself up. It caved in and disappeared again, as the ocean closed over it. If Freyja had charged into the sea at that moment I'd have let her.

To stay around a volcano I'd have to have had a death wish. I didn't have any such thing. I was alive, getting stronger, tough enough to carry a few burdens, strong enough to carve my own pathways now.

I was at the start of my own awakening. And no one, not even Freyja, whom I needed and loved, had the power to take that from me.

Seventeen

After she'd gone, reaction began and I hit a low time of deep loss.

Why didn't I realise that Freyja's feelings were changing? I replayed all the scenes since we'd met, from the first to the last and over again. I lost her. She left me. I threw her out. She made me. On and on, round and round.

I waited a week then tried to phone her. Her gran answered, said Freyja was out, she'd pass on my message. Waited two days. Tried again. The same response. After the third time, I didn't try again.

I thought about Freyja's friendship when we first met; our need for each other then; her strength in challenging me; my support for her when she dumped her story on me; her caring when I described Maria's death; her sensitivity to the early stages of my 'voices'.

Who was Freyja really?

If she wanted sex now, why not sooner? Why not at Easter? Why not then, if she'd missed me so badly since I left London to work for Harriet? But at Easter, we'd only just started waking up sexually. Our bodies had been numb until then – two years after Maria's death; one year after Gemma's. It seemed that I'd taken longer to come back to life than Freyja.

I'd not fallen in love with Freyja, though she was very attractive and I loved her dearly and I'd told her so.

I reasoned to myself: if Freyja's blocking my phone calls,

due to hurt, loss and rejection, her anger must be equal to mine.

For several nights after my third attempt to contact her, I dreamed of the twin sisters Fire and Burn swirling in a fire-dance in matching cloaks.

One morning I woke before dawn. My skin burned. It wasn't like the burning when I first met Roarie. That was grief and guilt, mostly. This time I burned with raw anger as well.

Now I knew I'd been angry, very, very angry after my bereavement. Freyja had known about her anger, but I hadn't known about mine. Not until now. But Maria had been hard to live with. In our row when I stayed home with Graham, she'd accused me of not wanting to help Bronwyn and Daphne realise their vision, or their politics.

I had been furious.

Now I knew it, lying in the dim bedroom, more aware, more ready to deal with it. Bluntly put, guilt hid my anger after Maria, and Freyja's explosion released it.

They say that in public disasters, the main emotion of survivors is anger. Rage at the loss; the sense of being out of control of the situation; being abandoned; being left to carry the load.

That morning in the early hours at Hermit's Hut, Wind came through my open window, from a night of swirling in the mist.

'D'you need a friend?'

'I hoped you'd come.'

'I came because you're angry. I know anger. The helpless rage I felt so long ago in Japan.'

'Rage at losing control.'

'Loss of self. Yes.'

'I'm falling backwards.'

'You'll survive. Believe me.'

'I'm burning again. I don't want to.'

Wind rested gently on the edge of my bed. 'Sad to find you in this state again.'

'I was doing fine.'

'It's not a straight line, Denny.'

'I try to tell myself that.'

'Tell Harriet. Let her in. Let her help you. Now come, come with me, I'll take you up on the moors, with Roof, in the mist, cool you down.'

'It's dangerous.'

'Then we'll follow the roads, with a torch.'

So we did.

High on the moors I watched the sky turn light, with the sun rising behind sky mountains of cloud. I watched the skyscape, peaks and summits, aware of three figures roped together on a mountain. Red and bright blue and navy, falling roped together.

I'd been falling, like a horror film, into a deep mine shaft full of bright hot flames, but Wind came to rescue me. Quietly, she roped herself around my waist. Slowly, she tugged me towards that high cool place, away from the fire's edge.

I looked out to sea, feeling the flames retreating, thinking of Maria, Bronwyn and Daphne. Now, I realised just how near the edge I'd be yet a while; and how much nearer the flames was Freyja.

On the moors I thought back to the suddenness of it all. Through Freyja, only last November, I'd met Lerryn, then Harriet, with a job offer.

Unwittingly, I'd done to Freyja what I'd done to Roarie Brewster – up and left. It made the bridge harder for Roarie, though we'd eventually spanned it. But Freyja was alive and present-day – real and twentieth century. Her anger must've been building up ever since.

Wind was gently by, perching on a large boulder, keeping me company, and now whispered: 'Sorry to interrupt your thoughts.'

'You're not. I'm glad I'm here with you.'

'Yes, but I must go now. Running out of words, m'dear. I'm off to collect and recycle.'

With that, Wind was gone.

I returned with Roof, to Hermit's Hut. Home.

* * *

I talked it through with Harriet, leaving out only my feelings for her.

'How did you deal with the loss of Pierre?' I asked.

'I did what you did. I kept myself to myself as far as intimacy was concerned. Although we were married for many years, Pierre and I were not lovers, not since our third child was born. We were, like you and Freyja, very close friends.

'When he left, to live in France with Jacques, I was, to use Lerryn's word, devastated. I ran away to Shropshire for a while.

'Publicly I went about my work. I threw myself into it. I was very fortunate, I hadn't lost my job or my home at the same time, and when I wasn't working I kept very busy with the garden.

'I was profoundly angry with Pierre. If I tried to reason with myself, I was left empty, like you feel now. Empty because it's not about rational thought. It's deeply emotional.'

I said: 'On the beach when the explosion first happened, I wanted Freyja to walk into the sea. I felt tough and strong. So what, I'd manage. It hit me later.'

'Give yourself time. It takes a long time.'

Wind returned that night.

'I want to talk to you about war,' I said.

'Which one? There's a cease-fire in the Gulf.'

'We live in a war world – large- and small-scale wars all over the earth. Freyja and I have our own war; our incident on the 'army' beach, has really shaken me.'

'Incident. Indecent. Indiscriminate. Oh, you get me going, Denny.'

'I know. I've no peace of mind either. Maybe it's because the army blew up that ship on a beach where little children play – I didn't tell Freyja, but nuclear families go there all the time. Nuclear. It's all linked. I've a head full of explosions and children and soldiers. Terrible dreams of children *being* soldiers. In real wars.'

'Ah, yes. Child soldiers. It's an international scandal.'

'Thousands. Dead and alive. Six-year-olds, abducted,

trained to carry guns. Nine-year-olds made to kill their own families. I have two sons. They were little once. At night my dreams are full of wars and horror.'

'Personal war breeds nightmares of international wars. Transmutation. Violence on different scales.'

'Yes. I'm shocked that I didn't avoid an explosion with Freyja. I zigzag. Anger and grief. To and fro.'

'You will survive.'

'The children don't. Some of them go mad. The Khmer Rouge used hundreds of them.'

'Their families killed before their eyes,' said Wind, then, 'do something.'

'I will. I don't envy you, being so world-wide. I long for world peace. It's a horrible, dreadful century.'

'Sure is. I have to go far out to sea sometimes, just to get a breath of fresh air. But you'll be OK. You're facing things, making links. That's always a good sign.'

'Of what?'

'Wholeness. Being real. Well, I'm off now. Got to go find some cumulus. Have to speculate to accumulate. Bye.'

One Friday afternoon, Lerryn, Tessa and Jules arrived unexpectedly, having shared the driving from London.

Harriet said to us: 'It seems Freyja's in some kind of crisis. I'm going to JoAnne's, so you can all have the hut.'

'You mustn't do that. This is your home.'

'And yours, Denny. You shall have some privacy. Besides, Truro's nearer to Plymouth, and we have theatre tickets. See you Sunday night.'

'You're very kind. Thank you.'

As the four of us talked, night closed round Hermit's Hut.

Lerryn began: 'We thought you should know she's leaving next week.'

'Next week? For Auss? What did she say?'

'That she asked you to be lovers with her; you hedged a while and then said you were in love with Harriet.'

'Harriet . . . Oh, she didn't. Oh, no.'

Tessa said: 'Denny, we came to give some support. We

knew it'd be a shock. Freyja's distant, isn't she Lerrie?'

'Yes. I'm her friend but I can hardly reach her. We didn't think we should simply phone you, not when you can't be open with Harry. We love you – the difference you've made to Harry – I've not seen her so happy, not in the whole of my life.'

Lerryn paused for breath and I interrupted: 'Harriet doesn't know. I'm trying to get past it.'

'It's none of my business how you feel about Harry, nor how she feels about you – it really isn't. It's not my business, and it's not why I'm here. Personally nothing could make me happier than to see Harry and you get it together . . . no, wait, hear me out . . . I shan't mention anything to Harry, and I shan't ever ask you about Harry and you. I wouldn't stand for anyone telling me who I can and can't fall for. One or two dykes in London tried to do just that when Lindsey and I split (Lerryn glanced at Tessa, who nodded) – it's nobody else's business – and that's the end of my little speech.'

I laughed. 'How many times did you rehearse that?'

'Lots.'

Jules said: 'She hasn't phoned you, has she?'

'No. She won't answer my letters.'

'I was fairly certain she wouldn't,' said Lerryn.

I began: 'Last Easter we had a talk. We didn't want to have lovers, but our bodies were waking up. Then in the summer, she said suddenly: "We're friends – our bodies are lonely, so, why not? Let's do it." '

'The way she put it to me, Denny, there was more to it than that,' said Lerryn.

'What sort of more?'

'She was searching for something. She thought she'd found it. She could make a new life in this country with you.'

'And what was I? An insurance policy?'

'She wasn't just using you,' Jules said. 'To her it was real. She didn't realise till she came back to London after your row. It's Freyja's stuff, not yours.'

Lerryn said: 'Jules is right. We all feel for Freyja, what she's going through. I tried to talk to her about friendship and boundaries but it's hard to get through.'

'I didn't want to reject her like that. I wanted a close friendship. We *had* a close friendship.'

Tessa said: 'Freyja is the walking wounded now, and in that state she's dangerous.'

'I wouldn't have thrown her out of Hermit's Hut but she didn't leave me much choice.'

'We know. And we know you've tried phoning her, and been blocked by her gran because she told me so,' said Lerryn. Weighing her words, she added: 'She also said things about you and Harry and the age gap that were insulting and made me furious.'

Tessa spoke gently, stroking Roof who put her head on Tessa's thigh: 'Jules and I invited Freyja over with Lerryn, but Freyja backed out. It was strange because I'd met her several times and it seemed odd that suddenly she didn't want dinner, didn't want a theatre trip.'

'She loves theatre.'

'Exactly,' said Lerryn, taking over where Tessa left off, 'Freyja phoned me, and all hell let loose. I mean – she went crackers . . .'

'About Harriet,' said Jules. 'About the age gap.'

'The age gap?' I asked. 'Oh, so it's that again.'

Lerryn said: 'She flipped, on and on about you and Harry. Freyja's so wrapped up in herself she can't think of anything else. So she had a go at me, "It's all right for you, Lerryn, with your art and your friends, and teaching with Tessa. Your life's full and busy, you'll be OK." '

'Strewth. Did she really say that?'

'She certainly did.'

I whistled, Lerryn swallowed, then said: 'Denny, I was with Lindsey for sixteen years. I keep myself *very* busy, and I don't need our friend Freyja telling me that I'm all right.'

'No. I loved her, but I've been to hell and back since Maria died, and I want to go forward. But not to be lovers with Freyja. I didn't want that. I've phoned. I've written. It's hard that she's leaving without contacting me.'

'It seems there's a lot about her that we didn't know.'

'She's right to go back,' said Jules. 'To face things there.

She's been doing some fair old dumping, in London. Getting a reputation. Causing a few disasters . . .'

Tessa interrupted: 'So I took Lerryn out to dinner. To talk. We talked for a long time about our friendship, what we'd been through, all the support when Maureen and I broke.'

'Then my break-up with Lindsey,' said Lerryn. 'Tessa wined and dined me in style.'

Tessa said: 'What concerned me was that in trying to help Freyja, others were being upset and harmed, so what I said to Lerryn was: "I know you're fond of Freyja, and you want to support her but I care about *you*. I'm *your* friend, and I want you to be careful. Watch her, Lerrie. She's a vortex. You'll be pulled in." '

'She won't do anything *very* silly, will she?' I asked.

'No. I don't think so,' replied Lerryn. 'It's a positive thing to go where it all happened, deal with it. I have her address.'

I jumped in: 'But it's not simple for you either, not with Lindsey in Sydney. Freyja going back in a state won't help. I'm sorry.'

'Don't be. There's nothing I can do about Lindsey. I hope I never see her again.' Lerryn paused, then said: 'Searching's a strange process. I've done a lot of it, still do. I don't think Freyja was searching for a "someone", a lover, in the summer. I think it was for part of a question, and a decision.'

'You mean should she stay or should she go?'

'Yes.'

'I should have seen it coming. But I didn't.'

Jules said: 'You can't read the signs unless you're near someone to read them. I know it's hard to take, that's why we're here, with you. Freyja will get through. Especially if she goes home.'

Lerryn added: 'She was searching and you were there. Don't blame yourself for that.'

'It's hard not to.'

'You mustn't,' said Tessa. 'Freyja's getting all sorts of wires crossed in London. August's part of a wider thing.'

'She wouldn't see me, would she, if I came up to London?'

'No,' replied Lerryn. 'I asked her. She won't.'

146

'I'm so glad you're here, all of you.'

'Shame we have to dash on Sunday, but no getting round it.'

'No there isn't. And – it's better for me to know about Freyja, otherwise it's crazy-making. Been there, done that.'

'Break up's always crazy-making,' said Tessa, 'whether it's friends or lovers. You've been through so much loss, Denny. But this time, you've got "group" again. We want you to know it.'

'Thanks.' Hugs all round. We were all quiet for a while.

Presently, Jules said: 'I was thinking. What about a bonfire on the beach?' Turning to me, she said: 'You've talked often about fire, the negative images, and the positive ones. The shore would be the earth. The sea, the water. We already have air. We'd make fire. We could do an ending ritual. Generate some good energy. Send it across the ocean. I've done one before. It was wonderful. What about tomorrow night?'

She was right.

The horror dreams did not return.

Eighteen

With each tamarisk tree I planted that autumn, and each escallonia cutting, I buried my feelings for Harriet deep in the Cornish earth. I wrote often to Beatrice, hoping that Roarie would come through on to the blue airmail paper. I felt Roarie would return as she had promised. I knew she would – when our time was right.

High up on the moors, by Men-an-Tol and Ding Dong mine, surrounded by sea, with birds circling and crying, I heard Wind in all her voices, in all weathers. I felt I'd come through some powerful things that had made me much stronger, though I still missed Freyja in close time – and Maria in distant time.

My grief for Maria had changed; the raw hurts were softer.

Meanwhile I tried instead to be a passionate friend for Harriet. I'd read about them – rich women of the eighteen hundreds who lived together, great friends but not at all erotic. Nothing sexual going on. Not that I really believed what I read. Surely some of them fancied each other, in love as well as loving friends, and surely some of them found each other completely irresistible? Like *Patience and Sarah*, though they weren't exactly rich. But they did make love, live together. Wasn't it fiction based on fact?

The questions teased me, but I didn't have any answers.

I buried my love and want. It was hard work – the ground was granite.

That September we left behind the campaign trail; took

time out for some fun. Car-boot sales: I found a frame for a favourite photo – Maria, Daphne and Bronwyn, in a playful mood. I spent days sanding and varnishing the frame, mounting the picture carefully. Auctions: Harriet bought a dozen old mirrors, all shapes and sizes. We cleaned and polished them, hung them around her room, grouping and regrouping them. They gleamed, winked, and sparkled. She took them down, rearranged them.

Finally she stood back, satisfied: 'Well, what d'you think?'

A dozen Dennys watched me, waiting for a word. 'We're all beside ourselves.'

When Harriet laughed I saw women playing on the moors, flying bright red kites. 'Sit down,' she said, still laughing.

I sat, halving my numbers. Half a dozen Dennys, all in Harriet's room: everyone in trouble, everyone in love.

'I don't want to grow old and wise,' she said, perched on the end of her bed, 'I want to grow old and play; have some fun.'

'Sounds good to us,' I said. 'Speaking from all angles, as we all say.'

'Are you sure you like my mirrors?'

'We'll get used to them, in a while. Now we've all got to get out of here.' I dropped to my hands and knees and crawled along, under mirror level, coming face to face in the doorway, with Roof. She barked and wagged and ran to fetch a slipper, glad at last somebody was teaching me to play again.

So that September we played. We walked by gleaming rockpools, looking into other worlds, complete sci-fi gardens under water. We moseyed round nurseries, planning for the walled garden behind the house; we watched sea birds through binoculars – on clear days counted waves crashing on distant lighthouses, miles away; and we searched junk shops for blue and white plant-pots.

I was five, seven, nine, eleven.

JoAnne sometimes came with us. She took pictures of Harriet and me. We swapped cameras. Then they laughed, arm in arm, for my photos of them. JoAnne was dark haired and dark eyed, with deep lines around her eyes where she'd been out in the sun, and suntanned hands with weathered skin. She often dressed in red and black, and disliked pastels, joking that's what she had in common with Alexis from *Dynasty*, and the only thing in common with Joan Collins – JoAnne was medium build with plenty of midriff, and when she hugged you it was a proper hug, substantial.

To me, those pictures said it all: JoAnne and Harriet – old flames. And me, new flame burning brightly. I shone in the photos, though nobody quizzed me, and surely it was obvious what was happening to me?

Try as I would to turn this into friendship, I had the unmistakable glow about me of a woman in love.

I thought: both of them know. Neither of them's grassing.

Beyond Cornwall, other people in my life were getting on with theirs. Phil was in Mauritius, making a go of it, apparently with the same girlfriend and the same job, which surprised me. He never sent his address but he phoned every couple of months, which was enough. Graham was happy, enjoying university, working as a painter and decorator in his time off. Cheryl and I phoned one another now and then.

In October, while Harriet was away in Shropshire with her family, I decided to sort through my boxes in one of the outhouses, an old granite building, with a low sagging slate roof and orange lichens.

Inside – an arachnologist's paradise – I was armed with a soft brush.

'Come on you lot: notice to quit.'

Spiders of every shape, size and colour scuttled in all directions as sunlight arranged itself in shifting oblongs from cobwebbed windows. I removed dust-sheets from cartons raised off the floor on blocks.

Like Russian dolls, my boxes fitted inside each other. I set up a trestle table, brushed it, threw a clean dust sheet over it, removed my gloves and slowly began to unpack, until the trestle resembled a window dresser's Christmas. Not all my boxes gleamed silver and gold like the one that Rosa returned to me, but some did; and others, minute and exquisite, holding no more than one pebble or one carefully dried flower, were covered in felt and fabric, paper and ribbon.

Roof lay awake under the trestle.

I swept clean a couple of boxes and stacked them. Finally I sat down. Aloud, taking a very deep breath I said: 'I'm ready.'

'Don't be scared, I won't harm you. Love won't harm you,' she said standing, wearing jeans and a sweatshirt, beyond the trestle table.

'I've been dreaming about you. I was walking with you again through the art gallery where we fell in love, the pictures so clear you could walk into them, through them.'

'I waited for you. I didn't want to disturb you. So I waited for today. Nothing to be scared of. We fell in love; love isn't wrong, it just happens, it just is.'

'To be with you . . . like this. I want to touch you, but if I do you mightn't be able to stay.'

'Just talk to me. Don't touch. I want you to be happy. I want you to love Harriet, to be happy with her. To touch *her*.'

'I'm changing. Facing up to things. To you and me. So I . . . I came in here, touched the boxes, displayed them. I . . . I hoped you'd come to me. I hoped you'd help me . . .'

'You don't have to shut me out. I live in the sunlight. I'm not the other side of night. I *am* daytime. If you're alone, I can help you . . .'

'Daphne.'

'It's all right, Denny.'

The October sunshine was strangely welcoming. I felt warm, cocooned, happy as I said: 'I . . . I dream you. I dream your mouth, your hands, your body. You're so real . . . Not Maria . . . I don't dream Maria . . . now now, not since I passed out. But even in that moment you watched me. I felt you watch me face Maria on that floor. I blocked you out. I had to. I couldn't handle it. I'm ready now.'

In front of me, separated by the table, leaning foward with her hands on the boxes she'd made, Daphne smiled. Her being there seemed comforting, as I said things . . . that I couldn't say elsewhere . . . that would be hard to voice elsewhere . . .

'I was in love with you,' I said.

'It was mutual.'

'I loved you. I wanted you. But it wasn't resolved . . . when . . . I don't know how your accident happened, no one knows. I was so guilty. I couldn't grieve you. I began to know how . . . when I came here, listened to Wind, listened to water, to rain . . .'

'I wanted you too, Denny.'

'I've a new friend, from the seventeenth century. I don't know who she is, not really. She comes from a special place. She gives me a place . . . somewhere I can go, if . . . Maybe she helped me come here, unpack the boxes, call you.'

'Face to face we are now, at last. You and I.'

'I don't know what'll become of me . . . with you . . . it feels right. Right to speak it. I couldn't tell it to Roarie, my new friend, not the same. I have to tell you. Face to face. You and me. We loved and it was real. Tell me, tell me we were real.'

'Yes, woman. I wanted you. Make no mistake. Now you're moving on again. Follow your feelings, woman. Go for it.'

'I want Harriet. I want to understand things. I want to know what's real.'

'It's all real. You and Maria, you loved each other. You and me. *We loved*. I want you to love again. If you're strong enough to call me . . . you're strong enough to love again. Now blow your nose woman, all that sniffing and snorting, you'll frighten the spiders.'

Daphne laughed as I screwed up my face, closed my eyes and blew. A wonderful laugh, a familiar laugh, with me, not at me. She laughed and was gone.

Nineteen

Shivering in the biting cold, Martha shields her eyes against the glare from the snow as she stands on the ice-covered steps of the mill, surveying the countryside.

It's November 1666. Travellers have come and gone from the manor, talking of clouds of death over London; of the rich who left for country homes while recovery and rebuilding takes place; of the poor who camp in the burned-out streets, in makeshift shacks and tents despite the freezing weather; and of the Dutch who seem intent on war with England, adding to the general sense of trouble and turmoil.

Now the manor is cut off from the outside world by snow and ice; the only tracks are those of birds and foxes across white fields. A fallen branch begs up through the ice like a hand. There is a bleak, stark quality to the scene, coloured in black, brown, grey and white. Martha's red shawl shrieks in contrast.

Every day the ice changes the view, rimes new edges, makes odd shapes, strange angles. Each snowfall blankets and softens some outlines, sharpens and defines others. There are patterns in the ice that Martha hasn't seen before. Dried grasses edged in frost lean over the solid millpond. Posts, not quite upright are higgledy, brown striped white, tops like skulls.

Signs of life are the smoke signals from a few inhabited houses and from several of the chimneys on the pointed roofs of Harland Heights, for the Harlands are back from Scotland. But the manor house is empty – Lord and Lady

Chingford Meade perished when the plague hit Shropshire. Village people plunder the larder, just as foxes plunder the hen house.

It is noon. From the south, towards London, the sun is a silver blur behind leafless silhouetted trees. Martha pulls her shawl tighter around her, unwilling to return inside despite the penetrating chill as she hugs her arms around her body. This is going to be a long hard winter. Nearby there are tell-tale humps where abandoned cabbages and rows of bad turnips are frozen under the snow. Lucy Turner says there weren't enough people to bring in the harvest.

But the scene is not silent. Behind Martha inside the mill are the sounds of wood on wood, wood on metal. Everyone who can is helping in the winter's task – the reconstruction of Chingford Meade mill. Sounds of chiselling and hammering ring across the valley, and to the east, beyond the forest, Martha can just make out two people, she thinks they are women, one taller than the other, watching the mill from the flat roof of the new wing of Harland Heights. From there the servants gathered to see the Great Fire of London. From there it is said the young mistress, Bennetta, forced into marriage with her cousin Alistair, himself brought back from the West Indies for that purpose, takes comfort of an evening watching the sunset, alone.

On the roof, Bennetta's personal maid, a young Black woman brought with Alistair's retinue from the West Indies, is asking for her freedom papers.

Lydia, the maid, stands, feet slightly apart, aware of being watched from a distance by a woman in a red shawl on the steps of the mill. Cold as ice inside, her face expressionless as she makes her demand, Lydia stands. She has rehearsed this for months.

Bennetta pretends not to understand.

Lydia repeats her words. She wants to live as a free Black woman in England. She is baptised a Christian. She can ride. She is an excellent seamstress, can make her own living.

Bennetta sees the words skim smoothly, polished, an oval stone across flat ice, fast and accurate.

154

Now Bennetta stops pretending. She's angry. Fire boils from inside, from her pelvis, belly and breasts, where she hurts, assaulted by a husband she didn't choose, doesn't love.

'Freedom. Don't ever talk of it. I have no freedom, can grant you none.'

'Ma'am, 'tis not true. You are my mistress. You may travel and play as you choose. 'Tis your house, not mine.'

'Don't dare talk so. You are my servant, my personal maid. So be it.'

''Tis justice is my desire, ma'am.' Lydia now speaks coldly, slowly. 'The master has power. Great power over the both of us. 'Tis true, as you say, but in the law of this land 'tis you be the one free woman, and I the unfree. So, ma'am, 'tis my freedom I be without, and 'tis in your own power to bequeath it.'

Angrily, Bennetta raises her right arm to strike her maid, whom she sees as insolent. Bennetta's arm is high in the air. Lydia does not move, does not flinch. At that moment the lace of Bennetta's sleeve falls back. Lydia's eyes go to a line of raised marks, dark blue bruises from Bennetta's wrist to her elbow.

Eye to eye, height for height, they stand. Bennetta drops her arm, the lace falls back, the bruises are hidden again. Lydia can imagine, as Bennetta now knows, how Bennetta's arms are pinned above her head as the master takes what he wants, when he wants, with no concern for her. Lydia has first-hand knowledge of Alistair's methods. She visits Roarie Brewster, for salves and lotions, to heal herself. Lydia has tinctures and remedies, herbs and mixtures that have rid her of two children already, since coming to England.

She used to visit Mary By-the-Well; but the flogging of the healer was watched by all the servants of the Harlands, from the flat roof of the new wing.

Later, Lydia sits alone in the chapel on the Harland estate, calling up the spirits to help her.

She watches as the sun moves across a stained-glass window, casting pools of blood, gold, sky and fire on the wooden pews.

155

The huge stained-glass windows, along both sides of the nave and behind the altar, glorify God, Jesus and the Harlands, since stained glass is expensive.

In calling up the spirits, Lydia holds her mind on the word 'freedom', its strengths and possibilities.

Freedom is fought for: successes are told and retold, slave to slave on the plantations, passed to each generation to encourage and sustain.

True stories of long, lonely journeys, safe place to safe place. Contacts with strangers, who might betray. Signs from the spirits who take their rightful place on the side of the slaves: white masters die from weird accidents; white mistresses are poisoned; white youths get fatal diseases.

Lydia has not toiled tending sugar cane; she has toiled tending white people. How shall she escape? How shall she reach freedom?

As if in answer to her questions, the light from a window shifts, falling directly on Lydia's face, and into her mind comes a picture – of a blackamoor highwayman rumoured to be working in the area. Servants in the kitchens at Harland Heights say he cannot be caught – he is too skilful – and they say it was he who cut free Mary By-the-Well.

As a young girl, before being brought to England, Lydia hears of freedom trails. Men, women and children die attempting to get to the trails. Better to die than be caught – set upon by vicious dogs, flung into boiling sugar, clamped into spiked collars.

Lydia is used to the fact that white people are rich, powerful and atrociously violent, wherever they are: at the fields, in the gardens, inside the great house.

But in England, to Lydia's surprise, she discovers there are also white people who are poor and treated brutally. Layers of white people, a mountain of white bones, the poorest taking the weight of the others. Lydia has new knowledge. Not all white people have Harland wealth, Harland whips and hearts of sour white pith. Not that she will ever trust white people. But she is astonished to find that they are also beaten until they bleed; worked until they are exhausted; punished until they are submissive, which they never truly are, so they never stop being punished.

In England, alone in the chapel, determined to leave and trying to plan, Lydia turns her thoughts from the punishments.

Blood and fire: the time has come, she thinks. Did not Mary, mother of Jesus, find a new shelter, a stable, in her time of need? So shall I.

She leaves the chapel, cuts through the herb garden, lifts the latch on the lych-gate, and this being her day off, she slips unnoticed into the woods that lead to Mary's cottage where Roarie now lives.

Although she knocks softly at Roarie's door, it is opened at once. Stepping across the threshold, on to the earth floor, swept clean, Lydia meets warmth from a fire burning in the brick hearth. As a sign from the spirits, she watches Roarie take a sprig of rosemary from a bunch hanging from the rafters, and place it on the fire. Its fragrance fills the room as they sit by the table.

Lydia has a glass bead necklace, a gift from Bennetta. It is not worth anything but it is pretty. She wears it hidden under her neckerchief. If the spirits want Lydia to go forward with her plan, they will move Roarie Brewster to speak of the necklace.

'You wish to ask my help but you fear I shall betray you.'

''Tis the truth,' says Lydia.

'You wear a glass necklace, hidden from view. 'Tis worth but a few farthings although it is pretty. You wear it not to please yourself, but to test me. For this reason: what you want is dangerous. If I should betray you, you would be flogged. A prisoner at Harland Heights till you die old and not free.'

'They do say you are wise, though young.'

'And you're here to ask for my help.'

'A contact. With the man who 'tis rumoured cut loose Mary By-the-Well.'

'That cannot be. The risk is too high. For both parties.'

Lydia listens. She does not answer at once but takes her time, watching the kettle that is hooked on a swinging bar and now hangs over the fire, boiling slowly.

When Lydia speaks she is sure, unhesitating: "Tis truth you speak. I know it here . . . and here.' Lydia touches her heart and then her forehead in a slow, certain gesture. To rely on a white woman is a terrible risk, and there are worse punishments than flogging if she is betrayed. For daring to speak to someone beyond the Harland walls she can be tortured into never speaking again, to anyone . . . for women in England who speak out, who scold, who find a voice outside their household, there is the iron helmet and the mouth bit. Silent screams and unbearable pain.

Watching Lydia, Roarie knows she is being tested. If she is caught helping Lydia, a worse fate will befall her than the flogging of Mary By-the-Well. For Roarie is not licensed by the Bishop as Mary was, a trained midwife, approved to help women in labour. Nor is she a valid apothecary, trading legally in medicines and herbs, tolerated by the College of Physicians only because there aren't yet enough of them to treat all the poor of the villages. On every count, Roarie is untrained, unlicensed, unapprenticed. For months she has been trying to reason this through, to find her own plan for finishing her apprenticeship and carrying on Mary's work.

"Tis a great risk to approach me. I am honoured by you, am I not?'

'A slow death in a great house. 'Tis a prison. I shall not smother my own fire by mine own hand. Wouldst rather die, walking to freedom. Be it dogs, or whips, to resist is to live.'

'When?'

'At the end of winter. 'Tis impossible in the ice and snow, is't not true?'

'Drifting snow would cover your footprints . . .'

'Aye. Would bury me also. By my reckoning only a fool does tryst with snow and ice.'

'So, the end of winter, then?'

'The end of winter. 'Tis far away but I must plan. I must succeed. Shall reach Chingford Meade Mill by midnight, by my reckoning.'

'At night? By the moon?'

'Perchance a clear night.'

'The path, 'tis known to you, Lydia?'

'Should my eyes be closed, I would know it. Will you contact – with him, who saved your teacher?'

'Yes, I will. I can tell you now of my plan. When I was young I desired to fire the Harland estate. Myself and a band of young strong lads from this manor. Two brothers of mine would be with me. They lie in the graveyard. I told my plan to Mary By-the-Well. Ne'er did I see her so angry. Wouldst I fight like the Harlands, she asked? Would I kill and plunder; and maim? Could I be her deputy yet talk so of murder? Mary By-the-Well spat at the fire. A huge gob hissed on a log, there in that hearth.

'Then I saw I would lose her from my life, if I dreamed only of fire and death. I fought my dreams, day and night, my dreams of armies, marching, killing. My tongue stayed itself; I talked of life and love, to her.'

'Do you dream now of firing the Harlands?'

Roarie laughs. 'I am not the child I was.' She laughs again then changes tone. 'Shall fight in other ways, but mark me, I shall fight. To rid the earth of Harlands – is it not to rid us of a plague? 'Tis my own riddle: shall I a warrior or a healer be? Are they not the same?'

'Freedom, 'tis my desire. Resistance, 'tis the marrow, the ember.'

Eyes meet and hold. Then Roarie nods slowly, saying: 'As to the highwayman – I shall make known to him the plan.'

'So. To the end of winter then, Roarie?'

'To the very end, Lydia. And a bright full moon.'

Next day, Roarie goes with Ruth and Martha to a meeting called by the Turners, Wainwrights and Claytons. Being townsfolk, Ruth and Martha are not familiar with winter in a place like the manor. They are not used to the rhythm of the seasons, and although they might chop firewood until their backs threaten to break, they can't harvest where they haven't planted.

They have enough money to buy tallow from Alice Clayton for making candles but they can't brew ale as they haven't grown hops; and they don't have any animals, except a few chickens saved from the foxes that roam the gardens of the deserted manor house.

The Turners, Claytons and Wainwrights are not so badly off, but with only one year passed since the plague, they are short of labour for all the outdoor work that's needed.

On the manor friendship grows between the remaining households, as they meet around the Wainwrights' hearth the first week of November, and begin to plan for a long hard winter.

Once again, as with the winter following the plague, the lives of the survivors are saved partly by the still room of the late Lady Elizabeth Chingford Meade. It is filthy with dust and cobwebs, but still stocked with almost two hundred jars and bottles, whereas in the previous year there were five hundred. Apples and pears are laid down in thick syrup; damsons, plums and loganberries in water. There are crystallised fruits and candied peels, with airtight wax seals; there are gooseberry wines and elderflower; quinces in jams and jellies; simple mead; and jars of honeycomb.

Christmas is a cautious celebration: this is the coldest, severest winter known for many years. News from London is of the poor sleeping in shacks and tents on the ice, their homes destroyed by the Great Fire. On the manor, everyone has a roof and walls and a bed; there is plenty of fuel; and the food although rationed is adequate, some of it delicious.

After the festival the work continues. Lucy Turner takes over William Brewster's loom, and with Roarie's help she warps up and prepares to learn the craft. The slam and bang of the shuttle and marches can be heard again as she practises during daylight.

Hannah Wainwright and Alice Clayton grind corn by hand, a laborious task. Anne Brewster milks goats and makes cheese, as she's always done. Hannah's husband, Tom, works with John Turner and Joseph Clayton, dawn to dusk, refurbishing the mill with Martha and Ruth.

Roarie supervises the older children, who haul quotas of firewood, and carry messages between the adults.

January brings the last of the mead and wine from the manor still room. Where it had reflected the light from shelves of dusty bottles, it now shows empty, upturned containers.

Outside, the ice shows no sign of melting.

February the second is Candlemas, usually heralding the end of winter. Not this year. The last of the rushes in the stores means the last of the wick lights. No work can be done after dark.

The oats are running low; sacks of dried peas and beans are almost empty; the onions are finished; and the last barrels of carrots stored in dry sand are eked out.

Annie Wainwright, who is six, begins to have trouble with her breathing. Roarie struggles to treat her, but it's no simple cough – a thick white membrane seems to clog the back of her throat. Roarie can soothe her, but she hasn't seen such a membrane before.

By the end of the next week, Tommy Turner who is four, can't breathe properly, joined by Sarah Wainwright, who is seven and Lizzie Clayton, who is Alice Clayton's only live-born child. The Claytons are the youngest married couple on the manor. They're tenant farmers – the land they farm belonged to the manor and will eventually revert to the crown if no one claims the manor house and its adjoining tenants' plots and cottages.

To isolate the sick children, and slow the spread of the attack, the four are carried across the snow into the Brewsters' old home. Lucy, at the loom, stays near them.

Beds are made up for them. A huge fire is kept going day and night, to warm them. They seem unable to swallow junket nor julep drinks, and their breathing is frightening to hear.

By the third week of February the four very sick children are steadily choking to death.

Mocking, like a giant wooden toy, the mill stands, locked in a white ice landscape, a solid millpond slightly above it, a frozen millrace below. The adults can't make it work without water; and sick children don't play. So it waits, a huge inert model, unmoving, its mechanisms iced where its axle meets the stone support each side.

The end of the third week of February, the ale is gone, and the well is frozen. Roarie boils the snow now, adding a few dried herbs; everyone takes fewer oats for a daily meal of porridge.

The first week of March, Annie and Sarah Wainwright, Tommy Turner and Lizzie Clayton die, strangled by the membrane's grip.

The ice shows no sign of melting. All the adults, men and women, help to dig the small graves, which have to be chipped from frozen soil under the ice and snow, near an apple tree in the churchyard. Then they carve the dead children's names into a heavy log, which they carry to the apple tree.

Annie, Sarah, Tommy and Lizzie are buried on a Sunday, under the apple tree. Prayers are said. There are two older children left in the Wainwright family, a boy of nine and a girl of eight. The Turners have one child left, a girl of three.

The living children, some of them remembering the plague year, watch stony-eyed as small bundles wrapped in white cloth are lowered.

Anne Brewster, Martha, Ruth and Roarie stand beside Lucy and John, Hannah and Tom, Alice and Joseph, who can't afford chiselled stones for dead children.

None of the adults can weep.

Next day they wake to the sound of slow dripping.

The ice has begun to melt.

Twenty

Now that Roarie and I were Speaking Paper again, it was easier for me to side-step my feelings for Harriet.

If my mind had been empty of its own interests, p'raps I'd have needed something to fill it – Harriet, for instance.

Now because of the seventeenth century, and the manor of Chingford Meade, I had a place to go, rather than a space to fill. While listening to music of an evening, I could easily walk in the folds of the hills and woods of my imagination. Contented to let time pass, and pass me by, I felt peaceful and calm, undisturbed by the fact that I shared words with a seventeenth-century weaver's daughter.

I no longer feared the voices; I welcomed them.

Nor did I ask myself if Roarie was real.

I knew she was not me: beyond that I didn't know, and didn't really need to know, so long as she came to me, across the bridge, often.

So it took me aback when, in the middle of listening to a Joan Baez record one evening in November, Harriet said: 'Could we talk, Denny?'

'Yes, of course. What about?'

'Cinderella.'

I thought: follow that, Denny. But how?

'I suppose it's that the panto season's come round again and we've been here almost a year,' she said. 'I was wondering how you really feel about me being a modern Cinders? Marries prince, gets castle.'

'Keeps castle, loses prince. You paid a high price.'

'I want to know how you really feel about it.'

'I've often thought of your life as a modern Cinderella story. There's no shame in wanting money, but you went through such loneliness. I can't bear to think of you being lonely. I know what it's like. You can't buy friends. We're friends. I know I'm paid to work here, but I think that we're good friends.'

'Have you thought of leaving?' She blanched as she asked.

'Yes . . . but I don't want to. Everybody has to think about the future. I came here to work, and now I know I could work other places, if I had to.'

'I suppose this is a review of the end of our first year here, together.'

'I'd love to stay, if you want me to.'

'Very much. It's because I think we're close friends, I want to tell you about my other friends, starting with JoAnne.'

'She never left Oliver, did she? But it's you she loves.'

'Sometimes, Denny, you're ten years ahead of me, and it's not to do with age.'

'Our friendship hasn't anything to do with age at all. Not in my book. So, you and JoAnne?'

'We were childhood friends. I went to London. JoAnne met Oliver. They were engaged. She came to stay with me so that we could do some shopping. She fell in love.'

'Did you fall for her as well?'

'Not really. Not in the same way. I fancied her, but it was very complex. I was in love with someone else.'

'Strewth. What did JoAnne do?'

'She fled to her aunt, who lived in Scarborough. I think Oliver thought she'd joined the foreign legion. Which she had, in a way. But he waited, and finally she returned and they were married. We didn't see each other for a while. We knew each other so well – eventually we could re-establish our friendship.'

'Meanwhile, you said you were in love?'

'Yes. With someone I'd met via the art world after I was married . . . a woman whose name I think you've heard: Anna von Schiller.'

I felt confused. I'd heard that name from Lerryn.

Carefully, I asked: 'What happened to you and Anna?'

'My lover fell in love with my niece.'

I drew in a quick breath, thinking rapidly then asked, as gently as I could: 'Lerryn doesn't know that you were lovers with Anna, does she?'

'No. Once I came very close to telling her, but something stopped me. I hinted that I was celibate, asexual. I recall my exact words: "Nothing there dear. Just not interested."'

Harriet added: 'Later, the intense politics around the miners' strike was followed by Lerryn's mother's death, then the split with Lindsey. The timing was never right.'

'These things are always about time, aren't they?' I thought of Freyja, the awfully bad timing.

Harriet said: 'I was with Anna a good while before she whirled Lerryn off her feet. But Lerryn never knew that. She was only nineteen when they met. Anna had never been to Herton Hall with me, and Lerryn had never seen us in the same bedroom.'

'But if you and Anna were seen together publicly, how come someone never told Lerryn?'

'Because in public Anna and I were merely friends. My sons were away at school. I had ample opportunity to be at Anna's place with her when she was in London. She never stayed at my home.'

As Harriet spoke I watched her carefully. She wore her old green cords and a soft sage-green jumper that suited her.

She said: 'At first, after Anna left me, I was angry and bewildered. I couldn't accept it, kept looking back. I went through a stage of hating her, and doubting myself, asking how could I have been so foolish as to be with her in the first place . . .

'It took me a very long time to work it through. When I had, I was able to mix with her in the art world again. She'd also suffered by then – Lerryn had refused to live with her, or follow her around the various continents where she has houses.'

We sat either side of the open fire, in comfy armchairs. Red wine relaxed me, though my mind flew like a wild bird.

Roof stretched between us, posing as a hearthrug. She so trusted Harriet that she didn't twitch when Harriet leaned over her to tend the grate.

'You're a good listener, Denny. I needed to hear your response to my Cinderella story, because I'm in trouble.'

'Trouble?' Why had she borrowed my word?

'After Anna, I never expected to want anyone again. I thought that wanting was over for me. Pierre had his partners; they were always men. I had my work: Herton Foundation for the Visual Arts, where Lerryn used to come and stay, and where she met Lindsey; the huge house in Shropshire – the garden was a copy of Sissinghurst; and the Chelsea flat. I have some ideas for what I want to happen with that flat; very glad I never sold it, but that's another talk another time.'

Harriet paused, then, almost thinking aloud, she said: 'It's a comfort to me that my sons are all happy inside their gilt-edged securities, running Herton Hall, and the Chelsea galleries and the Shropshire house, and their own homes, with their good wives and two-point-two children and family dogs.'

I interrupted her: 'Then don't knock it. You don't want them divorced or penniless.'

'True. But if they saw inside my head, they'd put me away.'

'They. Them. Takes me back to the bleak times before I met Freyja, and Lerryn, then you. They was my name for I don't know what, but I used to sit and wait for Them to come and get me. It's a sort of bleakness and terror I don't want to go through again.'

'Which brings me to the next thing. Whatever happens to our friendship, this place is yours for ever, Denny. You are the beneficiary of my will.'

'You mustn't do that Harriet. They. Them. They'd contest it. It's very kind of you, but it's not possible. If anything happened to you, I've made all my own plans. I'd go to Aotearoa for a while, to Beatrice. She has my money, safe in an account there. I can't touch it. That way I'm safe and my fare is paid.'

'Are you afraid they'd call you a treasure seeker?'

'Oh, they'll do that anyway, whether I stay or leave, money or not. The mere fact of being here in a job like this makes me vulnerable. I knew that before I took the job. If anybody bothers to talk about me it's easy to gossip that I'm only here as housekeeper to wheedle my way into your affections. Whereas, in fact, I'm confident now; confident to get this kind of job in other places. I'm independent now.'

'Then I'll share with you, Denny, what *I'm* afraid of. I'm afraid of my own wanting. I never expected to want again.'

Now, she looked at me, and I knew. I daren't move; daren't touch her. But I returned her gaze. Then she knew.

'You have your life ahead of you,' said Harriet.

'So do you. You might die tomorrow, or ten weeks from now, or ten years, or twenty. I might die tomorrow or ten years or twenty or forty from now. There is no insurance. Maria had her life ahead of her too, so did both Bronwyn and Daphne.'

Now there was tension shimmering in the room, like air currents under sea birds' wings. To misjudge this would be to drop between high cliffs, snarled into pieces in the teeth of the sea. We'd be washed up on some distant beach, our feathers thick with oil, our eyes staring into nothing. Many's the reckless bird we'd brought home for a decent burial.

But not to fly in the first place?

'I'm sixty-six in a week or two. There are twenty-nine and a bit years between you and me. It takes a great deal of imagination to leap across twenty-plus years.'

'Then leap.'

'I already have. I have imagined us.' She paused . . . 'We're both in trouble.'

'Double trouble.'

'We'd have to totally rearrange our lives; change every part of the household we've built so carefully here, all our work, our schedules. I couldn't possibly blur the boundary between me and someone in my employment . . .'

'Any more than I'd have nooky with my boss?'

Bad girls laughing in a teenage gang, sneaking into phone

booths, dares half-planned.

We didn't make love that night. On the edge of a beginning, neither of us had covered our backs.

I took Roof for her last-thing-at-night walk, not romantic at all. The fog was thick. We kept to the road. I walked with fast biting steps, using a torch. Visibility was about fifteen yards. Enough to stay safe, on the road, not on the moors or cliffs, and my face and hair were soon soaked.

Romance seemed a warm gentle lie in comparison to my love for Harriet. We'd talked of fire, not romance.

I slept soundly, waking to the unmistakable hoot of our fog horn – a trillion megawatt owl we named Minerva.

Outside my windows luminous layers of fog swirled a few feet above the fields, under a duvet of damp cloud.

In a thick tracksuit and warm slippers I padded into the living room. Harriet was already up. Through our wide windows the light was pale bright grey. The cliff edges were invisible.

Harriet, already busy at the Aga, offered tea and toast. Thanking her I said: 'Are we housebound? . . . I slept well – how about you?'

'Like a log. So happy. I know we've long discussions ahead, but what an amazing change this is in my life.'

Was it the way she looked, in her warm red dressing-gown and fleece-lined moccassins, like mine? Was it the way I felt, awake, alive, strong enough for a shared future, all its ifs and buts, that made it that moment we held out our arms? We kissed and kissed, until forced to stop by an athletic whistling kettle that hurtled across the Aga.

Over breakfast Harriet said: 'It's a strange way to start, but as I fell asleep last night I thought if we don't discuss the end, we can't begin at all . . .'

I interrupted: 'Not strange to me. If I can't face the end I can't start this. When I realised you'd been twice through bereavement, you touched me very deeply.'

Harriet said: 'Neither of us wants the other to be left, to go through that loss again. But we might have to . . .'

'In fairy tales lovers choose to end at the same moment –

turn into oak trees either side of an old doorway. It'd be nice to do that. Live years together, then tell our friends: "Get ready – tomorrow we turn into trees the same minute." '

'What a thought. You always surprise me, Denny.'

I replied slowly, choosing my words: 'This time I want courage to be aware: to be aware of every day with you, every year with you, in a way that I wasn't with Maria . . . Life wasn't precious enough. Not until it was gone. You're special, life's special, the time is here and now . . . I won't waste a drop, not this time.'

We held each other again, touching one another's faces, and kissing, minutes long. Where our breasts and bellies touched, our energy was wonderful: powerful: where the ley lines meet.

We worked side by side all day as we began a complete reappraisal. To outsiders it would have seemed a bore. All those sums, plans, schedules, but Harriet and I enjoyed it.

My job as housekeeper for Harriet was over. I wanted a regular job outside Hermit's Hut to secure my independence. Later I went to work for JoAnne who offered five mornings: computer graphics, word processing and some reception in her office.

Taureans like me are down to earth, practical, though there is fire in my sign, in several aspects. But common sense usually takes me over as far as money's concerned – no one I'm lovers with rips me off. A lot of people in Harriet's life were afraid even to try and match her. A Sagittarian, she could move fast as the arrow from her own bow, as I'd learned over Clause 28, and she was used to the business world. She didn't found Herton Hall for nothing. I wouldn't dream of being with her, as her lover, if I thought there was any chance of not matching her, speed for speed.

So, tedious as it seems, the details became significant, to quote Graham in his university voice.

Harriet would cover the phone bill: I couldn't compete – the phone grew out of her hand – she had friends in America!! I'd pay half the food, electric, water and so on, and my own poll tax when it hit me on the head. She'd pay for fancy food. I lived quite simply when I was in London. I wouldn't choose posh food if I was on my own. We'd sort out what was posh and what wasn't as we already had for shampoos and lotions. Harriet's 'friv'(olous) spending was fresh flowers, mine, my music.

We'd have plenty of time for loving, making love, playing. But you can't grow clematis up a wall if you haven't built the wall first and fixed the trellis.

That evening, I fetched from my bookshelves my copies of *Dream of a Common Language*, and *A Wild Patience Has Taken Me This Far*. We sat, by our living-room fire as fog thickened to December night.

I read some of the *Twenty-One Love Poems*, slowly, no need to hurry; and 'Integrity', one of my favourites, which gave the image of clematis rain-smashed, being wreathed back on a trellis.

We sat, a younger woman and an older woman, in love, reading poems: wise and aware of our bodies. We might have been any women lovers, anywhere in the world, any time, in any living-room, knowing one another's bodies intimately, having been lovers for years and years. Anywhere, in any living-room.

There seemed nothing new about it, though it was new to us together. It didn't seem rare, or even extraordinary. It seemed glad, honest, and very real.

That's how we began.

But Hermit's Hut was built on the north Cornish coast, and that's no place for sentimentality. Passion, yes. But if, at any time, I became starry eyed, or wore my heart on my sleeve, I'd turn a corner, snag my heart on a nail. Harriet, who loved the place as I did, called it 'a land of wild, uncompromising scenery matched only by a stark and brutal history'.

It was spring 1989, not long after we had become lovers that I came face to face with this history, during an unexpected encounter, in a strange and disturbing incident.

We had taken to visiting famous gardens, she and I. She called it our 'Tre-garden' phase. Usually I read the guide

170

books carefully before I went, but on this occasion I didn't, because the day suddenly turned out sunny and we set off in a hurry.

It was a wonderful day. We sat on a bench in a quiet enclosure in one such garden, surrounded by camellias in full bloom, and under them was a carpet of Solomon's seal, palest pink primroses – ones I hadn't known of until I lived at Hermit's Hut – and jonquils. Beside me, Harriet quietly listened to bird-song.

So much for sentimentality.

Into the enclosure came three people – a man, his sister and his wife, all of them pensioners it seemed.

The man was ranting, loudly and continuously. It was impossible not to hear all his words: 'Place was entirely built on slavery. All of it. Slave money. Entirely built on slavery.'

He passed by, out of earshot, still ranting, with his sister, but for some reason (I never found out why) his wife lingered.

'Excuse me,' I spoke up, quite boldly, 'I couldn't help overhearing.'

'Oh, he does it all the time.' She spoke with a full Cornish accent. 'Such a bore. Much older than me, you know.'

Harriet and I exchanged glances.

I said, 'He said it was built on slavery?'

'Oh, but it's true, my love.'

She told us the story of the family that first built the house, its subsequent sale to a slave owner, who founded the gardens, and its later sales and extensions.

Eventually the woman bade us goodbye. Harriet saw that I was shaking, and only then discovered I didn't know the history. Usually I was so clued up.

Around me, innocent trees and shrubs. Innocent blossoms.

Wild primroses where the dead are buried. Symbolically, that is. How many slaves for each flower? I was shocked at my own naivety, as I sometimes was if Wind caught me out, and challenged me in one of her 'My God, Denny, you're so unworldly' moods.

'Have to go home,' I said. 'Will you drive?'

She did, without asking any questions, assuming I didn't want to talk. Though I did want to talk – but not to Harriet.

I ran into my room, sat at my small table, picked up my pen.

'I'm here,' said Roarie, at once.

'I didn't read the guide book,' I began. 'I've just been to a Harland Heights look-alike, here in Cornwall. There was even a wing with a flat roof. If I'd seen Bennetta or Lydia on it, my head would've blown right off. As it is, I'm whirling round all over the show. I was so calm before. *Almost* sentimental.'

''Tis not possible to run from my times. My times are everyplace.'

'I know. I'm so glad you're here. I don't know how I'd live anywhere else – it claims me – it's so lovely. But everywhere is death. On the cliffs, in the ruined mines, in the sea, on the moors, and now in a bloody camellia garden. Literally. Bloody.'

'Aye. No place is clean. No clean money. 'Tis a land of extreme wealth, extreme power. Know it. Canst not run away.'

'They buried the slaves – or rather slaves had to bury each other – then They, the owners, planted gardens from the blood and bones of the dead. It dazzled me. So clear. Today. Dazzled me. Europeans steal land, people, minerals, materials, everything, even the flowers. Then they build a world bank so the people they steal from can borrow the money that's taken from them, and pay back at thieves' interest rates. And what for? For basics like clean water, and seeds. I can't believe I was so naive.'

''Tis not too late. Not for you. You're alive. Do something.'

'I shall. And I shan't bloody stop until all Third World debts are cancelled. And I mean cancelled. Can you imagine – if the Great Train Robbers offered their money back to the British government at a rate of interest? Oh, but you don't know trains, do you?'

''Tis all right. I like you, Denny. You bounce back every time.'

172

'I am so angry, that's why.'

'Yes. Fine words. Though camellias are not in my time.'

'Yes. I know. They were stolen later, and not from the Caribbean. But you know what I mean.'

'I do. But . . . wait . . . go to Harriet. Hold her. Be close this evening. Then rise at midnight. Pick up your . . . pen . . . Meet me, on the manor of Chingford Meade, as the snow melts. Midnight . . . at the very end of winter. And hope. For a bright full moon.'

Twenty-one

It's wet and windy the night Lydia makes her escape.

She puts pillows into her bed to resemble her sleeping body, wraps two extra blankets over her thick winter cloak, and creeps down the back stairs of the servants' quarters, past the dogs she doped at supper. The animals snore as she lets herself out into the white grounds.

Silently she crosses the laid lawns, skirts the physic garden, and the new glasshouses (Bennetta's latest venture) and enters the walled shrub garden. Once inside its walls she feels safer, even though she's still near the house. Passing through a lych-gate into the churchyard she says prayers as she reaches the tombstones. The names of the Harlands are blurred by melting snow. A stone moves – the figure of Roarie Brewster appears, and becomes solid.

They enter the woods together.

Their footsteps become yards, the yards stretching to rods and poles as they recognise and pass each landmark.

First the ice house, then the holly dip. Up the other side past ten fat oaks. From the oaks to the second holly dip, then the cross path, shaped like a crucifix. To the solitary beech next to two oaks. From there uphill for fifty steps, small steps as it is so steep. They have hardly slowed their pace and are steaming at the mouth. To the path shaped like an elbow. From the elbow three hundred steps over level ground to the dead tree covered in ivy. Three holly dips and four levels. Tomorrow night this will be impassable in the dark on foot with the fast melting of the snow. A final uphill stretch and then a long slow valley. Their ankles ache from the downhill trek, and bitter knives of wind are slicing their faces. They walk separately, concentrating.

Holding hands is impossible. The path is too narrow in places. Past the beech wood on their right with the ever-greens on their left. They have chanted the route to themselves so often since they first laid joint plans in midwinter.

To the badger's den then the stream, then along the banks of the stream until it meets the footbridge. There the stream flows to London and the path across the bridge leads to the long wooded hill down to Chingford Meade mill.

The woods are too dense here for the women to dare leave the path, and the night too hostile for anyone to be out, so they reason that robbers and footpads will be in the inns.

Rain intensifies when they are half-way down the hill to the mill-stream. Rain soaks the edges of their blankets, so they struggle to walk and hold the blankets around them-selves at the same time.

Down the track to the valley of the mill. Rain drips on their eyebrows and eyelashes, and they pull their blankets further over their heads, just able to see out through a tunnel of cloth. They've both been at work since daybreak and are tired and cold to the centre of their bones. They carry nothing except their savings. They wish they might have stolen a horse. How much easier the journey would have been.

Exhausted, they emerge from a beech coppice, to the low flat part of the mill. They have little idea whether they've made good time, arrived late, or too early with a freezing wait, at the mercy of night.

They listen for approaching hooves. Nothing. They move close to each other and blend themselves into still trunks. They can't see more than twenty feet through the darkness. So much, thinks Roarie, for a bright full moon.

Lydia hopes that her escape will be thought to have failed. Sheer foolishness will have ended her up in some ditch in the woods, or in a marshy hollow under melting snow. She slipped, in the dark, pulled down into a cold sucking grave.

The cold seeps on, inwards. From their boots to their calves, their knees to their thighs. From their hands to their wrists and arms. From their shoulders, creeping across their shoulderblades, until the blades of cold meet at their backbones and inch up into their skulls.

When John Wild finds them they're almost gone. He tries to shake them but they're unconscious from cold.

He hoists each of them side by side, face down over his spare horse, and wraps them with more blankets which he carries with him. He ropes the bodies around the horse, so its jolting won't dislodge them.

This is his land – the place he knows in every season, during each part of the night. It is his time. He's unafraid. The wind drops, and though the rain continues, it doesn't interrupt his work. There is no traveller abroad to watch him.

He mounts Naomi, leading the spare horse by a leading rein and turns for the route south, towards Wapping.

They wake fully clothed, in a narrow bed. Someone has put warm bricks around them. The blankets are warm, and weigh heavy. A small Black girl is beside the bed, touching Lydia and saying: 'Mother says make haste. 'Tis night, the moon's up.'

The little girl points to steaming bowls of broth on a table. Roarie grunts, easing up on her elbows. Every part of her aches.

'Night?' says Lydia, trying to stretch her stiff shoulders.

'Didst sleep the day. Thought you wouldst die. Mother says make haste.'

'Give her thanks. Shall be but a short time.'

The girl grins and nods and runs out.

They fall back on the bolsters. 'We're alive. We're alive.'

They rise, fold the bedding, drink the hot broth, feeling its warmth flow inside, and then they hurry out. They're young and strong. One night in cold rain and melting snow is not enough to blight them.

The little girl meets them on the landing and leads them

along a corridor that twists, down stairs to a street a few feet wide where John Wild waits. Each of two horses has sacking tied around its feet. John Wild is a tall man, with good shoulders, and wears a heavy black coat, riding breeches and tall brown leather boots, burnished, which shine in the pool of light from a lantern over the doorway. He's already seated on his horse, a dappled grey, and leans down to hand Roarie up beside him.

Lydia says: 'We owe you our lives.'

'You owe your lives to your courage.'

Lydia, who can ride, mounts the second horse. The women turn to thank the child but she has gone. Lydia follows John Wild, with Roarie clinging on behind him, out of the street.

The horses' hooves are muffled by the sacking, which slows them but prevents them from slipping on uneven melting ice. After several minutes' travel (tedious on foot and many times longer) John Wild reins in by a warehouse. He dismounts, helps Roarie down and signals to Lydia to do likewise.

The moon is rising steadily, casting bright light down on to the front of the warehouse. There are no clouds and it is bitterly cold. There's no lantern.

John Wild knocks at a small door set in huge wooden doors across the entire front of the building. A woman and a man come out, dressed in heavy boots and long cloaks. They have pale brown skin.

John Wild turns to Lydia and Roarie: 'These are my friends. They know the river like I know my horse. You can trust them. You will not know their names – for the safety of you all. Go well and arrive safely. They will make the next contact for you. We ask no payment. You shall be trusted on oath ne'er to fail to help others such as you.' After speaking to his friends once more, he turns and leaves.

Roarie and Lydia follow the woman and man to the back of the warehouse, down stone steps to a small beach where the banks of the Thames slope steeply and which would be covered at high tide. A post is set in the beach, with the sodden corpse of a thief tied to it. They turn aside in disgust.

It has been washed by the high tide three times, but not removed before the Thames froze over. Roarie knows that the heads of thieves are displayed on spikes by London Bridge, but has never seen them. Now she believes it.

They step into a small barge with oars. Their guides take an oar each and cast off, rowing confidently. The water is black under the rising moon, and lumps of black ice float by.

As they reach south bank Roarie and Lydia can make out a figure on a wooden jetty. Wooden steps lead down to the beach at one side. The bank is lined with warehouses, some with hand-operated cranes. Down river two sailing ships, iced in, lie at a tilt, waiting for full thaw.

Their guides whisper: 'Good arrival. Safe freedom.'

Lydia leans forward and says: 'Safe freedom.' Then she clambers out of the barge on to the jetty, followed by Roarie.

Candace leads them to the back door of the out-buildings of an inn. Roarie thinks she could never find this place again on her own. Wooden stairs clatter a shout on each step up to the first floor. Candace turns right, through a low doorway where Bess is waiting. The room is dim from rush tapers and low embers. Gabriell is asleep on the bed. From under the bed, later, is pulled a clean mattress for Roarie and Lydia.

Roarie stays almost a week at the tavern before taking leave of Lydia, Candace and Bess. Her part in Lydia's escape is recognised. So is her need to find Mary By-the-Well. But on that journey Lydia won't accompany her. She could, if she wished. Could work and live on the remote farm in the south, where also live the Ellisons, Tom and his sister, Sarah, and Sarah's child.

But Lydia is not sleeping well. In a final conversation with Roarie, in the stable yard as they help Gabriell groom the horses, she explains: 'Such a place, run and owned by a white woman, 'tis no refuge, no sanctuary.'

'How so?'

''Tis a place of visions and trouble. Free and not free. Did I not say the riddle was blood and fire?'

''Tis true. You did speak so.'

''Tis said by Candace and Bess that Frances Felham, the

widow, is good. Yet her farm is south of the manor house of Charlewood?'

'Aye. 'Tis many miles from here. But 'tis safe. Remote. Tom tends the sheep and Sarah works in the glasshouses. They be not purchased of plantation gains. 'Tis not Harland Heights.'

But Lydia replies: 'Couldst not rest there. Nor work there. Wouldst be a prison – open fields. Prison but ne'er a wall.'

'Shall you stay here?'

'Aye. Shall work with Candace and Bess. Candace shall find me a lodging, nearby. I shall work for freedom. Shall be part on't. The trails. These women shall be family now.'

'So? 'Tis good. 'Tis real. You are needed here. For myself – I shall find Mary By-the-Well at the farm. Shall learn all I can. I do not know how I shall fight. But mark me Lydia, I shall fight. Shouldst like to read and write. Perchance this Frances, if she be good and wise, as they say, shall make me a scholar yet.'

'So, 'tis goodbye. 'Twas good chance to meet you. Shall not forget you, Roarie.'

'No? Good. I shall ne'er forget you, nor this journey.'

'Go well. Safe freedom.'

'Goodbye Lydia. Safe freedom.'

It is spring 1667 on the manor of Chingford Meade. Slowly the village people start to recover their land after the freezing winter.

Alistair Harland's pursuit of Roarie Brewster and Lydia Harland is over. He finally accepts Bennetta's verdict that the young women have perished together in the melting snow, their bodies sodden at the bottom of a bog or pond. Harland's interrogations of the village people reveal nothing, because they know nothing. But after the hunt is over, news reaches Martha and Ruth at the mill, via a messenger late one night, of Roarie and Lydia's successful arrival at a tavern on south bank. And there's news too of uprisings – of quarrels between working people and landowners across Essex to the coast.

On the manor of Chingford Meade after the secret rejoicing that Roarie and Lydia are safe, people continue a new season's work. They rent oxen from the neighbouring manors, arranging to pay in goods or labour. They till and plant: oats, barley, rye, carrots, cabbages, onions, leeks, turnips, peas, beans and hops. Only the wealthy people drink wine, but even they are returning to ale and beer – to Anne Brewster's profit – because the wine which used to be imported on Dutch ships is now cut off while the troubles with the Dutch continue.

No wonder then, say visiting merchants and pedlars, that in London the rich are turning to coffee, and a fine trade can be done by running a coffee house. There the men gather daily for news of shipping and business. News from mouth to mouth and ear to ear is important, since newspapers of the day don't list the shipping or business affairs, though there are rumours that this may change.

The very wealthy who go to London for the theatre, or to dances and court occasions, may choose to dine at new exclusive dining places; but the lesser rich – known as 'the ordinaries' – they eat in streets like Fleet Street, where they sit at one long table and share the food and the bill. There they may drink sack from Jerez, and cider from Kent, gin from two hundred distillers of London, and usquebaugh from Ireland.

Interesting as the snatches of such news are from London, they don't alter the work that goes on from dawn to dusk as spring becomes summer on the manor. Now there are chicks and eggs again in the hen runs; calves in the byre, bought on credit from the neighbouring manor, to be repaid when they bring their corn to be ground free of charge at the mill; and blossoms on the fruit trees promise apples and plums.

Lucy and Hannah are both pregnant. Summer 1667 is once again a time of hope. But lest anyone stop working there are also graves in the churchyard to remind them that at best life is hard graft, and at worst a precarious balance.

Talk swirls and changes between them all as they work. In this way they make the language as well as receive it. They adopt some words like coffee and chocolate, and alter others. Usquebaugh becomes whiskey; lord of the manor becomes squire; villein becomes labourer; Lammas becomes harvest-home; but not quickly, because this is the country still, where change is slow and cyclical, despite the upheavals and crises of everyday life.

Ruth thinks of this, and language, and how she would love to be the one who can read, and how she no longer dreams of tall ships with herself at the helm. But sometimes, when the fields are on fire, long strips of flames burning off the stubble to make way for a fallow field next year, she will recall snatches of the sailors' tales, of ships and adventures, and fires thrown up from under the sea. She will stand, holding in her arms a small child of one of her friends here, and she'll shudder with memories of the fire approaching Rising Hill Mill, and worse, the witches' fires in the horror stories of her mother's mother's generation. Some stories straddle town and country, as her friend's child straddles her hip.

To Martha however it seems that Chingford Meade Mill in the late 1660s flows with cycles of water. The mill-wheel turns; and brings slow cycles of seedtime and harvest, equinox, midsummer, equinox, midwinter, equinox, transforming the landscape from green to brown to green again.

Leaning on her hoe in the field beside the mill, the first summer there, Martha turns slowly surveying the rebuilt mill; the mill-race falling away into its stream; the stream flowing on to the River Lea. She turns back to watch the fields. As she thinks about the land, a hare bounds across her path. But Martha is not pregnant, so it poses no threat.

Past the fields are the houses at the edge of the manor, and the deserted manor house that no one is coming forward to claim. No one seems to have won or lost it in a gambling debt; no son has survived for it to be passed to by the rules of firstborn – a common enough word, thinks Martha for all its high sounding. No daughter seems to have survived to inherit sideways now that the brothers are dead.

Perhaps someone has put a curse on the place; so that anyone who might have inherited it – a distant female cousin even – fears to move in lest new people in the manor house be struck down as were the former ones.

There is so much turmoil and news about land and enclosures that it's small wonder Martha thinks now and then about the empty manor house. Most days she ignores it, because she is housed herself and happy with Ruth as her lover. Martha has no desire to have children and watch them die, and she has no need whatsoever for a man in her bed. John, Joseph and Tom are friends, who work hard and have rebuilt the mill. A community is growing, and the Turners, Claytons and Wainwrights will have plenty more children, for whom times may, hopefully, be easier.

Hannah runs the dairy; Alice works in the fields; Lucy is becoming a fair weaver, though the craft takes years to learn. Now that there is more contact with the neighbouring manor, Lucy has found a weaver who will advise her. Martha's glad. As she puts together all the parts of herself, the first summer after fleeing from the Great Fire, she wants happiness for her new friends. She misses Roarie badly, but Roarie could not help Lydia and then stay. People have to survive as best they know how. Sometimes it means leaving behind everything that is known, as she herself has done. It is enough that Roarie is safe.

Meanwhile there is so much to learn. Lucy, Alice and Hannah are teaching her: when to plant and when to wait, working the rythmns of the seasons and the moon; because the land and moon are felt to be closely linked in the country, and you have that to learn if you arrive ignorant from London. The work goes on.

Twenty-two

In the spring of 1989 I joined several environmental campaigns, preparing for 1992. EEC guidelines for clean beaches, sewage dumping at sea, and drinking water issues were at the forefront after disasters such as Camelford, when aluminium sulphate entered the water supplies.

Through these issues and through work, I became close to JoAnne, who accepted my relationship with Harriet, glad for us that we were so happy.

At Easter, Lerryn, Tessa and Jules came to stay with us.

Tessa and Jules needed time for themselves and time to paint, free from London pressures. So we three went to Mevagissey, to visit Lerryn's widowed father.

He was a kind and gentle person, and I liked him. Now retired from work as a hospital porter, he was still strong and agile. The lines of his face told of years of sea fishing in a small dinghy. His eyelids had turned red as white people's do, who're constantly exposed to direct wind.

On our fishing trip Harriet sat quietly near Lerryn, listening to the pull and suck of the sea.

I thought of Daphne. She seemed very close to me. I realised in the dinghy that I was most aware of Daphne when I was near water, or high on the moors gazing towards the distant sea.

I'd called for her only once – in the outhouse, with the boxes, but I was often aware of her, a comfortable awareness.

I remembered her voice: follow your feelings, woman.

Now, I trailed my hand in the water: Tiamat/Themis was the fish who gave birth to the universe, mother of the original four elements: water, darkness, night, eternity.

She was the Deep; and the Deep was the word for Womb.

In south Arabia, she was part of Ishtar: her eyes flowed with tears. Her womb was a great reservoir of blood: the eastern shores of the Red Sea are still called Tihamat by the Arabs.

In India, she was part of Kali: goddess of destruction, treasure house of compassion; giver of life; fount of every kind of love through her agents on earth, women.

Tiamat, Tiamat, four-fifths of the earth's surface is water.

I looked at Harriet, opposite me in her brother-in-law's boat. From the very beginning of our relationship, I'd talked to her about Daphne, and my recognition about both Daphne and Maria. I spoke of my voices, and all the elements – fire/air/earth/water. She listened as I told of unresolved feelings, and coming to terms with never being able to resolve them.

Had I really been breaking up with Maria? I don't know. But we'd loved one another very deeply, and very well, for a very long time. My love for Maria had been real. I didn't need to deny the rough patches; or give myself nightmares of what the future might or mightn't have been. We'd had real love, between real women, ups and downs, reality.

My love for Maria was based on everyday routines, raising our children, sleeping each night in the same bed, waking each morning to each other's face, each other's voice, knowing each other's touch. Lips, mouths, breasts and hands. Thighs and bellies and deep inside safe and secret places. Places I now knew with Harriet.

From my vantage point in the dinghy I watched the land: I thought of Daphne. With her I'd known Fire. Very different from my love for Maria. I was Earth and Fire; Daphne was Water and Fire. Then I thought of Themis, stones, bones of the earth mother. From the stones rose up the new bones of the people.

I had new bones. New bones for a new person: me.

I could feel Daphne near me, the whole time I was

thinking. I didn't need to know if the experience in the outhouse was real; any more than I needed to ask if Roarie Brewster was real. So long as I was voiced, I was real, and both of them, in their own ways, helped me find my voice.

Harriet caught my eye and smiled. She too was deep in thought. She wanted me, with Tessa, Jules and Lerryn, to sell the Chelsea flat; contact Rosa, Daphne's ex-flatmate (whose number I still had); and set up a fund for Daphne. Daphne's vision of a sports centre could be started, at last. Once the contact with Daphne's Black friends was made, Lerryn and I – as white women – would withdraw. Harriet's name wouldn't be involved; she saw her role as providing the cash.

Not for nothing had Harriet founded Herton Hall.

Before our boat trip I had made her promise never to leave Hermit's Hut to me.

'But why, darling? It would give me peace of mind, to know you were provided for.'

'You wouldn't have peace of mind if you saw me struggling with all the class stuff that comes up from the bottom of my pond.'

'Class stuff?'

'I can't handle inheritance. Any more than Lerryn can. It makes me feel unequal – I can't do the same for you. If I could, maybe I'd feel different. Stands to reason – I'd be a different person. As it is, I'd be in a quandary. It would be wrong for me, on my own. I'd have to sell Hermit's Hut, break my heart. Strangers invading the rooms. Men in the beds!!'

At that she laughed and laughed. 'All right Denny, I promise. I'll use all my imagination . . . as Wind would say to you . . . I'll come up with a new solution. All right?'

'Brill. I love you.'

After the boat trip, we stayed overnight in a B & B, did a cliff walk next day, then drove home to Tessa and Jules. Time together, for talking, playing, painting, listening to music.

My diary said: And so to bed. With Harriet.

In May Harriet went to London for a week to stay with Lerryn, to say what she'd wanted to say for years. I didn't ask her how she'd say it.

In May 1989 soldiers fired on students in Tiananmen Square. It was an intense time. Some of my fire dreams returned.

In June, the Ayatollah died. I went into a week of dreams, re-living my fears about Philip during the Iran–Iraq war, though it was almost a year since the cease-fire there.

There was also a terrible gas explosion in Russia, setting off another string of fire dreams. But each time, I was stronger, better able to understand and face them.

That summer a drought deepened each day. Vans toured Devon and Cornwall asking people to use water very sparingly. 'Save water' notices appeared on small posters by busy roadsides, in car parks, in doctors' surgeries, in libraries, and on municipal buildings.

We lugged water in bucketfuls from the bath to the gardens; tipped the washing-up water on to the thirsty patio tubs; and worked with the jingle: 'if it's yellow let it mellow; if it's brown flush it down.'

Meanwhile the sky was cloudless blue, day after day, and I felt I was already retired, living in the south of France.

Nights were warm. Harriet wasn't sleeping properly, which was unusual for her. When she finally fell asleep, after midnight, she tossed about and sometimes muttered in her dreams.

One morning, looking particularly drained after yet another bad night, she said she needed to see someone about it, would take the car, and would shop for a picnic.

'I'll drive you,' I offered. 'I need some things in Penzance anyway.'

'Thanks darling, but no. I want to be alone, and I've no idea how long it will take.'

'You're not usually more than an hour,' I said, thinking she was going to the doctor's. 'I don't mind waiting.'

'Denny, I know you don't, and I know you want to help, but I really do want to do this alone.'

'All right. I'll take Roof out for a long walk. She won't want to go with us later, if we're going by car. I'll make bread. That'd be a change. Haven't baked bread for ages.'

She kissed me goodbye and I busied myself until late afternoon when she arrived back, much calmer, with the car boot full of supermarket boxes and carriers for our picnic.

An hour later we sat on a high rocky outcrop near Botallack, looking down to the sheer cliffs. The infamous Crown Mines pointed up like index fingers from clenched fists.

To me they always looked like a dose of death, but they fascinated and called me too. Their perfect geometry and precision were part of that. The colour of the stone, the beauty of the local flowers, couldn't fail to impress. Just as the people who climbed them to build them couldn't fail to fall off.

It was now almost seven. To the west an all-seeing red eye, enormous, above an orangey-pink sea. Long streamers of gold and orange blurred in a blue marble sky.

I munched bread and brie; Harriet didn't eat. She cupped both hands around a wine glass full to the brim with red wine.

'I went to see a clairvoyant. Today in Penzance.'

'Oh, I thought it was the doctor's.'

'No, not this morning.'

It didn't seem right to speak, so I waited, opening a bag of prepared watercress, and swigging from a bottle of mineral water. Harriet had downed half her glass already. If she was hitting the wine, I'd better lay off it and drive us both home.

'There's a lot to say. Will you hear me out, darling?'

'Of course I will. Whatever's the matter?'

'I've been sleeping very badly, as you know. I've been having premonitions. Time closing in around me. Gifts I want to give; things I want to say. Preparing us both.'

'For what? You're frightening me, Harriet.'

'I feel that I am going to die soon.'

'Die? What d'you mean, die? How soon?'

'Very. So I went to see Fenella.'

'Fenella? Hell, you must be serious.'

'I am serious. I thought we had many years together. Five,

187

ten, fifteen. Many. But my dreams have been so urgent this week. You're trembling, darling. You asked me how soon. I feel it will happen before the end of the month. It's a particular time, the anniversary of the outbreak of the Second World War. I have death on my mind.'

I said: 'And the Devil took me up to an exceedingly high mountain.'

'Pardon?'

'The only phrase I remember from Sunday school. I only went twice.'

Questions in our eyes. Harriet dry-eyed: myself blurred in a mist of nerves.

'Listen, I'll tell you everything,' she said.

I nodded, reached for a paper serviette, blew my nose.

Harriet said: 'I've seen you sorting your photos, holding them, searching them – all your complex feelings about Maria, Bronwyn, Daphne . . . I watched as you began to reconnect with Roarie Brewster, trying to finish the un-finished business there, which if you hadn't suddenly left London when you did, you maybe would have had chance to finish . . .

'I want you to finish that writing about Roarie. Turn it into a manuscript. Get it published.'

'Published?'

'Yes. Work on it actively, when you mourn me, when I am gone.'

'Gone? You're not going anywhere. You're perfectly healthy. This is all silly. A few bad dreams and you wind both of us up, and bring up the past, which I don't want. How do you know what you say you know? You could be wrong, wrong.'

'I don't know how we know these things; I don't know what material substance premonitions are made of. Which is why I talked with Fenella. I was out in my timing. My mind wasn't accurate. We have only a few weeks left, Denny. You must hear me out. We must prepare.'

'I don't understand. Prepare. Even if it was true, how the hell do I prepare? You're here alive, and I'm in love. And you ask me to prepare?'

Harriet spoke patiently, gently, very kindly. 'Yes. That is exactly right. That's why I brought you here. I am asking you to help me, to help us, prepare.'

I sat, shaking.

She took my arm, pointing out to sea: 'Look, Denny, at the fire in the air, reflected in the water. Feel it. Don't be misled by sunsets. There is death here, as well as life. One goes with the other. Prepare. This time don't let it smash your psyche to pieces, as it did last time. This time, prepare. We have not as long as I'd thought, nor as I'd hoped. If I had the answers as to how we know these things I'd not be so mistaken in my timing, would I?'

'I don't know,' I whispered.

'How did people know where to place the stone circles? How did they know that stones gave directional signals to sailors? How did they know where the healing energy would be, and which of the stones they should trust? I don't know. If we had such answers, Cornwall would have a different story.'

For her sake I managed a weak laugh. 'You're trying to tell me you dowsed the well in the wrong place?'

'Stones out of alignment. Yes I am. We only have a few weeks left. I didn't know that until this week, nor precisely, until today.'

I breathed deeply for a few moments, trying to stop the shaking. She put her arm around me. The tomato-eye burst in the sky. Blood spilled over the sea. I saw death: red flooding death. Tears flowed down my face.

She said: 'The word you want is active: action.'

I concentrated on each of Harriet's words. She had my total attention. She continued: 'Lerryn taught me that. She loves you, and will be a comfort to you.'

I interrupted: 'Harriet, she'll be devastated.'

'Yes. And she knows that aunts are not immortal. You'll be very good for each other, the two of you.' Harriet thought for a moment then said: 'Lerryn will always be a political person. Woman. Our ancestors, hers and mine died here, under this ground. In the tin mines. My ancestors owned nothing except a felt hat with a candle stuck to it. Candlefire spreads over the sea in front of us, each sunset. Under the sea are dead miners, pirates, sailors and slaves. Male and female; Black and white.

'So, the oppression of my ancestors, under this ground, with no light other than a single candle, can you imagine that – that oppression has been transferred on to other oppressed peoples. I think the beauty of this place should be shared too. And not before time.

'I am leaving Hermit's Hut in trust. I'm hoping you and Lerryn, JoAnne, Tessa and Jules will be trustees. I'd like it set up as a women's space for art, music and writing. For women to be able to stay, free of charge, on working holidays. The place to be available for you to live in, perhaps as caretaker, for the rest of your life, but not owned by you . . . since you made me promise.'

Harriet took my hand. She said: 'Mourn me *actively*. If you don't mourn you can't move on. And you must move on, my love. Emotionally, I mean. I want you to live, be happy . . .

'Write Roarie's book, finish it, get it published. Write it so that the living can use it. That's what it means to keep the home fires burning.'

Harriet died peacefully at Hermit's Hut, whose windows look over the Irish sea, as it moves to meet the Atlantic. A coastline that has claimed many ships. She died in my arms fifty years after the Germans invaded Danzig, now Gdansk. A port, a ship-building place. She died before the autumn when the two sides of Berlin were reunited; when the Czechs took to the streets waving banners, demanding action; when the whole of Europe was changing through the actions of ordinary bods like me.

The funeral was quiet, secular, with Harriet's sons and daughters-in-law and grandchildren. I met Pierre, who came to pay his respects. A memorial service, immense, with artists from all over the world, was organised by the family, the part of the family that I wasn't part of. I met Harriet's ex-lover, Anna von Schiller, who came from America.

Then, with Lerryn, Anna and JoAnne, Tessa and Jules, as requested in Harriet's will, I scattered her ashes on the cliffs: 'in the wind and sand, where my song began'.

Then I set to work. Active: action. I travelled with Roof to London, and stayed with Lerryn while we met solicitors, and arranged the trust fund for Hermit's Hut. I met and talked with Tessa and Jules, trustees, who had plenty of ideas for the use of the house and land.

Once the fund was set up, and the admin group started to meet, I was extremely busy, glad of the action.

I stayed some weeks in London – going to libraries, making notes, visiting bookshops, talking, thinking, gathering images, ideas and impressions, collecting maps, articles and books.

Leaving Roof sometimes with Lerryn, I travelled to Epping Forest, Walthamstow market, Tulse Hill, Brixton, Brockwell Park and the Sussex Weald, where Frances Felham's remote farm might have been.

Harriet lay around my shoulders, a warm Celtic shawl. I was in no hurry to remove her. I wasn't lonely as I'd been after Maria, Bronwyn and Daphne. Life was precious, each day full.

In November I returned to Hermit's Hut. Lerryn was up and down to Cornwall to see me; JoAnne was a short drive away; and Roof was by my side. Nightly, on television, I watched the events in Czechoslovakia and debates about changes in East and West Germany. During the days I sorted Harriet's belongings and her papers. I wrapped treasured objects to be stored; I filed her papers and boxed them (some for her sons, as she requested, others for me to keep; and others for recycling).

I felt her close to me, supporting me, helping me stay strong.

At Christmas I chose to be alone with Roof. I watched every news bulletin on Romania; communicated every day with Roarie, who never once failed me; and read the history tomes and articles I'd brought with me from my trip to London, which Harriet had wanted me to do (she called it my 'research' trip).

In New Year 1990, I accepted JoAnne's offer – that she would look after Roof for several months at her home in Truro. I knew I could trust them together.

Tessa and Jules applied for unpaid leave from work; so during late spring they'd live at Hermit's Hut, to finish their paintings for a forthcoming exhibition in London.

At Easter, Lerryn would use Hermit's Hut, and after that she'd arrange times there for other women artists, musicians and writers.

My arrangements complete, I flew to Aotearoa, to Beatrice.

I was on a beach in Auckland when we heard of Nelson Mandela's release. Full circle, I recalled the demos with Maria – shouting 'Azania, Azania Now. Free Nelson Mandela.'

Travelling with Beattie to South Island, we heard the Mandela concert, Easter Monday, broadcast around the world. It was the first months of the last decade of the twentieth century. Significant changes – not much to celebrate: apartheid's walls still firmly in place; Amnesty's files thick with horror; fires blazing across the rain forests.

Arms linked, Beattie and I walked and talked: old friends, sharing our past, bringing memories through today, for tomorrow. Clichés patched, darned but not worn through: new decade, new hope, world peace, an end to torture, imprisonment, disappearances, hatred, oppression.

How we talked, Beattie and me!!

In wild places, beautiful scenery: backdrop for our very small-scale personal dramas. But we weren't unimportant and we knew and spoke it. Jokingly we might call ourselves specks of dust in the sweep of time, but we knew the galaxy was made of specks like us.

My manuscript was finished and left with publishers in London.

Before I left England, I picked up my pen each day to Speak Paper for a few minutes with Roarie.

Sometimes I went over and over the tales she'd already

told, changing and altering the words, re-listening to the women as they lived their lives, talking and working. Other times Roarie asked me to close my eyes, watch the story as she revealed it.

It is New Year 1668, on Felham Farm to the south of the manor house at Charlewood.

Roarie's hopes of becoming a scholar are not coming true. Nor are her longings for her teacher Mary By-the-Well. Her joy and happiness at arriving safely at the farm last May, in time for May Day celebrations, of finding Mary alive and well, and of becoming friends with Frances and the other people at the farm, all of these are past.

Now Roarie works for Frances, whereas before she worked for her father and for Mary By-the-Well. Frances has no desire to teach the newcomer to read; for she is herself a writer, claiming long hours of solitude at her casement window, watching over the people working for her on the farm.

She is a good woman, in so far as no one is badly treated. But she owns and organises; that's how she views her life and land.

There's no room here for a weaver's rebellious daughter.

Longings and dreamings. Roarie makes a decision . . .

The words trailed off. I sighed, being used to this by now.

'Where are you?' I asked.

'Lying in bed, alone, here on Frances Felham's land.'

'What's the matter?'

'Mary By-the-Well loves me not. I have no shawl. You have a warm shawl for your shoulders, is't not true?'

'Yes. I'm calmer than I was after Maria died. I'm safer, myself. You helped me, though I don't know where you really came from, nor who you really are. But I needed you and you were there. Now it's my chance to help you.'

''Tis ne'er my home here. Mary By-the-Well wraps her body in her child, wears him like a cloak; sleeps with him in her bed.'

'Are you outside, beyond her touch?'

'Alas, I am but her apprentice. Her midwife skills she

193

keeps for sheep. No woman here is heavy with child.'

'Can't you finish your training there then?'

'I desire not to deliver sheep. Didst journey so far, for this?'

'You're leaving?'

'Shall return to the manor.'

'Why? Surely that's the last place that's safe to go?'

''Tis home. 'Tis the manor I long for.'

'Was it a mistake then, to leave?'

'No. 'Twas good chance. Didst meet Candace and Bess. Didst see London. Didst learn much of laws, of King and edict.'

'Yes. There was an edict of Queen Elizabeth in 1601. There were so many Black people in London she tried twice to have them rounded up and sent back. But both proclamations failed. I don't like numbers games, but my books are useful. I'm angry Frances won't take the time to teach you. It wouldn't hurt her.'

''Tis the way of rich women. I trust them not.'

'Mary's staying? Are you losing her friendship?'

''Twas a dream. 'Tis gone. I am forsaken.'

'What will you do on the manor?'

'Make trouble.'

Roarie and I laughed briefly over this, for she sounded so stroppy and yet so forlorn at the same time. Then I said: 'But won't the Harlands get you, if you go back? Be careful.'

'Harlands be departed. To plantations. Alistair desires to return. Dost force Bennetta to 'company him.'

'To the West Indies?' I asked, aware that in my time it was called the Caribbean, but wanting to make translation easy for Roarie. She replied that it was a long way by ship, especially for Bennetta who was 'heavy with child' again after two stillbirths. It seemed typical to me of Alistair's harshness, that he'd put his wife at risk for the sake of his own plans. But of course should anything happen to Bennetta, Alistair would take a second wife, until he had all the sons and daughters he wanted.

I said: 'So, you're going home? Your Aunt Anne'll be amazed when you turn up.'

'She loves me. Meet me . . . on the manor of Chingford Meade . . .'

It is 1668 when Bennetta Harland dies aboard ship, and is buried at sea with her dead baby.

Harland House remains with the Harland family until the end of slavery (one hundred and fifty years later) changes the Harland fortunes. The house and gardens are bought by a rich Essex merchant, early eighteen hundreds. The name Harland dies.

Brewster lives. One line in a printed book.

It is the night of full moon, April 1668, that they gather, eight of them, bound together by work and daily life, on the manor of Chingford Meade.

Five are women, three are men. Linked by tough, rough threads of poverty and toil. The Chingford Eight: Martha Faryner, Ruth Bates, Roarie Brewster, Lucy Turner, Alice Clayton, John Turner, Tom Wainwright, Joseph Clayton.

Hannah Wainwright and Anne Brewster watch over the children.

The Chingford Eight don't gain fame – because they're not caught – there is no mention in William Holcroft's book, which he kept as verderer of old Epping Forest.

Sure footed and swift treading they make their way towards the first fence, their knives gleaming silver in the bright night.

The fences are made from uprights beaten firmly hard down into the earth, their cross-pieces lashed with sinewy strong cord. No dogs have been put to guard the enclosures which stand as a symbol of scorn for the poor. But the Harlands are on the high seas, on their way to their plantations, and now is the chance, while Harland Heights is managed by a few servants, to claim back the land.

Approaching the first stretch of fence with the rest of the Eight, Roarie Brewster lets her mind move over the Harland list of misdeeds against servants, villagers and commoners.

Broadsheets and songs tell the tales of the common people, who need their common land. As in every struggle there are gains and losses: the Chingford Eight gain time. Time for animals to graze the forest; time for firewood to be carted; time for community to grow.

Roarie gives a last long glance at the moon, no cloud, crossing the open sky, no shadows to restrict the work of the group. Pausing, she lets the next of the group catch up to her. He does likewise, then with one touch of her hand on his arm, a signal which he passes along the line, they move forward to begin. Two hold an upright while another slices the cords. The uprights are left in place; cross pieces are removed and piled neatly. Two uprights to be done at a time; for there are six working and two on guard; and the night's work is organised, silent, rapid, thorough.

Across Essex, resistance to enclosures continues, and appears in the history books.

But there is other resistance too.

Sumach trees don't lie.